SON OF SORON

STONEBLOOD SAGA: BOOK ONE

Prologue

VELAINA DIPPED HER finger into the drink then slowly ran the wet digit across her lips. An old habit, one her mother's family had ingrained in her. The dinner was in the royal courts, the drink a simple fruit juice for the expecting mother and her considerate husband. While the rest of the guests drank wine, a servant had filled their goblets with the nectar. Suddenly she felt it, a startling and unexpected tingle in her lips. *Poison* she thought to herself as she leaned over to her husband Soron. "My dear I am not feeling well. Would you take me home?"

Soron gave his young wife a puzzled look, knowing something was out of sorts. "Of course," he said.

Her mind was racing at the realization someone was trying to kill them. She signaled the servant who had poured their drinks to come to the table.

The young serving girl came over with a smile. "What can I get for you, your grace?"

Velaina studied the girl closely, sensing no guile or sinister intent. "Where did you get the juice you served us?"

The girl replied honestly, "The man in the kitchen said you were with child and would not drink wine, that you would prefer this instead."

"What man?" asked Velaina.

"I... I don't know your highness. It happened so fast I never got a look at him. He just put it in my hands and told me you would prefer it instead of wine. He said there was only a little of the juice and to only serve it to you and your husband." The servant looked at the jug of juice suspiciously, worried she had done something wrong. "Did I make a mistake?"

Again she sensed innocence. The girl was not trying to murder them. Velaina smiled, "It's okay, the mistake is not yours." She poured her goblet of juice and her husband's back into the jug. She handed the jug to Soron as she rose from the table. "Take that with us my dear, we wouldn't want anyone else drinking it."

Soron frowned and furrowed his brow as he realized what she meant. His marriage to Velaina had made many unhappy in both families. The impending birth of their child may have awoken old angers. Soron looked about the room. He smiled as if nothing was amiss. His protective instincts were fully aroused. Attentively he helped fasten his young bride's cloak, as they graciously excused themselves.

The journey back to their cottage was made in silence, with an eye to every shadow, an ear to every noise. Behind their locked and barred door, they collectively sighed in relief. Soron gathered his wife into his arms, hugging her, comforting her. The city of Venecia was no longer a safe haven. Their marriage had caused divisions, created enemies. But, until they knew who was behind the attack all they could do was to be careful and alert. Venecia was now a dangerous city for them.

...

The salty coastal air mingled in with the scents of the market. The blend was exotic and yet familiar, it was one of the things Soron liked most about Venecia. Today as he strolled through the market with his lovely Velaina he smiled, the previous night's near fatal events momentarily forgotten. Glancing at the blonde-haired, blue-eyed goddess he called wife, he noted the color in her cheeks and the sparkle in her eye. When his glance went down to the protruding belly, he saw an unmistakable sign of her carrying a special package inside. Motherhood suits her, he thought to himself. She is as lovely today as the first time I saw her.

His musings on the bliss and happiness brought into his life by this wonderful woman were cut short by pain in his hand. His lovely wife was squeezing the life out of it. Velaina had always been able to sense the emotions of others, a trait shared among a few of those with magic blood; motherhood had heightened this mysterious ability. Her clenching of his hand was a warning. Someone in the market had evil intentions toward them.

Now aware of her concerns, Soron casually looked around. The multitude of vendors and throngs of citizens mulling their way through the large city market had now caught his attention. He did not need to share his wife's magical sense to note the pair of men ahead of them, who were trying not to stare as they stalked Soron and his young bride. Stopping at a spiced meat cart, Soron stalled. He inspected the cooking spiced meat, haggling with the vendor all the while watching for signs of other possible dangers. Two more men who had been walking in the same general direction as they were had suddenly stopped walking when Soron stopped at the food vendors stall.

Soron smiled at Velaina as he took a bite of his hot and savory chunk of charbroiled venison. Pretending to make funny observation, he smiled then leaned in to whisper, "I see four of them. What does your magic tell you?"

Velaina gave a half-hearted attempt at laughter, understanding her husband's ruse. She leaned in close and whispered back, "Five. There is one farther back in the crowd. Are we going to be okay?"

Soron gave her a reassuring smile. "Of course we are my love. I waited my whole life for the joy of having such a lovely wife. Nothing in this world will thwart me from seeing my child born. Besides, five men is not enough, not nearly enough." Soron was not idly boasting to his wife. On more than one occasion, he had been in a battle where the odds were stacked even higher against him. His being alive today—along with a multitude of scars across his body—were testimony to his battle skills. Knowing the number and intention of his enemies before their impending attack was a huge benefit to Soron. He could now manipulate the circumstances to increase his odds of victory. His first priority was the safety of his wife and unborn child.

Leaving the food vendors stall, he steered Velaina in a new direction. Before, they had been meandering through the markets, heading north towards the city center. Now he veered west toward the nearest stable. As they approached the building, Soron was able to get a few quick glances of the men following them. The assassins were closing in. They could tell the stable was the intended destination and likely thought it was a good place to spring their attack.

Walking into the cool, darker and confined space of the stable, Soron quickly surveyed his surroundings. Against one wall leaned a pair of tools: a pitchfork and a shovel. These would have to suffice, he thought to himself. He was carrying his dagger but other weapons would help. He grabbed the shovel in both hands and drove the handle down across his raised knee, snapping off the end of the shovel off. He handed both parts to Velaina. "If anyone gets close to you use the metal end as a shield and spear them with the jagged end of the handle." Soron paused, looking around. "Hide in that first empty stall; they won't be able to get to you without passing me."

Velaina silently took the makeshift shield and spear from her husband. In the two years they had been together, she had never seen this side of the gentle giant she loved. She knew his history as a warrior but never witnessed the intensity of his anger or any hint of his violent past. She could sense the change in his mood today. The deep inner rage for the unknown assailants plotting to harm his family was disguised by a cool veneer of calm. That calm, a product of training and experience, gave him the level-headedness to harness his internal rage. Velaina no longer felt fear, only pity for the families of the men about to die. The assassins deserved no mercy.

Closing the thick oak door of the stable stall behind Velaina, Soron turned his focus to the coming battle. First, he took out his dagger and whittled the bottom of the pitchfork until it was sharp. The stable tool so handy for moving hay was now a two-sided weapon as deadly as he would need against most foes. Then with the loose soil and hay of the stable floors hiding the deadly pointed addition he had made to the already dangerous tool, he stood waiting.

The stable doors slowly opened. Carefully, four men slid into the building. Silently they stalked closer, pulling out clubs and swords, making no pretense of being in the stable other than to deliver death. As they approached Soron, they formed a horseshoe around him. The stall door protected his back but he now had attackers on both sides.

"Gentlemen, tis a fine day that brings us here together at this moment in time," said Soron in a solemn voice. "If you don't mind I would like to say a small prayer for those about to leave us for the next world and whatever gods occupy it," with his head slightly lowered as if in prayer.

The thug to his left gave a grunt of dismissal before replying. "You can save the sermon, your highness. Northern prince or not, you are about to die and your body will be thrown to the pigs. No royal burial for you." The would-be assassin smirked as he shifted his sword between his hands.

Another of the men spoke, "Now Rory, don't be so hasty. This is a nasty bit of business no matter how you look at it. Having the gods' mercy might not be a bad thing. Someone *is* going to die any moment now. Only the number remains in question. Let the prince say a word or two."

Soron scanned the faces of the other two men. The first seemed to be nodding in agreement with the second man, while the last warrior's stoic face showed nothing. Soron took the silence as a sign to continue. "Right then, may all the gods witness this. As we stand here today, four souls are going to the beyond. The crime they attempt: murder of a woman and unborn child. May the fate they suffer in the next realm be slower and infinitely more painful than the end I bring to their worthless existences today."

The attackers were taken aback. They had thought the prince would ask for mercy upon himself and his family, not say words to damn them. As they realized the significance of his words and started to react, it was already too late.

As the grunter to his left moved to attack, Soron flew into action. With his left hand holding the pitchfork, he blocked the swinging sword. As the tines of the pitchfork caught the incoming sword, Soron smoothly, with practiced hand, pulled his dagger out and stepped into the assailant. His dagger slid into the man's belly. The attacker's eyes bulged as the blade worked its way through his innards. While the man slumped forward dying, Soron reversed his direction, pulling back hard on the pitchfork.

As he lunged backwards, Soron stabbed the second attacker in the throat with the sharpened handle of the pitchfork. The assassin had not noticed the deadly modification before the wood punctured his throat. Using his momentum Soron spun around towards the stoic attacker, throwing his dagger into the man's chest. The man looked at the blade in his chest then up at in Soron in disbelief. Without delay, Soron quickly grabbed the sword out of the hand of the second dying warrior.

The fourth warrior already had his sword speeding through the air towards Soron. Soron was able to raise his borrowed sword in time to partially block the attack. His enemy's sword sliced into his shoulder before his blade rose to counter. Soron pushed the attacker back. The man stumbled back, unused to dealing with the extraordinary strength of a northerner, he was caught off guard by the forceful push. Soron surged forward, bringing down an overhand attack. The off balance mercenary tried to block the attack, but the mighty force continued down into the man's head despite his attempts to stop it. Pulling the sword out of the assassin's skull, Soron took a step back and recovered his dagger from the body of the once stoic third man. Despite the four dead men at his feet, Soron stood ready, weapons in hand, waiting. Finally, slowly entering the stable, the fifth attacker made himself seen.

The man wore a long grey cloak with a hood; the cloak hid the man's face and body well. The mysterious man undid his cloak, letting it slide to the ground. Although the cloak was gone, the man's identity was still unknown; however much could be told from his physical appearance. The well-toned muscles, encased in a honey-brown skin, hid behind a veritable map of tattoo's covering the man's entire body. Even his face and clean-shaven skull were covered with intricate designs. Soron had seen many sailors with tattoos and had heard of the tribes of island warriors that would celebrate the death of an enemy with an additional marking. The tattooed warrior stood there, his eyes going over the scene in the stable, looking at the carnage of blood stained hay where the four bodies rested. He then looked at Soron standing defiantly before the stable stall that he was blocking. Finally the warrior spoke in a low and surprisingly warm voice. "The man who hired me said he was sending these men and I would just make sure the job was done. I told him these men were a waste of time. He should have sent for a half dozen of my tribesman. He laughed and said these men had never failed and I should not worry so much."

Soron was not fooled by the friendly tone of the warrior's voice. He knew from experience that when a snake is rattling its tail is not when it is most dangerous. When the noise stops, that is when it attacks. This warrior, like a deadly viper, would soon strike.

Ignoring the warrior's attempt at conversation, Soron simply prepared himself. He lowered his body slightly, putting the weight of his large lithe body on the balls of his feet, relaxing his hands while keeping his eyes focused on the warrior.

The warrior smiled, this northern prince was no fool. He pulled out his ornate silver handled scimitar. Stepping sideways almost like a dancer, he moved rhythmically from side to side as he worked his way towards Soron. In an explosion of cat-like speed, the tribal warrior lunged at Soron, his blade slicing through the air. Soron's sword adeptly blocked the attack, while the threat of Soron's dagger kept the warrior from moving any closer. The men stood there trading parries, a flurry of attacks and counter-attacks that displayed the deadly skills of both men.

The tattooed warrior drew first blood, catching Soron with a quick strike that sliced a shallow but long cut across his thigh. Neither man slowed at this successful blow. The tribal assassin continued to press the attack, his scimitar sliced through the air only to find the cold steel of Soron's blades blocking each attack. The warrior, thinking his opponent should be slowing soon, spun around in a pirouette. The risky maneuver brought him alongside the northern prince and should have ended with his scimitar in the large man's back. Instead, the dancing blade found nothing but air. Soron had countered his maneuver with a spin of his own. His dagger found a home between the warrior's shoulder blades.

As the assassin dropped to the stable floor, Soron slumped against the stable wall. His wounds were superficial, but the loss of blood and physical excursion of battle had exhausted him.

Velaina opened the door to the stall and reached out for her husband. Ignoring the bodies on the floor, she grabbed the assassin's cloak off the ground. Taking Soron's dagger from him, she cut the fabric into long narrow strips to secure his wounds. Silently she worked while her husband regained his breath. With the bleeding stopped, they cautiously headed home, keeping a wary eye on the shadows for further danger.

Back in their cottage, Velaina cleaned Soron's wounded shoulder and thigh, and then applied a salve. As she carefully worked on the small wounds, they discussed the attack. Velaina had sensed the men's intentions during the walk. All five attackers had the same goal: death of her, her husband and their unborn child. She shared this insight with Soron. "Those men were hired to kill the three of us, I could read their emotions. My death was more important to them than yours Soron. They want to prevent the birth of our child. Two attempts on our lives in two days. Someone wants us dead very badly."

Soron sighed, he had feared as much. Someone had gone to a lot of effort; poison, then a group of four assassins with a fifth warrior as a backup in case they failed. Whoever wanted them dead was a dangerous enemy, and since they wanted Velaina dead to prevent the birth of their child, it seemed likely that the root of the attack had to do with the forbidden crossing of bloodlines. The question was whose. His father was a northern king, with many enemies. Her father was a Baltan king, in a land where magic and intrigue were commonplace. The threat could have come from either family. They had hoped living here in Venecia would keep them arm's length away from the politics and superstitions of their families. That hope died with the attack. "We shall leave in the morning."

"Where shall we go?" asked Velaina.

Soron looked at his royal wife with a sorrow filled gaze, saddened by the turn of events forcing them from their home. "East, we will go to the one of the small villages south of the Applomean Mountains. Those villages don't belong to any kingdom. We shall go and live as commoners for the safety of our child."

Velaina embraced her husband. To the east they would go. She placed a protective hand across her baby bump.

Chapter one

LYING ON THE COOL mossy forest floor, Nathan wondered what the heck just happened. One minute he had been running through the forest chasing his friend Ava, the next minute he was looking up through the trees into the blue sky above. While he sat there trying to regain his senses, he noticed how interesting the sky looked from this angle, sprawled out flat on his backside. The delicate white clouds deviously danced through the treetops while the sun wrestled with them, fingers of sunlight trying to push their way into the trees. Nathan would have stayed there a while enjoying the artistic display had not giggles and the shadow of the girl standing above him brought him back to reality.

"You okay?" Ava asked demurely, as she tried not to giggle. Her concern for his well-being was suspect. He detected a distinct lack of sincerity in her query.

"Ugh, my head hurts. What the heck happened?" Nathan had a sneaking suspicion that he knew what happened but waited for a reply anyway.

"You were running past that big cedar when you tripped over a stick," said Ava.

Ava was not smiling but Nathan saw a look of mischief written all over her freckled face. The dimples were a dead giveaway despite her best attempts to look contrite.

Nathan, still lying on the ground, tilted his head back and looked behind him to the big cedar in question. Sure enough, a long stick sat at the base of the tree. He was sure the stick had not been there a few moments ago. "Where did that come from? I totally didn't see that there at all."

Ava broke into laughter, no longer able to hold a straight face. "Well it may not have been there the whole time. I might have been holding it and accidentally lifted it when you came around the tree."

Nathan groaned. Her lifting the stick just as he was running by certainly did not sound like an accident. "That is not playing fair, tripping and trying to kill me is not part of the game."

Ava smiled to herself, getting away from Nathan was getting harder all the time; he was getting bigger and faster. Luckily, she could still outsmart him and was willing to play dirty to win. "Well you always catch me if I don't cheat. Besides, you are barely bleeding. You are certainly not dying... I swear sometimes you are the biggest wimp ever." Ava reached down and wiped a small bit of blood off his cut lip. "All better. Now let's go, we are almost there and I want to pick flowers." The 'there' Ava mentioned was a small meadow hidden within a fortress of thick pines. A gentle flowing creek sliced through the meadow and, at the bottom end of the meadow, ran into a small dark pond that was great for swimming and fishing. It was their special place.

"Since when do you pick flowers?" asked Nathan. He tried to picture Ava as a demure lady, dressing fancy and picking flowers, but the image didn't fit at all. Ava was anything but ladylike.

"Oh shut up, I promised Rose I would bring her some flowers. It was the only way to keep her from tagging along," said Ava. She didn't mind bringing her little sister once in a while but sometimes it was nice when it was just the two of them.

Ava grabbed Nathan's arm and yanked him to his feet. Side by side, they walked through the forest to the waiting meadow. It was a gorgeous sunny day and despite Ava's commands to get moving, they were in no hurry.

While Ava picked through the assortment of wild flowers growing throughout the meadow Nathan carefully tiptoed his way across the top of a mossy log, which had fallen across the creek. Keeping his arms out wide for balance, he carefully walked one foot directly in front of the other over the slippery moss covered surface.

"If you fall in, I will laugh so hard." Ava said while she sat down beside the pond, placing the flowers at the water's edge so the stems stayed wet. She gave Nathan a dirty look that warned him not to make any more comments about the wildflowers. "Hurry up and get to your side of the pond. I am going to kick your butt." There really was no winner to this game but her competitive nature made everything a contest.

Nathan laughed to himself at Ava's bold exclamation. *As if*, he thought to himself as he claimed his usual spot, parking himself beside his left over cache of pebbles. They were sitting on opposite ends of the pond playing their customary game of splash, a simple game of throwing rocks at each other's feet attempting to get the other player wet without the rock hitting the shore, when Ava froze mid throw. Not wanting to make a sudden move, she slowly lowered her hand and spoke to Nathan in a soft deliberate voice. "Nathan turn around. There's a wolf behind you."

Nathan read the expression on Ava's now pale face. This was not one of her normal jokes, which she often tried to play on him; there was a touch of fear in her voice. Slowly he turned and scanned the edge of the forest. Ava was not lying; a big grey wolf was sitting there looking right at him.

Nathan, surprisingly calm, looked back at the large predator. The wolf stopped its advance. For what seemed like forever, the wolf and Nathan just sat there staring at each other. After several minutes, the wolf walked towards Nathan.

Now nervous and starting to get scared, Ava spoke, "Nathan-"

Nathan cut her off mid-sentence before she could suggest some plan involving him jumping into the pond and her throwing rocks at the large and potentially dangerous beast. "Shhh, it is okay Ava. He is not going to hurt me."

Nathan did not know how he sensed it, but he was certain that the wolf posed no threat. Even as it continued walking closer and closer, Nathan did not panic. Finally, the beast was right in front of Natthan— so close he could reach out and touch the magnificent beast. The wolf had golden eyes, glossy healthy fur and glorious black and grey markings. The animal was now near enough to Nathan that he could hear its breathing. His heart pounded with excitement. Nathan was fascinated by what was happening. The wolf stopped and sniffed at Nathan then studied Nathan's face. Nathan could tell the wolf was curious about him. He was not sure why, but it was almost seemed like he could understand the wolf, as if he could read the thoughts of the creature. Seconds passed before the wolf turned and walked back into the forest, looking back only once, as if it too was unsure of what to make of this meeting.

Once the wolf disappeared back into the forest, Nathan turned and looked at Ava. Some of the color had returned to her face. He gave her a confident grin. "See I told you it was going to be okay."

Ava could not believe what had just occurred. Nathan was not normally that brave. He had just sat there while the wolf came right up to him. "I can't believe that just happened! Weren't you even a little scared?" asked Ava.

"No," Nathan said before pausing for a moment. That wasn't totally true, he thought to himself. "Well, I was scared when you said there was a wolf behind me and your face turned white, but when I looked at the wolf the fear went away… I just knew it was going to be okay." Nathan's face showed he was just as bewildered by this as she was.

Nathan and Ava walked back to the village discussing the strange event that had just taken place. "It was so weird Nathan. Like the two of you were talking to each other. I've never heard of a wolf walking up to a man like that before."

Nathan agreed that he had never heard of such a thing either. And to himself he admitted that yes, it had kind of felt like the wolf had been talking to him. But that wasn't right either; it wasn't talking to him as much as connecting to him. Strange… strange indeed.

Chapter two

SORON SWUNG HIS hammer, striking the hot metal sitting on the anvil. He enjoyed the work. The methodical pounding of the iron was soothing to him. Soron took pleasure from turning iron into useful tools or, when the opportunity presented itself, into artistic creations. Elderwood was a small village. If not for the traders passing through, he would not have enough business. Luckily, the traders who frequented these roads sought out his talents. He had a reputation as a creator of fine jewelry and tools.

Soron created items favored by traders for their black color and exceptional quality. Despite his being a foreigner, any question of his origins had long ago been forgotten by the long years he and his family had spent in the village.

Today, Nathan joined his father in the workshop. Nathan at fourteen was just now growing bigger than the other youths in his village, a marker of his northern heritage inherited from Soron. But one look at his blue eyes gave away that, while his father came from the north, his mother came from even farther away. Velaina's blonde hair and blue eyes stood out as much as her husband's size. Her beautiful blue eyes hinted at her lineage being from Balta, a kingdom in the continent of Mithbea.

Soron handed the pair of tongs, which held the metal rod, to Nathan.

Nathan eagerly took over. He loved watching his father work, but much preferred it when he got the rare chance to put his lessons into action. He jumped at the opportunity. The biggest challenge with using the forge was the intense heat. Once the metal turned a dark orange, Nathan knew it was time to take it out of the heat. Next Nathan carefully sprinkled graphite and phosphorus dust over the molten hot iron rod. He then placed the rod on the anvil and hammered the metal.

Soron watched carefully as his son worked on the metal. He frowned for a moment as Nathan let the metal twist. He did not interrupt his son, as he was curious to what his intentions were.

Nathan rarely pushed the limits of his skills as he did today. As the metal continued to twist, a pattern emerged. An intricate pattern of folds appearing to look like braided metal formed. The process was slow and tedious. Sweat poured off his brow as he took a metal chisel and engraved the final touches on his work.

Soron said nothing while Nathan put the bracelet into a bucket of water. The water steamed as the metal cooled into its final shape. Finally, after a few minutes Nathan brought out the bracelet and nervously handed the finished product over to his father.

Stepping outside of his workshop, Soron held the bracelet to the light to examine it closely. The bracelet now looked like woven vines with tiny leaves along the side. *Impressive,* Soron thought as he inspected his son's work. "It is beautiful," Soron told his boy as he handed back the bracelet.

Nathan nodded his head and smiled.

"A very tricky design. What are you planning on doing with it? Giving one of the village girls a present?" Soron teased.

Nathan blushed and looked sheepishly down at the bracelet. "I didn't know if it would work or not, I just wanted to try, and no it's not for some girl. It is for Mother, tomorrow is her birthday," Nathan said.

Soron grabbed the boy by the shoulder and pulled him in for a hug while messing the boy's dark and shaggy hair with his free hand. "It is a wonderful job and a present worthy of a queen. Your mother will be proud to wear it."

After Nathan finished at the blacksmith shop with his father, he spotted Ava coming out of her family's house. He walked over to her. "Hey Ava."

She smiled. "Hey wolf boy, let's go for a walk."

Nathan did not mind her teasing; she was his best friend and despite her sharp tongue was always there for him. They walked through the village, stopped and chatted with the widow Noggin.

She was on her front steps sweeping up dirt a patron had dragged all over her plank floors. "Hello Nathan, Ava. What are you two up to?"

 "Oh nothing much, just going for a walk, maybe head towards the creek," Ava replied.

"I am going to make some pies tonight. If you bring me back some apples I will pay you in pie."

Nathan and Ava jumped at this deal. Widow Noggin was an excellent cook and made the best pies in the village. "You got yourself a deal" Ava piped up for the both of them. Nathan grabbed the large empty basket from Miss Noggin and ran to catch Ava, who was already running towards the orchard.

As they picked fruit, Ava climbed up one of the biggest trees. She liked to climb to the middle and top branches where, she insisted, the best fruit came from. Nathan knew it was just an excuse to climb, but there was no point arguing about it as long she picked apples while playing on the high-up branches. While working they discussed the previous day's adventure.

"I thought that wolf would eat you, and then I would have to drag your half-eaten carcass back to the village to show your dad that a wolf killed you and not me."

Nathan laughed. "Mom is the one you would have had to worry about. She knows all about poisons, she would make you a tasty pie and poof your belly explodes and you are dead."

Ava scrunched her face up. "That's gross Nathan."

"Hey, you were the one who was carrying my half-eaten carcass into town."

Ava laughed. "Yes but you getting eaten by a wolf is possible. Your mom poisoning me is ridiculous, she likes me." As she explained the flaw in Nathan's logic, she picked a worm-eaten apple and threw it at Nathan.

 Nathan dodged the projectile, taking a seat, refusing to get into an apple tossing fight with his friend. He had lost way too many already. Besides her quick wit, one of her best qualities was that she threw with more accuracy than any boy in the village did. Any contest involving throwing was a losing proposition. "Well, I really don't think I was in any danger. It seemed like the wolf knew me." Nathan knew it sounded strange but he really had sensed that the wolf posed no threat.

"I don't care, it is just really weird. Have you told your parents about it yet?"

Nathan was not sure he wanted to try explaining to an adult how a wolf walked right up to him, looked him over and then walked away. It sounded a little unbelievable. "No, but I suppose you are right for once. I will tell mom about it."

Another apple whipped by Nathan's head. He barely ducked in time. "What do you mean 'for once'?"

Chapter three

VELAINA LOVED THE days she got to spend with Nathan. She and Soron shared the responsibility of training their son. On Soron's days, they worked in the blacksmith shop, on hers she took her son out into the forests and swamps to learn about the different plants and wildlife. Velaina came from a family of healers and herbalists. Her potions and salves sold to healers all over the continent. Her herbal skills were as much in demand and as valuable as her husband's metal works.

Today they were on the edges of the Great Northern swamp. A vast isolated murky and vile land thought by most people to be cursed. She knew this swamp released a large amount of methane. If you weren't careful it would cause you to pass out, usually into shallow water were drowning often followed. A few foolish travelers and injured animals had died this way and the bones left future travelers to wonder at the deadly swamplands. These bones were at the heart of the curse stories but Velaina discarded the stories for the misinformed gossip they were.

After collecting some of the swamp reeds that grew along the banks of the dreaded swamp, Velaina and Nathan retreated to higher ground to have a quick lunch, they sat together under tree watching the birds flying above and diving into the swampy waters, preying on the fish beneath the surface of the murky waters.. Later they would continue further into the swamp in search of other valuable herbs. Many such as bilbub ferns, a dark purple flowered plant with a sweet almost candy-like aroma grew only in the treacherous lands.

Velaina opened her small basket and brought out their lunch as they sat under a large willow tree, enjoying the shade it provided from the bright sun above. As she handed Nathan his lunch he took the sandwich from her outreached hand and returned a small handsomely wrapped package in its place.

Velaina, surprised at this unexpected offering, looked at the package wrapped in balsam leaf and twine. "What is this?" she asked.

Nathan smiled at his mother. "You didn't think I would forget your birthday did you mother? It is your gift."

Velaina was very proud of her thoughtful son. With curiosity, she opened the package; inside she found a beautiful bracelet. In the shade of the tall willow, the dark metal seemed almost black, yet the speckles in it caught the leaf filtered sunlight and sparkled like tiny stars on a dark night. The intricate pattern of woven leaves reminded her of ivy curling around the base of a young cherry tree.

"It's gorgeous, Nathan, thank you so much. You must have done a lot of bargaining to get your father to make such a bracelet that won't be sold." Velaina put the bracelet onto her arm. The dark metal contrasted perfectly with her light golden brown skin.

Nathan smiled with pride. "No mother. I made it for you myself. Father let me forge my own rod yesterday."

Velaina cast her eyes back and forth from her young son, who was beaming with pride, and the beautiful piece of artwork that now decorated her arm. She knew Nathan was not lying to her but the bracelet was a very intricate and detailed piece of work. She could not help but be impressed that her young son had done this himself. After the initial shock of discovering the depth of his talent, she realized that it shouldn't have been that big of a surprise. Nathan was a clever and creative child. His northern strength mixed well with the creative mind and dexterity of hand that came from her people.

While watching her son, Velaina thought about the many hours training and education that she and Soron spent on their son. One day he would need all the skills they could pass onto him, but that was a darker thought for another day. Velaina pushed that thought away. It was far better to bask in the beauty of the day, be thankful for their quiet life, and enjoy her son's wonderful gift. Life had not always been so good. Tranquility was to be enjoyed.

"Mom, I need to tell you something." Nathan gave her a serious look as he spoke. "The weirdest thing happened to me. The other day, Ava and I were sitting in the meadow by the pool..." Nathan paused for a second to gather his thoughts.

"Nathan, Ava is a beautiful girl. It is natural for you to like her, I just hope—."

Nathan looked at his mother "What? No, mom. That is not what I am talking about. Nothing happened between Ava and me."

Velaina gave a sigh of relief; whatever Nathan was going to tell her now was not nearly as terrifying as where she had thought this conversation was going. "Sorry son, I thought we would be having a birds and bees conversation. I'm glad to hear it is not time for that yet... Now what was so weird?"

Nathan gave her a funny look. The birds and bees? What was she talking about?

She laughed, sensing his discomfort at this idea. "I'm sorry son. Continue your story."

He cleared his voice before continuing. "We were sitting on opposite sides of the ponds just playing around when Ava tells me there is a wolf behind me. I turn and there is a big grey timber wolf sitting there watching me. I stare back at it just watching. Then it slowly walks right up to me, sits there for a few minutes, sniffs me a couple times then turns around and walks back into the forest. That was the weird part. What do you think it means?"

Velaina's heart raced, despite her calm exterior. She had expected that one day she would have a conversation like this but still was unprepared now that it was happening. Pretending to be calm and indifferent, she replied. "Well it means that the wolf did not feel like having you for lunch, and for that I am grateful. If something ate you, who would make me such nice jewelry? Now let us pack up, it's time to head home," Velaina replied as she gave her son a big hug. Picking more herbs would have to wait. Velaina needed have to have a discussion with Nathan's father before she admitted the truth of the wolf to her son.

...

Later that night while Nathan slept, Velaina shared with Soron the news of Nathan's encounter with the wolf. She relayed the event as Nathan had described to her, along with her sense that Nathan had held back explaining the full story. "It is likely that the wolf sensed magic and was attracted to him. It will probably happen again with other animals."

Soron absorbed this information. They had talked about the possibility that this might happen one day. Velaina was a'kil, an Ingla word for magic blood. She had gifts the villagers knew nothing of, such as the ability to sense people's emotions. This ability was how she always knew when Nathan was lying. Soron's family also had a history of having a'kil among them. The chances of their son being born with magic blood had always been a concern.

Being a'kil was not bad, most born with the gift were happy to have it. However, it also came with great risk.

The problem was that most Solotinians feared magic and over the years most a'kil were killed or driven off. Most a'kil hid their talents or moved to safer, more magic-tolerant lands. Velaina and Soron had chosen to live in a small village outside of any of the kingdoms partly for that reason. If Nathan was a'kil, it was better to live in a small village where hopefully no one would fear him if he started to show signs of magic. Even in a small village, there were many who shunned magic as evil. Nathan's life would be changing drastically soon.

As Soron pondered the repercussions of this information, Velaina continued to think about Nathan's encounter with the wolf. Animals being attracted to and forming bonds with a'kil did happen, so the wolf was a very good indicator that Nathan was in fact an a'kil. Soron had already known that Nathan might be magic blood, like her and others of his own family. Lately, Soron had been thinking that Nathan's ability to make black steel and how easily he shaped it were much too good for someone his age and size. Being a'kil would explain this.

"Your bracelet that Nathan made is far better than any fourteen-year-old should be able to make. Truth is, it is better than even I can make. I have suspected for a little while now that there was some magic involved. The wolf only confirms it. Nathan is a'kil," said Soron.

Velaina looked down at her bracelet. It truly was a beautiful piece and magic or not she was proud Nathan could make something so wonderful. But this was still a troubling revelation. Being a'kil in Solotine was dangerous. "Do we raise him here or take him to Mithbea?"

They both pondered this question. They were all happy living in Elderwood and, for now, were safe. A few of its residents, such as the previous blacksmith, resented them. But for the most part, the villagers were their friends now. If Nathan developed other magical powers, or people started noticing the ones he had, they would probably need to go to Mithbea and the kingdom of Balta. Mithbea was a land where magic was more common and better accepted than Solotine.

Finally, her husband answered the question. "For now, we stay. I shall start training the boy in weapons. If his magic continues to grow, then you can start teaching him about it. But for now, we will leave it. If things change, we shall go to Balta."

Chapter four

"WHEN YOU ARE DONE with your breakfast don't bother putting your shoes on. We are working inside today," said Velaina.

Nathan was surprised by this. The weather was nice outside and rarely did they stay in on such a nice day unless she had a particular lesson in mind. More often than not, those lessons would wait for a wet or cold day. Done eating, Nathan joined his mother.

"Yesterday I made up several potions. Today you will identify them," said Velaina to Nathan as they entered into the small workroom. It looked like a small storage room filled with shelves full of herb, barks, bags of different ground plants ground into powders, bottles of fluids and medicine-filled jars. On the main workbench were four large vials.

Knowing that this was his project for the day, Nathan took his time and examined the vials one at a time.

The first two vials took Nathan very little time to identify. Within minutes he recognized the ingredients. The first two vials were common concoctions that Velaina made to sell. "Lavender, honey and white birch bark in spring water, used to ail a sore stomach or headache. Used for cleaning wounds, but best to boil it down to a salve for that. The second one is black current, pine needle, and swamp pod mixed in cedar sap."

Nathan smiled. he knew by his mother's silence that the next two vials would be much trickier. With this in mind Nathan took his time with the third vial. Looking closely at the vial he studied the dark red, almost purple, fluid. He gave the vial a small swirl and watched the fluid swish around in the vial.

The fluid moved quick and easily but was a slight bit thicker than the contents of the first vial. Again, he went through the practiced motions of holding the vial away from himself while he uncorked it then wafted its scent up towards his nose. The familiar fruity and pungent aroma filled his nose. Nathan frowned; this one seemed too easy. Was she trying to trick him? He decided to go through all the identifying steps before making a judgment on its contents. Nathan took a mint leaf and dropped some of the mystery fluid onto it. Carefully he folded the leaf and rubbed the drops between the leaf halves paying particular attention to keep the potion off his skin. He took a close look at the mint leaf. Against the dark green leaf, the stain appeared almost black. The leaf veins a dark red.

Next, Nathan went back to the shelf behind the table and selected an empty vial. He took a jug of spring water and filled the vial half-full of water and added two drops of the fluid to the water. He let the drops sit for a minute and watched the fluid slowly start to disperse into the water. He vigorously stirred the mixture until the water turned a light purple.

A deep frown set into his face. Nathan walked to a smaller cabinet in the corner of the room and took out a small bottle. Returning to the workbench, he added a small drop from the bottle into the vial. In an instant, the water turned from a light purple to a hazy orange. Nathan looked up at his mother in surprise. "It is poison and a really strong one!"

Finally Velaina moved from the wall where she had been quietly observing Nathan as he worked on the vials. "Yes, it's elderberry wine with velmadine leaf extract. It looks, smells and tastes like ordinary elderberry wine yet the smallest sip is strong enough to kill a man."

Nathan was surprised to hear this. He knew his mother had a vast knowledge of poisons and the remedies for them but never had she given him a poison to identify.

"What's in the fourth vial?" asked Velaina.

Nathan looked again at the vial of poison then looked into his mother's piercing blue eyes. "The fourth vial is crushed ramble cactus and juniper needle in apple cider."

Velaina smiled and nodded. "That is correct, but how did you know without looking? "

Nathan finally relaxed a bit and returned her smile. "It's the antidote for velmadine poison. It had to be in apple or plum cider for the acidity to be right. And since there was a chance I might have drunk it, you would have used the apple cider. If I had drank the poison you would have felt bad about me spending the next couple hours retching and vomiting. You would have used the apple cider so I wouldn't spend rest of day complaining about throwing up nasty plum juice, not to mention the after-effects on my bowels."

Velaina smiled softly at her son. She hated to give the types of lessons where the results could be so unpleasant. Sometimes the only way to learn about how different remedies and poisons worked was to feel them. A few years prior, during Nathan's unguarded curiosity period, Nathan had a bad time with a remedy that required plum cider to choke it down. Worse than choking it down was the hour spent bringing the concoction back up. He never looked at plums the same way after that, nor did he trust sweet smelling concoctions in glass vials.

"If we don't learn from our mistakes," Velaina prompted...

"There is no use in making them," finished Nathan. "Why do you make poisons, mother?" he asked. "Do you get requests for them?"

Velaina studied his face. The look was earnest. "I do not sell poisons. My art is intended for healing. Healing sometimes requires potions to negate the effects of poisons for those evil ones who would poison their foes or friends for power or money. If ever in a hostile land, or an unknown place, dip your finger in any offered wine or drink. Touch it only to your lip and wait. If your tongue detects an off taste, if your senses tingle or your tongue feels numb, pretend to spill your drink." Velaina thought back to that incident long ago where that very habit had saved all three of their lives.

Nathan heeded her words. "'Tis a good thing I'm not rich or powerful. No one needs to kill me to gain a kingdom. It is quite safe to drink the wine in these parts!" he teased, naively unaware of the discomfort his teasing caused his mother.

Velaina took a deep breathe. Life had not always been quiet and peaceful, nor were there any promises it would remain that way. One could hope, but considering their secrets, preparing for unwanted eventualities was wise, if not a necessity. Nathan had a sheltered existence thus far. She could only hope it stayed that way.

Chapter five

IS THERE ANYTHING BETTER in the world than warm apple pie? Nathan thought to himself as he took another bite of the delicious dish. Earlier that afternoon, Ms. Noggins had let Ava know that today she was making good on her promise of pie in exchange for the apples they had picked for her and that she and Nathan could come by in an hour or so to get them right out of the oven.

Sitting at one of the few tables in Ms. Noggin's Inn, the Burning Candle, Nathan and Ava had a whole pie sitting in front of them. Well, a whole pie, minus the two rather large pieces the pair were devouring.

"One piece each, right?" Ava mumbled between bites.

"Yes. We will save the rest for after we get back from the games." Today was Sunday, and every Sunday the children of the village would gather in the forest and play bartoh. Bartoh involved a lot of running, so being stuffed full of pie would be a very bad idea.

Ava finished her piece of pie, licked the last few flakes of pastry off her finger, and gave Nathan a big smile. "Okay maybe just two pieces," she conceded before cutting herself another large piece of the warm, delicious desert.

Nathan took the last bite of his first piece and was reaching for a second piece before he even finished the first. "Right, but this is it. No more pie before bartoh…"

"I can't believe we ate the whole pie," said Ava. She then let out a loud burp and rubbed her belly in satisfaction.

Nathan chuckled, "Nice one! You are such a lady."

Ava almost looked offended by this statement as she reached across the table and gave Nathan a push. With a thump, he hit the ground, falling off his bench.

"Oof. Hey, why did you do that?"

Ava sat up straight and in her most prim and proper voice, spoke. "A lady never appreciates her manners being questioned by a servant." She then let out another even louder burp.

Nathan groaned. "Hmmph, servant my eye. Give me a hand up I'm too stuffed with pie to get up on my own."

They both laughed as she got up from her bench grabbing Nathan's hand, yanking him to his feet.

"Come on let's get down to the forest," said Ava.

Bartoh was a simple game. Two teams each had a scarf, which would be hung around a tree on their side of the creek. The first team to get the scarf across the creek won. Each team comprised of a troll, a witch (or warlock as some of the boys insisted on being called) and knights. If a troll touched you, then you were dead, unless someone saved you.

Only a witch or warlock was able to save dead players. Touching a dead player revived them. The player was now able to walk back to their side of the creek. Once they got back across the creek, they were alive and able to go back to hunting for the scarf. Each team had one witch and one troll, everyone else was a knight.

This particular Sunday, Nathan, Ava and Rose joined a team with Jordan, a small quick boy Rose's age. They were playing against Tomas, Regan, Sharon and Edward. Tomas and Sharon were both sixteen, while Regan and Edward were younger, like Rose and Jordan. Nathan, stuffed with pie, volunteered to be his team's troll; he figured hanging back and guarding the scarf would be much easier on his poor rumbling belly. Rose wanted to be the witch, leaving Ava and Jordan to be knights.

Once the scarves were in hanging on any tree within a hundred feet of the creek, the game would start.

As the game began, Nathan picked a old fat cedar tree to hide behind. It was only a couple paces away from the birch tree where they had placed their scarf. Nathan was confident from this position he would be able to see any knights racing up to grab the scarf. The bonus of this position was being able to rest his pie-filled belly while he waited for the enemy knights.

It took a quiet ten minutes before Nathan noted the first person start to come close enough to see the scarf. With a quick peak around the cedar, he saw Regan. Regan was almost to the scarf before Nathan jumped out and attacked. Despite the heavy lump of delicious apple pie sitting in his stomach, Nathan would have been more than quick enough to catch Regan if the younger boy had made one more step towards the scarf.

This was not the case though, because as soon as Regan noticed Nathan, he turned and bolted back towards the creek screaming "TROLL...." Nathan smirked; Regan was overly dramatic and loved to run off in terror at the first sign of a troll.

The next one to make an attempt was Tomas. The older boy had heard the screeching of Regan and quickly honed in on the scarf. Nathan had already returned to his hiding spot and was in position when Tomas came running up to the scarf. Just as he had when Regan appeared, Nathan sprung out to attack the knight before he could grab the scarf. While Regan had bolted off in the other direction, Tomas kept running towards the scarf. Nathan quickly positioned himself between the scarf and Tomas. Tomas made no move to change his direction. In fact, he ran harder once he saw Nathan get in front of the scarf.

Nathan readied himself. As soon as Tomas changed directions to try get around him, he would reach out and tag him. Any second now, any second now thought Nathan but the second never came. Instead of trying to get around Nathan, Tomas simply lowered his shoulder and ran right through him, knocking him hard into the ground. It was the second time this week Nathan found himself on his back looking up into the sky.

"What the heck, Tomas. You didn't even try to turn," said Nathan in frustration as he rose to his feet.

Tomas simply smirked at the younger boy. "Oops, I am sorry about that. But since you tagged me and I'm going to be here until a witch can rescue me, we should talk."

Nathan wanted to accept this apology but the smirk and tone of Tomas's voice were leading him to think it was not a very sincere apology. Warily, Nathan replied "Alright, sure. I tagged your shoulder with my face. Now what do you want to talk about?"

"I've been trying to get Ava to come spend time with me. She keeps saying no, that she has plans with you. I want you to stop bothering her so she has some free time."

Nathan did not believe it; this horse's ass had run him over on purpose and now was telling him to not hang out with Ava? As if he thought to himself. "Look, Tomas, who Ava spends time with is up to her. If she wants to spend time with you, I have no issues with that. But I'm not going to stop spending time with her on your say-so."

Tomas's smirk quickly turned to a sneer. "You're not getting it, Nathan. I am not asking you, I am telling you." With that, Tomas threw a punch right squarely onto the Nathan's already wounded jaw.

Nathan, caught unprepared, once again ended up on the ground. Tomas quickly took advantage and jumped onto Nathan's chest, pinning him to the ground. Tomas landed a couple more stiff jabs to the face while he held the younger boy down. "Are you going to leave her alone?"

Nathan, despite being in an indefensible position, did not intend to cower before his new rival. "Hell no!" Tomas rained down several more punches to Nathan's face.

As Sharon came running up to revive Tomas from the dead, she found him not lying on the ground pretending to be dead but on top of Nathan striking him. Sharon quickly made her presence know. "Cut that out you two. Tomas get off of him right now."

Tomas leaned down and whispered into Nathan's battered ear, "Better keep your mouth shut about this. Stay away from Ava or I'll thrash you again." Tomas got up, looked over at Sharon and gave her his best I'm innocent shrug. "Sorry about that, Nathan. You tagged me hard and I got angry. Here, get up," said Tomas as he reached towards Nathan.

Nathan, too groggy and hurt to bother arguing with Tomas's version of events, took Tomas's pro-offered hand and with a nod started to walk towards the village. "Okay, no problem Tomas stuff happens."

And, with that, so ended Nathan's least favorite game of bartoh ever. Nathan avoided the other kids and headed home.

As Nathan purposely set his path along a route that would avoid the other children, he pondered what had happened. Tomas had always been a horse's ass, that was nothing new, but usually he reserved his aggressive behavior for the older boys. When had Nathan become a threat to him? Nathan pondered. And when had Ava suddenly become such a lightning rod for comments? Lately both his parents had made comments about his relationship with her! Now, so was Tomas. What was he missing? Tomas always flirted with the older girls, pretty girls like Sharon. Did Tomas think Ava was pretty? Nathan reflected on this for a moment. Sure, she was the smartest kid around and pretty funny. She wasn't as curvy as Sharon but she certainly had an athletic and distinctly female body. I suppose if you like freckles and a button nose, flaming red hair and smoldering dark eyes... Oh damn! Nathan thought as realization hit him. His best friend was beautiful. No wonder life was getting complicated. Beautiful girls were trouble. Life would be easier if his best friend weren't a girl.

Chapter six

SORON AND VELAINA were sitting at the table when Nathan arrived back home. Nathan went out of his way to avoid them and head straight to his room.

Soron noticed that Nathan kept his head down and had avoided looking at them. When Velaina asked him if he would like something to eat, he said no, he was full from pie and just wanted to go to bed early. Soron saw from Velaina's raised eyebrow that Nathan had not told his mother the full truth. Soron gave the boy a couple hours to himself then went to see him in his room.

When Soron went to check on him, Nathan was lying on his bed but not asleep. Even in the low light of the bedroom, Soron could see Nathan's bruised and bloodied face. Ah, his first real fight. Is it just his pride that is wounded or is he injured? Soron thought to himself as he went over and sat on the corner of his son's bed. "Want to talk about it?"

Nathan had long ago stopped trying to figure out how his parents always seemed to know when something was wrong, especially his mother. When he could not avoid talking, Nathan had found the best way to deal with his parents was to just be honest.

"I got into a fight with Tomas today. I don't even know how it happened; one minute we were playing bartoh, the next he is sitting on top of me punching my face in, telling me to stop spending time with Ava."

"Ah, Tomas is a little jealous of you and Ava, is he? Well, can't blame the boy for that," said Soron with a little smile.

Nathan gave his father an incredulous look. "Father, do you not see my face? How can I not blame him for that?"

"I didn't say he might not deserve blame for his role in the fight, I meant his jealous is natural. Ava is an interesting girl; why wouldn't he be interested in her? Tell me, son, what bothers you more: that you were beaten or that he wants you to stop seeing Ava?"

Nathan pondered this one for a minute. He was a bit embarrassed and his face hurt like heck, but he had no intention of leaving Ava alone to allow the buffoon to court her. "I'm not sure, father… it's a little bit of both."

"Okay, son, one thing at a time. Are you going to avoid Ava so that Tomas stops rearranging your face?"

Nathan grimaced at his father's blunt question but did not hesitate to reply, "He can try rearranging my face every day. I'm not avoiding Ava because of that jerk. "

Soron grinned. His son may have lost the fight but he certainly was not a coward. "Now, I can't help you with the girl, but I can certainly help you prevent having your face look like that every day. Tomorrow, we will start changing up your training. Hold on for a minute, I will be right back."

Soron slipped out of his son's room, returning a couple minutes later with a small package of salve.

"Here. Put this on your face so the swelling goes down before your mother sees it. If she saw you tonight we would be burying poor Tomas tomorrow."

Nathan couldn't help but laugh, his mother probably would have over reacted. But he wasn't so sure about the way his father's choice of words. "Poor Tomas? Why poor? I didn't even land a punch."

Soron gave a hearty laugh. "Trust me son, if I know anything about woman, Tomas is going regret his actions today. Ava is not the kind of girl I'd want to get on the bad side of."

Nathan thought about it. Maybe his dad was right. Ava had a ferocious temper at times. This made Nathan smile just a little bit. It probably was 'poor Tomas' after all. As

Soron got up and went to let leave the room, Nathan called out "thanks Father."

Standing at the door for a second to look back at his son, Soron thought about how fast his son had grown. "Get some sleep; you are going to need it."

The next morning Soron woke Nathan up early and took him for a walk. Velaina had not yet woken and Nathan was grateful for this. Having told his father about the fight was one thing; his mother was an entirely different story. While the swelling of his face had gone down considerably, it was still puffy and bruised. He was happy to avoid seeing anyone right now.

Soron had Nathan take him to the spot in the forest where he had fought Tomas. Nathan showed him the tree where the scarf had been, and the cedar he had been hiding behind. Next Nathan described how Tomas had run into him, the brief conversation and the rest of the fight.

"Tell me why you lost the fight?" Soron asked.

Besides getting the wind knocked out of me, sucker-punched and pinned to the ground? Nathan thought to himself before replying. "The fact that he is older and bigger probably had a lot to do with it."

"Yes and no, son. Yes, the element of surprise was a factor. Tomas running you over was an effective attack but that wasn't the end of the fight. The fact that he caught you off guard with a punch was a failure to judge your enemy. Tomas being older means little. While he is certainly heavier that you, I rather doubt he is any stronger. He got you in a position where his extra weight neutralized your strength." Soron paused for a second to let this information sink in before continuing the lecture. "Surprise attacks are just that, a surprise. So there was nothing you could do about that. After that point, how you react will dictate the outcome of combat. Fighting with your hands is no different than fighting with weapons. You need to know your opponent and fight to your strengths and not his. Since you are not going to stop talking to Ava, it is very likely that Tomas will try again. Most of the damage he inflicted was after he pinned you to the ground. Let me show you how to counter that."

For the next couple of hours Soron, taught Nathan the basics of wrestling and striking. By lunchtime, Nathan was exhausted so they stopped for the day and headed back home. As they walked back, Nathan asked his father where he learned to fight.

"The north can be a dangerous place; all young men are trained to defend themselves. I had good trainers," said Soron.

Nathan knew from previous attempts to get his father to talk about his past that this was all the he would say on the subject.

When they got home, Velaina had a pot of hot soup waiting for them. As Nathan came to the table, she came over and inspected Nathan's face. "After lunch, put some more salve on, and then again before you go to sleep. Now eat your lunch."

Nathan was surprised and relieved. He had expected a much different reaction. His father must have talked to her about the one-sided fight last night. Nathan looked over at his father who gave him a quick wink before focusing on his lunch.

"Ava came by while you two were out. She said for you to meet her by the pond this afternoon."

Ava would often come by after her daily chores were done so that was nothing out of the ordinary, but he suspected that Ava had heard about Tomas. She probably wanted to hear from him what happened. Nathan finished up his soup, thanked his mom for the meal and messenger service. He put some more salve on the bruises and headed out to the pond. Half way to the pond it occurred to Nathan that his mom had made soup so it would be easier for him to eat. He made a mental note to thank her later. He appreciated not being coddled. Perhaps his mother realized he was not her little boy anymore. She had made more than one joke about how fast he had been outgrowing his britches. Now to meet the second most important female in his life and hope it went as well as it had with his mother.

Chapter seven

AVA WAS NOT THERE when Nathan got to the pond, so he laid down on one of the big flat rocks that surrounded the pool and basked in the sun. Between his face being sore from fighting Tomas and his body hurting from training with his dad, Nathan felt happy to take a short nap and relax his aching body. He yawned. He reminded himself to chew some henta leaf to relieve the pain before going to sleep in the evening.

When Nathan awoke from his nap he was no longer getting the full light of the sun, something blocked the rays of warming heat and light. Opening his eyes, he found Ava standing above him studying his face. "That looks like it hurt," she said matter of factly.

"You think my face looks bad? You should see his hand. Now that fist took a beating, let me tell you," Nathan quipped. "Now do you want to get out of my sun please? I was enjoying my nap."

Despite Nathan's attempts at humor, Ava did not smile or laugh. She sat down. She lay down beside Nathan so they both got the pleasure of the warm afternoon sun touching them.

"So are you going to tell me what happened?" asked Ava. "Sharon told me she found Tomas on top of you punching you, and then you disappeared." She did not look at Nathan. She just closed her eyes and waited. The sun warmed the dusting of freckles across her cheeks.

Nathan gave Ava the full story from getting knocked to the ground to being pinned and then Tomas's threat about Ava.

"Fie! Tomas is disgusting," said Ava when Nathan finished his account of what had happened.   She continued, "He is a pig. He was with Sharon before and she liked him but he kept trying to touch her and kiss her. Finally, she told him to get gone. Now he is trying to get all friendly with me. The fact he thinks beating up you will help his cause is so stupid. I am going to kick his creepy arse for this." Ava's anger was apparent from the way her volume rose with each statement.

Nathan didn't need Ava getting involved in this. "Please don't attack Tomas. Let me deal with him," Nathan begged her. It was bad enough he had lost the fight, having Ava try to make it right by attacking Tomas would be humiliating.

Ava turned so she faced Nathan as they sat on the warm rock. "Well, I don't want this happening again," she said, reaching out and gently touched his face. She grimaced as she turned his face to inspect it further, tisking then adding, "You are ugly enough without getting your face smashed up."

Nathan produced a small grin. Her gentle caress felt nice. "What are you talking about? I was already too beautiful; these war wounds make me look more manly and rugged. All the ladies are going to love me now. I should be thanking Tomas."

Ava's gentle caress of his bruised face was quickly replaced with a swift punch to the arm. "Watch it, mister, or Tomas won't be the only one making your face manly and rugged."

Nathan felt relief. This had gone better than he had envisioned it, and having Ava caress his face felt good. Maybe things weren't so bad, he mused to himself. For the rest of the afternoon, they just sat there enjoying the sun. Occasionally the silence would be broken by a short argument about what each unique cloud looked like, but by their standards, this wasn't an argument. It was merely an ongoing dialog to interrupt the comfortable silence.

Chapter eight

RAUL VENTEGO'S FEET hurt! His high quality Morthon leather boots were excellent for riding but left a lot to be desired when it came to walking. From now on, he would travel with a second pair of shoes just in case, he thought to himself as he walked down the road.

Half a day's ride north of the village of Birchone, his horse had come up lame, and so he walked. For two days now, he walked to keep the horse from suffering further injury. He looked forward to reaching the village of Elderwood, where he could get the horse looked at by the blacksmith and spend a night at the local inn. If he remembered correctly, they served darn good pie there.

Raul was one his way to Progoh, the largest of the nine cities that comprised the kingdom of Tarnstead. Raul along with his brother Paulo ran a large trading company in Venecia. Once every couple of years one of the brothers would make the journey up from the coastal city through the eastern plains and into Progoh.

Searching for new vendors and goods to send back in return for the goods they sold.

This trip, however, he was also acting in an official capacity as an emissary of the Venecian council. Bandits were starting to cause serious losses for many of the wealthy families that ran Venecia; losing money was not a popular pastime in Venecia. Raul was carrying a letter to the king of Broguth, demanding action as much of the bandit activity was situated just outside the lands surrounding the kingdom of Broguth—the very roads he walked on now, Raul mused to himself. He regretted the impatient decision that had led him to leave the safety of his company's well-guarded caravan. The blasted group just traveled too slowly. Now, with a lame horse, he was in a precarious position. With luck, he would reach Elderwood soon. Tired of the walking he decided that when he reached Elderwood he would wait there for the caravan. That would give his horse a day or two to rest and he would enjoy some of that town's famous pie.

...

Edmar, a short, shifty-eyed bandit scout, quietly yet swiftly moved up to the large oak beside the road where the bandit leader Ungar waited. For three days now, Edmar had been scouting the road from Birchone to Elderwood and had found several interesting targets. The one with the most potential was coming up the road now.

"He is coming around the bend now, and will be walking up the path in a minute," the scout reported. Ungar was, even by bandit standards, a vicious man and the scout did not want to cross him, so he quickly finished his report. "He is well dressed, southern style. He has a high-quality saddle on a good-looking horse with two saddlebags. His horse has a sore front right hoof and, for at least the last day and a half, the southerner has been walking to save the horse."

Ungar nodded, quietly absorbing the quality scouting report. All of Ungar's men were good woodsman and fighters, many having deserted or served time in the king's army. The gent would be tired, an easy kill. The horse would be valuable if its front hoof had no permanent damage. If the hoof was bad, no matter, the rest of the horse would fill their bellies nicely.

"I want that horse and it's about time I had a decent saddle. Kill him. Don't give him any chance to escape." The bandit scout was used to this type of order. Often, if the intended victim argued about being robbed, he ended up dead. Apparently, this poor sod was not even going to get the chance to argue, the scout thought to himself.

A minute later, as Raul walked up the road into the clearing before the oak tree, he caught a slight movement to the side of the tree. Before his brain could recognize the danger, the arrow was in his heart. Quickly the bandits descended onto his lifeless body, looting his possessions and grabbing the reins of the horse.

Ungar slowly walked up and stared down on the recently deceased stranger, feeling no remorse or pity. "What did he have?" he grunted to the bandits looting the body.

"A couple gold coins and a letter for the king. It seems our friend here was an emissary from Venecia," came the reply from one of the men.

Ungar seemed not to care as he ordered the men to drag the body off the road into a ravine. Politics and kings irritated him. He cared not what was in letter, but he stuck it in his shirt. He was illiterate. He would have someone read it to him in private. Gold coins and a horse was a good day's work; he was rather happy with the outcome of today's heist. Little did he know the chain of events that killing this messenger would lead to.

Chapter nine

VENECIA, THE LARGEST of Solotine's southern cities, was a sprawling diverse group of communities rolled into one thriving city. As a port city, it was the central hub for traders from the continent of Mithbea and the far western lands. Grains, fruit, wood and wine would come from the eastern Kingdom of Tarnstead. Minerals and cotton, clothing and other materials would come from the nearby southern lands. If something was worth trading, it would come to Venecia. But the rulers of Venecia had a problem. Traders, the lifeblood of Venecia, were refusing to travel to the kingdom of Broguth. Bandits and pirates were harassing and killing traders and, more importantly, cutting into profits.

The council of Venecia gathered to address this very problem. Trade with Progoh and the other cities of the kingdom of Tarnstead was becoming increasing less profitable due to losses from bandits. The ruling party in Venecia was the council, a collection of merchants, a few key tribal leaders, and landowners that together governed the city.

Four weeks had passed since Raul Ventego, a prominent member of the council, had left to discuss the issue with the king of Broguth. He had been expected back in three weeks, his brother Paulo Ventego, as he spoke before the council. "And what of my brother? Do we just sit here and wait for his return? If bandits or the king of Broguth has held up or injured him, I demand action."

Other members of the council nodded and spoke in agreement. Council members being killed or imprisoned was a very unsettling thought. Raul was a good swordsman, a strong man capable of looking after himself quite well. Perhaps the bandit problem was more dire than they realized. Either something foul had happened to Raul or they had angered the king of Broguth with their ultimatum to make safe the distance between the cities or be cut off as a trading partner.

Barouta, leader of the Chundo tribes, a strong and aggressive nomadic tribe known for their proclivity for war and horsemanship spoke next. "I will send a troop of my finest warriors. They will find Raul and deal with the problem."

Baron Tarozan, a prominent landowner, was one of the more level-headed of the council members. He feared his fellow council members would allow Barouta to take the problem of bandits and turn it into a war. Barouta often spoke of the advantages Venecia would gain by conquering the lands to the north and east. He often said Progoh needed new leadership and a change of fealty. The baron cleared his throat and spoke. "Make it a small troop Barouta; we don't need you starting a war."

Barouta coldly looked upon the baron. "Barouta does not start wars, he ends them," and with that, the meeting was over.

As Barouta left the city, he turned to one of his lieutenants Ashuna, "Take fifty horsemen, find Raul and if you can't, find an answer from the king."

"Yes my lord, and if the Raul is in the custody of the king?" asked Ashuna.

"If those fools have given me any reason to press for war, I want ample proof. But do not be too aggressive with the king. If war is to come, it will come." Barouta almost smiled. He welcomed the idea of war with the eastern kingdom. "We will not start a war without provocation." Barouta stroked his braided beard. He hadn't specified how little provocation he would ignore. Allowing too much lenience was a sign of weakness. He dismissed his lieutenant. He was bored with peace. A war stirred his blood, and winning a war brought wealth and status. It had always been the way of the Chundo. Alliances were hard to balance and shifted often.

Chapter ten

THE WARM AFTERNOON sun felt good on Nathan's face as he sat by the creek. Nathan, sore all over from the last few days training with his father, was glad to have gotten a reprieve today. This afternoon, his father let him quit his training early. Nathan thought he would go find Ava and head out to the pond, but his mother had other ideas. She wanted fresh fruit for their supper and since Nathan wasn't working with his father this afternoon, he got volunteered to pick some fruit from the orchard. Not that Nathan minded terribly, it was several hours until dinner so he was having a rather enjoyable time alternating between picking fruit and stretching out in the sun. Nathan's basking in the sun was soon interrupted by a familiar and increasing annoying voice.

"So you ratted me out? You little shit. Ava won't even acknowledge me now. I am going to beat the snot out of you, you arse-licking mixed-blood bastard."

Nathan sighed and quickly got up, despite being sore. He had been expecting to run into Tomas sooner or later, so he was not surprised by Tomas showing up.

Warily, he corrected Tomas. "Actually she found out about it from Sharon, but that doesn't matter, I told her what an ass you are anyways. I am not going to stop being Ava's friend because you have designs on her. If you are stupid enough to think beating me up is going to help you get her attention, that is not my problem."

Nathan watched as Tomas's face went a deep red and his fist clenched. Nathan was not going to be caught off guard this time. He squared his feet to the older boy and relaxed. He would not start a fight with Tomas over Ava. But if Tomas thought he would be beating him up easily, he would be in for a surprise.

"Oh, so I am stupid? You are the one with a purple face. I am really going to hurt you this time." Tomas was already swinging his fist as he yelled at Nathan. However, this time things went much differently.

Nathan, expecting Tomas to take a punch at him, easily slipped under the wild haymaker. Nathan countered by planting a jab to Tomas's face, causing blood to gush from his nose. Enraged, Tomas yelled and continued to throw wild punches with everything he could muster. Nathan, using his father's lessons, kept dodging and weaving, delivering stinging jabs to the face and hooks to the kidneys.

Tomas now had a swollen eye and a fat lip to go along with his bloody nose. Frustrated by his lack of success throwing punches, Tomas tried to tackle Nathan. Again, Nathan was well prepared for the change in tactics and was anticipating the attack. He pivoted, grabbing Tomas by the head and back of the pants. Using his momentum, he sent Tomas tumbling to the ground. Nathan followed Tomas to the ground, delivering a hard knee to the older boy's soft belly, driving the wind out of him. Tomas was completely defeated and did not try to get up. "Don't try it again, Tomas, or I won't be as nice next time." Stepping away from his fallen opponent, Nathan let out a deep sigh of relief. It gave him no pleasure to beat Tomas, but it did give him great pleasure to know he could protect himself. All the work with his father was worth every sore muscle and bruise.

Nathan took up his bucket of fruit and headed home, leaving Tomas on the ground in a heap, trying to regain his breath. Turning back, Nathan couldn't help but adding "and if I were you I would avoid Ava for a while. She isn't interested in you at all."

After Nathan left, Tomas sat on the ground stewing over his defeat to the younger boy. Tomas hated Nathan with a passion, born from a lifetime of listening to his father Ned complain about "those damn foreigners". Before Soron had moved into Elderwood, Ned had run a small blacksmith shop himself. His metal was cheap and poorly made, but that did nothing to stop him from taking advantage of unsuspecting traders in need of repairs or goods. When Soron opened his shop, it took little time for Ned's blacksmith shop to become customer-less. All Tomas's life, he heard how that damn northerner and his Baltan witch wife were a plague on the village.

Growing up with such jealousy and prejudice, it was natural for Tomas to take a dislike to Nathan. He never had reason for that dislike to grow into anything more until Ava thwarted him. Tomas always had a way with the girls. His quick smile and confidence made him interesting and he took full advantage of it. It was only when Ava rejected him that he turned his attention to Nathan. When Tomas realized his competition for Ava's interest was Nathan, he thought it would be easy to scare off his competition. He miscalculated. The skinny kid was not a wimp after all. The bigotry of Tomas's family now combined with jealousy. The seeds of hate his father had planted now grew. Tomas got up and headed for home. This was far from over; he vowed to find a way to hurt Nathan no matter what the cost.

Chapter eleven

NATHAN WAS SITTING at the pond waiting for Ava. So far, he was having a pretty good day. The previous night he had told his father about the second confrontation with Tomas. Today as part of his lessons, they once again went through the fight, this time analyzing what he did right. His father had said he was proud of Nathan for trying to resolve the issue without violence. He also praised Nathan for properly using his lessons. But, as Nathan watched Ava approach, he could tell from her body language that the following conversation would not add to his level of happiness. Ava had both hands on her hips, a sure sign of her irritation.

"You were fighting with Tomas again," Ava said with a certain tone to her voice, which she reserved for when Nathan did something dumb.

Nathan sighed. Yep, she was not happy at all. But this was so not his fault, he thought to himself before replying, "It's not like I wanted to. I was picking apples for supper when he confronted me. He called me a rat for telling you about our first fight and then started swinging."

Ava groaned in frustration. "Boys are so stupid."

"Hey, ease up on the boys part. I did nothing wrong." Nathan would not be taking the blame for this mess. This was Tomas's doing and he should take the blame.

Ava sighed, removed her hands from her hips, and came over to inspect Nathan. "Your mother's healing salves are amazing; I can't even see where he hit you this time."

"What are you trying to say? He didn't hit me this time." Nathan felt like a piece of meat as Ava poked and prodded his ribs, his chest, moving his head around looking for any telltale signs of bruising.

"Oh, well, Sharon ran into Tomas and said his whole face was swollen and bruised, and he had a big black eye and a cut lip. I figured you would have the same or worse," said Ava.

Nathan tried to not sound like he was bragging. No point setting her off again. "Nah, after the first fight, my father started teaching me how to fight. After sparring with him, Tomas is not much of a challenge, actually pretty bad. I doubt he'll ever try again."

Ava showed her surprise at this revelation. "Your father was a fighter? He certainly is big enough. I've just never seen him do anything but work in the blacksmith shop and he is always so friendly," said Ava.

Nathan thought about this for a while before replying. "He doesn't talk about it much but I get the feeling he actually was a warrior for a long time. If you ever see him with his shirt off, he has all sorts of scars on his body. I think he has seen a lot of fighting."

"Oooh, your father with his shirt off, I would like to see that, all those big muscles...," Ava teased.

"Not funny Ava, that's my father you're talking about."

Ava just laughed "Oh relax, as if anyone has a chance with your dad while your mother is around. She is so beautiful. Come to think of it, both of your parents are beautiful. I wonder what happened to you? Do you think you were adopted or maybe they just dropped you on your face as a baby?" Ava sprinted behind a tree as she taunted Nathan.

Nathan laughed and chased after her. He might be bigger and stronger but Ava was as quick as a rabbit and hard to catch. He was getting better at it when she wasn't using branches to trip him up. Nathan yelled at her as he ran, "You know I am not adopted. How many blued-eyed villagers are there? Just mother and me, and I am much too smart to have been dropped on my head."

A few moments later, Nathan was again looking up into the sky, groaning at his bad luck. How did she always manage to trip him up? Did she plant branches in strategic spots before teasing him into chasing her?

Ava leaned over top of him. "Too smart to have been dropped, eh?"

Nathan just groaned and admired the sky.

...

Soron grew up in a world of violence. Northern Solotine was a harsh and violent land, its inhabitants as forbidding as the land itself. In the north, resources meant more than just wealth, it meant life. Those who controlled the mines controlled the ability to make weapons. Superior weapons often were the difference-maker in battles being won or lost. Controlling the mines meant fighting for them, and Soron had fought often. Soron was Nathan's age when his father sent him to the mines to learn the secrets of northern steel and how to become a warrior. Lessons in steel and blood came often for Soron. By twenty, Soron had seen, and caused more death than many warriors ever partake in a lifetime.

Now, he was content to live in the small, peaceful village of Elderwood as a simple blacksmith. But with the discovery of Nathan's magic and the increasing number of bandit attacks in the area, Soron was putting aside his own aversion to combat to teach Nathan the skills that may well one day keep him alive.

As Soron reflected on his own childhood, he watched his son work through the progression of footwork, blade block and attack combos he had been teaching him. "Eyes up, son. If you are watching your feet, you are not watching the enemy."

He is too much like me at his age, thought Soron. He enjoys this too much. Training with weapons had always been enjoyable to Soron, as a young boy he always found the physical training to be challenging yet fun. The desire to absorb his trainer's knowledge and prove his worth as the son of a tribal chieftain had pushed him to be the best. Training was fun. Actual combat was not fun, it was bloody, violent and left a mark on a man's soul. Soron could still remember the face of the first man he killed. Bloodshot red eyes and a bulbous nose, the look of shock on the man's face as a boy half his age pulled his sword out of the dying man's chest.

I can prepare him for battle, but how do I prepare him for the sour taste of victory? Soron pondered, while watching the boy swing his daggers in a smooth rhythm, like he was moving to the beat of a song.

The large northern, sword-breaker style daggers were unique and almost never seen south of the Applomean Mountains. At two feet long, the blades were shorter and wider than a normal short sword. Often northern warriors would use one of the daggers with a large sword. But for Soron's purposes they were perfect, giving Nathan a strong defensive weapon easily carried yet not completely offensive in nature.

The daggers featured a thick up-curved cross-hilt and three grooves cut into each side of the wide blade at the base just above the cross-hilt. When a sword would strike the blade, it could slide down toward the cross-hilt until it got caught in one of the grooves. When a strong man turned his wrist, the sword came right out of his opponent's hand. A very strong man like Soron often broke a poorly made sword this way.

For Nathan, a strong yet agile boy with excellent hand-eye coordination, learning to fight with two of the sword breakers would give him a skillset he could master now before he gained his full size and strength. His training would give him an advantage over most adult fighters. Used by someone with the proper training and skill, the two daggers would be as deadly as any sword.

While Soron hoped Nathan never had to use his training in combat, he felt a certain amount of pride in how quickly Nathan progressed with the blades. In the smithshop, working metal, Soron often could see how his own northern bloodlines were giving Nathan great strength and size for a lad of his age. Out here in the open training with the daggers, Soron saw the speed and agility for which Velaina's Baltan bloodlines were known.

This combination of power, speed and agility gave Nathan a frightening natural ability as a warrior. Soron was glad he and Velaina chose to raise the boy in the small village of Elderwood. If Nathan had grown up in the north with his own people, he would probably become a great warrior. Great warriors often died young or lived with terrible memories of the battles they fought.

Nathan did not have dark thoughts about learning to fight as his father had teaching. He enjoyed learning the block and parry combinations, and how to stab and slice with the large daggers, and how to thrust his dagger forward once an opponent's sword struck the blade, forcing the sword down towards the hilt and the waiting grooves.

Once the sword slid into the grooves Nathan quickly got used to snapping his wrist. He was at the point where he could actually turn the sword in his own father's hand. A hand far stronger than any future warrior or bandit he might face. While Nathan did enjoy working as a smith, being outside for the fighting lessons was always better. As Soron attacked him with his large wooden practice sword Nathan worked on blocking his father's strong attacks.

When they first started training his father's brute strength simply overpowered Nathan, but as he learned to angle his blades and counter thrust, he found he learned how to hold off his father's powerful attacks.

However, finding a way to counter-strike against his father's longer reach and superior technique was proving to be a much more difficult task. Soron continued his aggressive attack, pressing harder and harder. Nathan continued to use the right blocking techniques despite the ferocity of his father's efforts. When Soron ended the days training, he was satisfied that Nathan was ready for a new opponent.

Before the training went any further, it was time for Nathan to forge daggers of his own. The wooden replicates his father had made were excellent training tools but to truly master the techniques he would have to get used to the proper weight and balance of his actual blades.

Nathan took his time, honored that his father let him forge his own weapons. The forging of these blades wasn't much different than other knives he had done in the past. The biggest difference was the blade being bigger and wider, with the sword breaking grooves above the hilt.

As Nathan pulled a blade from the fire he applied the graphite and phosphorus that strengthen the metal into something special. As the first blade cooled he repeated the process on the second blade. Soon two perfectly made daggers were sitting on the workbench waiting for his father's approval. Nathan knew the blades were excellent. The balance was perfect and would only require a little work with a whetstone before each edge was razor sharp. Besides the bracelet he had made for his mother, the daggers were his finest work yet.

Chapter twelve

COUNT MAVANE, OF the city of Salba, had a problem, actually several problems. All of which revolved around the main issue: bandits. As the farthest west of the cities under the rule of kingdom of Broguth, Salba did a lot of trade with the villages and cities to the west and south. But those travel routes were not part of the kingdom and thus not patrolled by the king's army.

For years, Count Mavane petitioned King Parth to increase patrols in the lands surrounding Salba and along the main roads to the south. Unfortunately, armies cost money and patrols are not cheap. So until now, the king's army had protected only the city of Salba and the roads east to the capital. As Count Mavane predicted, the lack of patrols led to an increase in the number of robberies along the trade routes. Bandits became more aggressive as they realized no reprisals would come as long as they attacked only along the western and southern trade routes.

Count Mavane did have a small contingent of men-at-arms and scouts under his control. They would visit the nearby villages and assist them when possible, but this presented a small deterrent to the more aggressive groups of bandits. With the recent increase of attacks along the trade roads, the king finally had decided to dedicate some the king's army to address the issue. The king's solution was the count's latest problem.

King Parth was sending a small battalion under Duke Evollan to deal with the bandits. Duke Evollan, a fierce and loyal warrior, had served with great distinction in many battles during the wars to unify the eastern kingdom. This gave the duke great stature with the king and a place in the king's war council. But while fierce and loyal, Duke Evollan was also a boorish and arrogant man. He was quick to anger, and not known for being the most intelligent member of the royal families. Count Mavane privately had often wondered if some of the older royal families had a little too much inbreeding. Duke Evollan was known for winning battles, not for diplomacy.

Count Mavane thought killing and apprehending bandits seemed a task even Duke Evollan could handle. The problem being that the small villages to the west and south were not part of the kingdom, and often had stronger ties with other regions. Dealing with these villages would require diplomacy. Something Count Mavane feared Duke Evollan was not well-equipped to handle.

As Count Mavane pondered this newest problem, his main steward, Bannah, entered the room. "Bannah, have we received a reply from my note to Duke Evollan yet?" Upon learning that Duke Evollan was leading the small battalion, the count sent a message offering use of his local scouts to the duke. Count Mavane hoped having his men, familiar with the local villages and roads, would keep Duke Evollan from causing too many problems when dealing with the different, friendly but independent communities.

Bannah replied quickly, "Yes, my lord I'm afraid we have. Duke Evollan has refused your offer and wants you to remember he answers only to the king. He is not subject to local lord authority and, as such, does not need or want your assistance in this matter."

Count Mavane had feared that the prideful Duke Evollan would not respond well to his offer. He grunted and frowned at the thought. His scouts could be the difference between innocent people haphazardly being accused of wrong doing. With disgust in his voice, he replied "Well, let us hope then that Duke Evollan is as adept at defeating bandits as he is at storming castles." The count sighed. He suspected this was not going to be the case.

Chapter thirteen

AFTER HIS SECOND FIGHT with Tomas Nathan's life fell back into a normal rhythm. He spent his days in the old routine of lessons with his parents and book learning with the other children of the village. During his spare time, he would take his practice daggers out into the woods to work on his form. He was determined to get past his father's defenses at least once. Soron would use different weapons during their sparing sessions—staves, pikes, sword and shield, sword and dagger, and war hammer, but the most common was simply a single sword.

Most bandits and warriors used only a single sword; carry weight was important to looting and traveling. So, Soron trained Nathan mostly with the single sword. Normally, the sword-breaking nature of the daggers was enough to defeat someone using a sword. But Soron, adept in the use of the daggers, was able to counter Nathan's attempts to lock up his blade. Continually attacking and using his superior length to keep Nathan from scoring any vital blows. Nathan was determined to beat his father's defenses at least once. In his mind, a maneuver began to take form.

Fortunately for Nathan, he did not have to wait long to attempt the maneuver with his father. The very next day, Nathan and Soron were sparing again, and again Soron was able to thwart all of Nathan's attempts to get past his single sword defense. Then, the moment Nathan had been waiting for came. Soron came on the attack, backing Nathan up. He used a downward strike that Nathan would normally have blocked with his left dagger, forcing the blade off to one side while he attempted to counterattack with his right dagger.

This time, Nathan pivoted on his right foot swinging his body out of the way of the sword swinging down at him. Bringing both blades up, he crossed his daggers and let the sword strike the blades. But instead of trying to push the sword off to the side, he turned his daggers and forced the sword to continue on past. As the sword hit the ground he pushed down on his daggers keeping the weapon momentarily pinned to the ground.

He used the momentum of pivot to swing his left leg around and behind the legs of Soron. As Soron pulled back on the sword to release it from the wedge formed by the ground and Nathan's daggers, Soron's own momentum forced him back onto Nathan's leg. This caused him to lose his balance and take and awkward step back to regain his balance. During the step back Nathan kept his left blade on the sword, now pushing it off to his left.

Still balanced on his right foot, he pushed up and forward, bringing him close enough to his father's body to lightly strike him in the chest with his free dagger. He finally scored a clean hit on his father, the first time he had ever been able to do so.

Soron had to laugh. It had been a long time since anyone scored a hit on him during a training session, and to have a fourteen year old do it was un-heard of. "Excellent job Nathan, but I didn't teach you to use a leg sweep or to use your daggers to push a sword into the ground. How did you figure out to do that?"

Nathan smiled, and replied, "It was the only thing I could think of that might get you off balance long enough for me to get close enough to strike. I knew it had to be quick enough to prevent you from seeing it coming, and then just stepping over my leg and chopping it off."

Soron was impressed by his son's ability to recognize the short comings of his own weapons and create an attack without being formally taught it. "Using two daggers always give you an advantage when it comes to quickly blocking and turning attacking blades. But against a skilled opponent or multiple opponents, you will have to use your body to gain an advantage on the attack. That leg sweep was a good move against a single opponent. Another option is to pivot like you did but instead of following the sword down, let your opponent's momentum bring the sword down to the ground. It won't stay stuck like it did when you used the daggers but it will free up your daggers for a quick-spinning attack from two angles."

Soron was proud but Nathan still had a long way to go. The training was progressing well. Nathan was now at the point where he was not just reacting to attacks but formulating his own counters, a very good skill.

As Soron and Nathan continued sparring, they failed to see the set of eyes watching them from the distance, eyes that carefully noted the skill which they displayed.

Chapter fourteen

DUKE EVOLLAN AND HIS company of soldiers had been patrolling the stretches of roads outside Salba for several days now. Upon arriving in the area, the duke and his men purposely avoided entering Salba. Doing so would only allow the meddlesome Count Mavane to give suggestions on how to approach the bandit situation. He was sure the count just wanted to ride his coattails on this endeavor. Duke Evollan did not need some minor lord from a low-bred, outlying western city telling him how to deal with bandits. The accolades for this tedious venture were going to be his and his alone.

For one long and unfruitful week, they had been scouting along the roads west of Salba. Signs, in the form of decomposing bodies dragged off the well-traveled roadways and pathways, were noticed only because of noisy scavenging birds. With the few bodies they found, the corpses remained nameless, stripped of anything of value, flesh eaten by birds and other scavengers. The duke left the bodies to the forests, unburied. Unscrupulous bandits along the northern road that led to the village of Elderwood had been busy. The duke was finally closing in on the bandits, and all signs led toward the area around the village of Elderwood.

Earlier that day, the duke had sent out his scouts and they were now returning to camp. As he ate the barely adequate roast pheasant and sautéed wild onions, the duke pondered the lack of amenities. On the next excursion the king sent him on he would take a larger contingent of his house staff. A duke should not have to suffer such hardships as he currently was. Taking a sip of his wine, he listened to his first scouts report. "There is a small village to the northwest of here, sir, about a mile through the forest. From what I could tell, mostly berry-pickers and the sort, but I did see a large northern warrior and a young man sparring in a meadow at the edge of the village. Both looked to be skilled warriors, not the sort I would want to run into on a forest road." The duke took this information in, a northern warrior and a local sparing together. This could be the important.

Bailmont, his captain, an efficient if not overly blood-thirsty soldier, echoed this thought, "A northern warrior living in a small village south of the mountains? And training a local? If that doesn't sound like bandits I don't know what does."

Hearing Bailmont's words further solidified the idea in the duke's mind. That idiot Count Mavane had a whole village of bandits being trained by a northerner right under his nose. Before Duke Evollan had time to think through his faulty logic, a second scout rode into camp.

The scout, having been on the wrong end of Bailmont's temper before, quickly delivered his news. "Fifty or more riders are coming up the southern road and fast. They all look like tribal warriors my lord. They will be here by mid-afternoon."

Duke Evollan thought about this for a moment. The southern lands were full of tribes known to be fierce warriors. If these horsemen were part of the group of bandits working out of the village, he and his men would be hard pressed to defeat them together. The duke was no stranger to battle tactics. He quickly surmised the path to victory was to attack first, destroy the village before its reinforcements could arrive. "Bailmont, gather the men, we attack the village now, before those horsemen can help them."

Several of the men looked carefully at the duke before one replied, "Yes my lord, but are you sure? There are villages around here that trade with Salba. Maybe this village isn't bandits."

Bailmont, eager for battle, scoffed at this idea. "You heard the scout, a northerner sparring just outside the village miles from where travelers are regularly being attacked? No, it has to be a bandit village. And if we get caught between them and those horsemen, we will be in danger of being defeated. We attack."

The duke nodded his agreement with Bailmont. Bailmont was a particularly vicious killer. Putting him in charge was a mistake the duke would live to regret. But at this moment, all the duke could see was the praise and glory he would receive.

As they charged the village, Bailmont yelled, "No mercy. No survivors. We shall teach them a lesson that will strike fear in every bandit throughout this kingdom." Bailmont was not worried about reprisals. If any of the villagers were not bandits, they could blame it on the bandits themselves. The duke had never worried about his tactics before. This would be no different.

...

Soron and Nathan were in the blacksmith shop when the screaming started. They quickly went out the door just in time to see a villager drop from a soldier's arrow. Soron reacted quickly. "Nathan go next door, grab the Dollan's kids. Do it quickly. Take them to the great swamp and wait there. If we don't come, you wait a week before returning." As Soron spoke he turned back into the blacksmith shop, grabbing his hammer and a knife he just finished repairing.

Nathan was scared but did not want to leave. "I can fight father. I can help." Soron turned and looked as his son. Nathan was grabbing his daggers.

"I know you can, son. But part of fighting is protecting those who can't. Grab Ava, Rose and any more children you find on your way. But you must get to the swamp quickly. I am going to find your mother." Soron paused for a moment. He was trying to speak as fast as possible, as clearly as possible. So much he needed to say and too little time to explain.

"Son, there is a lot about my past and your mother's past that we haven't told you about. I don't have time to explain, but someday when you are older, I want you to go north of the mountains and learn of your heritage." Soron put the dagger in his belt and grabbed an axe he had sharpened for a neighbor, arming himself further as he spoke.

As Soron returned to the door, he carefully looked in all directions, scouting for an escape route for Nathan, hugging himself carefully against the walls he advanced to the corner of the building. Nathan followed his father's lead, stretching out flat against the wall.

Soron saw enemies advancing. Holding his son against the wall, he continued speaking as he calculated how many eyes would be in their direction. "You have birthrights and one day will have to choose to accept them or not. It will be your choice and I will be proud of you regardless of the choice you make. When you go north, tell them you are Nathan Stoneblood, son of Soron Stoneblood. Whoever you meet will take you to our people or try to kill you—either way, be ready. Your mother and I are proud of the man you are becoming; when this is over we, shall explain everything." Soron saw that the time to move had come. "Get ready to run on my command. I love you, son."

Soron watched the closest soldiers engaged in combat with his fellow villagers. Once he saw them all with their backs turned, he gave Nathan a push. "Go now."

Nathan's heart pounded as he sprinted the seemingly forever distance to Ava's house.

Seeing Nathan escape the notice of the closest bandits, Soron charged out from the edge of the blacksmith shop. Velaina was in danger! He could see her across the village helping a wounded neighbor. The soldier closest to him was hacking down a villager. He never saw the mighty swing of the hammer coming down upon his head, his death unfairly swift. Soron skirted the village, running as hard as he could, commanding women and children to run and hide as he hacked and slashed through the unknown assailants, fighting his way towards Velaina.

Nathan had no time to ponder his father's cryptic message about birthrights and his last name; he was focused on getting Ava and Rose, then getting to the swamp. His ears heard the pounding of hooves and the clanging of metal and the cries of villagers in the distance as he burst through the Dollan's door.

Edward and Suzie Dollan were elderberry pickers. At this time of day, they were either still out in the forest or at the creek on the far side of the village, rinsing the berries off. While they were working, their two girls stayed with Edward's father. Edward's father was one of the oldest villagers and his family had lived there for generations. For years the children of the village had been affectionately calling the elder Dollan "Bends" a none-too-subtle reference to the old man's walking gait. The Dollan house was just across from the blacksmith shop. Nathan was there and in the door in moments.

As he burst through the door, Nathan was relieved to find the girls inside with Bends. He hurriedly exclaimed, "Bends, I've come for the girls. I've been ordered to hide them in the swamp! "

Bends was already brandishing an ax; the girls behind him with fearful eyes. The sound of pounding hooves and screaming struck terror in their hearts. The frightening sounds were drawing closer. "We have been expecting you, Nathan. Your father and I discussed what to do if something like this ever happened. The girls are packed and ready to go, take good care of them." Bends handed Nathan a pack with food in it before turning to the girls. "Rose, Ava, go with Nathan!"

The girls looked up wide-eyed and terrified but nodded and followed Nathan to the door. Bends made certain it was safe for them to dart into the nearby cover of the pig hut. It was near enough to the bush to provide the children with cover. Bends ordered, "Run, run as fast as you can. Do not look back."

They ran with hearts pounding. They ran 'til they were out of breath. With most of the noise from the attack coming from the east side of the village, Nathan led the girls in the opposite direction, deeper into the woods, following deer trails and wild hog trails. When the sounds coming from the village were faint in the distance, he then made his way northeast toward the Great Swamp.

While Nathan took the girls into the swamp regions, the battle in the village did not take long. A few of the village members were ex-soldiers from the east or the southern cities. But for the most part, the villagers were farmers, elderberry pickers, wine-makers and other simple folk. Against trained soldiers, they had no chance. Within minutes, most of the defenseless villagers were dead.

Duke Evollan's men led by the bloodthirsty Bailmont did not make exceptions for gender. By the time Soron fought his way to Durant's farm, he found Velaina trying to defend the injured Durant from a small group of attackers. She swung a scythe like a sword, courageously attempting to keep the soldiers from slaying the defenseless farmer. Her blonde hair whirled as she fiercely fought off her assailants. But before Soron could reach her side, a soldier came from behind and thrust his sword into her back, the blade pierced through her heart. As she stood there dying, their eyes met one last time. While the light quickly flickered and faded from her eyes, Soron stood frozen for moment watching as his love fell to the ground.

Soron roared with rage and despair. Within seconds he reached the group of soldiers around the fallen body of his beloved Velaina. He sliced through the soldiers, his rage-induced attack destroyed all in his path. His hammer crushed through helm and armor while his axe found throats and hearts. But as the last of the resisting villagers died at the hands of the duke's men, soldiers still thirsting for blood joined the fray against the blood soaked raging northerner who was decimating their numbers. Even with several arrows in his chest the tall northerner continued to slay the attacking forces. More deadly arrows found their mark. Mighty Soron fell. His once towering body fell across the lifeless body of his soul mate. Sword wounds had weakened him. The arrows killed him. Over twenty of the king's rogue soldiers lay dead by his hand.

Nathan was deep into the woods leading the girls swiftly away from the conflict when the souls of his parents were passing from this world. At that very moment, he felt a pain throughout his entire being that he could not explain. He lifted up a tearful and exhausted Rose. Her arms were scratched as were Ava's. Rose was slowing them down, so he swept her up and piggy backed her. Already, Nathan was thinking of shelter, water and food.

Ava was silent, speaking only to reassure Rose. She too was thinking about the necessities, and her parents and her grandfather. Being with Nathan and Rose was her only consolation.

Nathan was acutely aware of the wind direction as they approached the treacherous swamp. The deadly vapors would follow the wind and kill them if they could. He calmed his breathing once again. If strangers followed them and strayed from the exact paths they were taking, the swamp would vanquish them, claim their bodies and use the decaying bodies to nourish the dark and forbidding trees. It paid to know the swamplands, to follow where animals traveled safely.

With every visible villager dead, Evollan retired his bloodied troops, leading them back east of the village and into the forest. If the southern riders were allies of the village of bandits, it was far better to meet them in the forest and not on open ground where horses would give them too much of an advantage. The duke was not overly concerned that the village of bandits and murderers consisted mostly of now dead farmers and berry-pickers, women and children alike. The attack at Elderwood was to be another crowning glory. While the duke might now be willing to concede to himself that the village was not full of bandits as his original assumption had been, it mattered not. His justification would be that the villagers were supplying the bandits with food and weapons, profiting from a liaison with murderers and thieves. As long as the bandit raids eventually stopped he would be well rewarded. Any rumors of unjust massacres would be swept away as hearsay, rumor from jealous sources. Evollan congratulated himself for his cunning. He prepared himself to deal with the mysterious riders advancing.

Chapter fifteen

ASHUNA WITH HIS FIFTY horseback warriors arrived at what was left of the village of Elderwood. They had been riding hard, not to join in on an attack on Duke Evollan and his troops, but to make it to Elderwood before dusk. Elderwood was the last village on this northern road before it turned east towards Salma.

Ashuna intended to buy food for his warriors before continuing on the way to Salma. When Ashuna and his men rode into the still burning village their faces were grim. At first glance, it appeared bandits, ruthless murdering bandits, had struck the once peaceful village. But the assortment of bodies on the ground told a different story. For some unknown reason, soldiers had struck this village. He sent scouts to look in the woods for survivors. Survivors were found; terrified, hiding in the woods. Something very dark and evil had happened here.

When Ashuna got to the body of Soron, he did not need a villager to tell him what had transpired here. The bodies of the soldiers lying around the arrow ridden body of a great northerner told him at least this part of the battle was not so one-sided. This man, above all, was a warrior.

Ashuna had his men help tend to the wounded while others buried the dead. He sent a few scouts back out into the woods to find out who perpetrated this attack. It did not take long for the scouts to find the company of soldiers fortified in the forest east of the village.

It seemed the soldiers in the woods were waiting for the Chundo to attack. When Ashuna and the warriors finished tending to the wounded and burying the dead, they remounted and went toward the east to see what this company of soldiers intended to do. Ashuna had important business in the eastern capital and had no time to deal with this. He sent a rider to the edge of the forest under a white flag to arrange a parlay with the soldiers. A meeting was negotiated.

Duke Evollan came cautiously to the edge of the forest to meet the leader of the horsemen. Ashuna rode up to the edge of the forest and greeted the duke. "Greetings, my name is Ashuna and I am an emissary from Venecia, enroute to Progoh. "The duke looked at Ashuna with a degree of disdain and distrust. "An emissary traveling with fifty horsemen, to me that seems excessive."

Ashuna gave a small acknowledgement to the duke's math skills. "Yes, well the last emissary never returned from visiting Progoh. Apparently, these roads aren't safe. My men are simply here to discourage any bandits from attacking me."

Duke Evollan relaxed. "Well you needn't worry. My men and I just finished dealing with a large group of the bandits causing problems in the area. Your travels should be safe from here to the capital." The lie rolled off his tongue easily.

Ashuna did not let his face reveal the disgust he felt. The stink of deceit was stronger than ever. It would be satisfying to cut the lying tongue out of the officer before him. Ashuna's sharp eyes missed nothing. The duke was truly an idiot to think the village was the source of the bandit problem, but he held his tongue. "Indeed, I was just at the scene of the battle in the bandit village." The sarcasm in Ashuna's voice was creeping out. "I hope you don't mind, but we buried all of the dead including your men." Ashuna put emphasis on the word men. He had no time to challenge the dastardly duke. Killing the waste of skin would have suited him just fine, but he did not relish starting a war at this particular time.

The duke did not notice the distain with which Ashuna was trying to hide as he spoke. "Thank you. We would have done it ourselves, but with a large group of horsemen coming from the south, retreating to the woods seemed a prudent plan." The duke smirked and gave a final goodbye to Ashuna sending him off to Salba. The southern warriors leaving now were one more problem he would not have to deal with today.

...

Late the next day, Ashuna and his men reached the city of Salba. Ashuna was brought to see Count Mavane immediately. "Welcome to Salba. How has your journey been?" Word of the events at Elderwood had not yet reached Salba. But none-the-less an emissary riding with fifty warriors had Count Mavane on edge. "The journey has been fine. There was a small delay yesterday. But other than that, no issues," replied Ashuna, unsure what role the kingdom of Tarnstead had in the recent events. Count Mavane could feel the tension in the room. "Oh did you encounter trouble? Bandits?" asked the count.

Ashuna watched Count Mavane as he explained, "We encountered a battle scene at a small village west of here. The village apparently was full of bandits and then we had a small encounter with a company of the king's army. They had just finished fighting the 'bandits' and were waiting in the tree line for us. Ashuna could see the color leave Count Mavane's face as he heard the news.

"Did you see these bandits?"

Count Mavane hoped that there was some mix-up here but Ashuna's next comments completed filling his heart with sorrow and shame. "Well, to my untrained eye, it appeared to be a village full of farmers and berry-pickers. And one northerner who almost defeated the king's men on his own, but your Duke Evollan assured me it was a marauding horde of bandits. So I can only assume I am mistaken in thinking the king's army is attacking innocent villages."

The count had feared that Duke Evollan would do something stupid. But he never dreamed that the man could be so ignorant as to attack the village of Elderwood. The thought of Duke Evollan's men killing the northerner living there was even more terrifying. "This northerner you spoke of, he didn't have a blonde woman with him by any chance?" Count Mavane had a hard time getting the words out his mouth was so dry.

Ashuna sensing that Count Mavane was not at all pleased with this news became a little more detailed in his description of the scene he found in the village. "Yes. Not more than twenty feet from where the northerner died was the body of a young blonde-haired woman. She died trying to defend an injured farmer. Am I wrong in assuming you know the place and the people there?"

"I know the northerner and his wife. He was a friend. The village you speak of is called Elderwood and its people are no more bandits than you or me" replied Count Mavane with sadness in his voice. "Your news is quiet distressing, Ashuna. Forgive me, but I am going to need a brief amount of time to deal with this. Then I can join you and your men in a feast to honor your arrival to the kingdom."

Ashuna understood then that the massacre of the villagers was not a plan for the expansion of the kingdom of Broguth. But an incredibly stupid blunder of the arrogant Duke Evollan that he met on the road. Ashuna graciously answered back, "Take whatever time you need. The sooner this unseemly business is resolved the better."

Taking his leave, Count Mavane quickly assembled his staff. He directed the scouts to go to Elderwood as soon as possible. He wanted them to confirm what happened and provide any help they could. He sent a rider to inform the king of the tragic news. Next he sent another rider to Duke Evollan requesting he immediately come to Salba. A wagon with supplies and a doctor were to leave for Elderwood as soon as possible. His stomach was hurting as it often did when he worried. He remembered how many times he had sent for stomach calming potions from the lady Velaina in the village of Elderwood. Then Count Mavane began writing two letters. Two letters he hoped could prevent a war.

Three days passed before the arrogant Duke Evollan finally arrived in Salba. He purposely had taken an extra day to arrive, angered that a lowly count had presumed to summon him.

"Count Mavane, I thought I made it clear I did not want your involvement if this matter. I have already encountered and defeated a large number of bandits. Now I would like to get back to the task. Why have you dared to summon me?"

Count Mavane's scouts had already reported on what they found at Elderwood so the count did not have to swallow any of the duke's lies. "No. What you have done is slaughter the majority of an innocent village. Not only did you slaughter innocent farmers and berry-pickers, Men, woman and some children. But you also, through your sheer stupidity, killed Soron Stoneblood, northern prince and his wife Velaina, a princess of the kingdom of Balta. You have single-handily placed the entire kingdom in jeopardy of war with the villages of the western lands, the southern kingdoms and the entire North."

Duke Evollan, still too arrogant and stupid to understand what was happening, replied snottily. "Impossible, I dealt with one village of bandits and peasants. That rabble? They were hardly worth mentioning, except for the one northern bandit who killed a fifth of my men."

"That one northern bandit that you speak of was the village blacksmith. If armed with more than a hammer and a knife he probably would have killed half your men. But he was not just a blacksmith. He was Soron Stoneblood, son of Theron Stoneblood king of the northern tribes. He and his wife had been living in that village for thirteen years," said Count Mavane.

The reality of the situation finally started to sink in for Duke Evollan. This campaign, to gain him favor and riches, was a disaster. War with the kingdom of Balta would be costly if it came to pass, but war with the north would leave the kingdom in ruins. The northern clans were a fierce nation and with slain prince for cause, they would pillage the entire kingdom. The duke would be lucky if the king didn't have him executed for this. "I suggest you head back to Progoh as soon as possible. Beg the king's mercy because you are going to need it Duke Evollan." Count Mavane spoke with utter distain. The actions of one man had ruined the lives of many and threatened the lives of countless more. Count Mavane turned on his heel, walking away from the duke, unwilling to look at evil one moment longer than necessary.

Chapter sixteen

IT'S NO WONDER father sent us here, Nathan thought to himself as he led the girls through the treacherous lands. The Great Swamp was a group of marshes, swamps and ponds that intertwined in the lowlands among the forest at the base of the Applomean mountain range. This meant that there were large areas of firm, solid land hidden within marshy areas, muskeg and quicksand. Travel in the Great Swamps was a dangerous business if you did not know the territory or were in a hurry.

Anyone coming looking for them would likely be unfamiliar with the area and have to move slowly. Some of the trails that Nathan was taking were so narrow you needed to walk single file, else risk being sucked into the thick swamp waters.

Looking up into the trees, Nathan could see the glowing hues of red and orange. The sun was falling over the horizon in glorious color. This beautiful sight was a warning that that darkness would soon follow. Nathan encouraged the girls to pick up the pace. They were not too far from their destination, a small island of high ground only a few hundred yards deep and a quarter of a mile long. The island, secluded and dangerous to travel towards, was a perfect place to stay.

They arrived, tired and wet, at the small island late in the afternoon. Nathan and Ava worked together to build a small camp fire. Nathan encouraged the girls to eat some food. He explained that they would be staying there for days, so they needed to make themselves a shelter to stay in. Ava nodded in silent agreement; she kept her fears and trepidation over the fate of their families to herself. Rose questioned why they had to come to the forest but seemed to accept that it was the safest place to be. The girls were young and scared but old enough to understand, and it seemed Bends had told them what to expect and how to act.

As they sat around the fire, Nathan organized his thoughts about how to deal with this situation. Ava, the older of the sisters, was the same age as Nathan while Rose was much younger. Nathan, not sure how much the nine-year-old understood about what had happened in the village, hoped to avoid talking about it. No point in worrying the girls even more by thinking about things beyond their control, he thought to himself.

Much like her older sister, Rose was loud, boisterous, bubbly and happy. Even today, she was trying to find positives in the situation. "Camping is fun. Are we going to do any exploring?"

Nathan smiled at her glad to have her thinking of anything but the village and her parents. "First. we are going to build ourselves a castle and then we will explore." Nathan gave Ava a wink, while Rose perked up.

"A castle?" she asked.

In the middle of the small island was a small cedar grove. Nathan had spotted one large cedar that had two dead tree trunks leaning up against it. With some smaller tree branches and limbs they could easily build a good sized shelter that would keep them dry and warm. "You see that tree?" Nathan pointed towards it. "We are turning it into a castle."

Working fast to take advantage of the little remaining daylight, Nathan and the girls gathered sticks and branches. Using bigger, older pieces to build an outer structure around the dead trees that leaned against the towering cedar. Then they used smaller, still-green branches to make a roof. Within a few short hours, they had a well-built little lean-to with two rooms: one for the girls and one for Nathan. The shelter was warm and cozy. The crisp, clean smell of pine needles filled the space, a refreshing change from the, at times, nauseating smells of the swamps.

Nathan was exhausted physically and emotionally, and was ready for sleep. Having said goodnight to the girls, he retired to his little section of the shelter. He was almost dead to the world when Ava came to him. "Are you awake?" she whispered.

"Barely, I am almost asleep now. How are you?" said Nathan groggily.

"I'm ready for sleep, too. I just wanted to say goodnight properly, now that Rose is asleep." She gave him a big hug, holding him for what seemed like forever. Nathan felt Ava disengage the hug. As she lifted herself up and away from him, she stopped to place a gentle kiss on his forehead. She whispered "thank you" before retreating to her bed and a well-earned sleep.

The next morning they ate a breakfast of berries and some of the biscuits that Bends had packed for them. Rose demanded to know when they would start exploring. Nathan explained, "After breakfast we are going to explore. While we are exploring, I am going to teach you some of the lessons mother taught me."

Rose was curious. "What kind of lessons, Nathan?"

Nathan looked around and spotted a good plant to use as an example. "See that big purple plant with the pink flowers?" The girls looked to where Nathan was pointing and both nodded. "What can you tell me about it?" asked Nathan.

Rose's forehead crinkled as she studied the plant "I'm not sure…, but it's very pretty."

Nathan smiled. "Yes, it is. Ava, how about you? Can you tell me anything about the pretty purple plant?"

Ava gave Nathan a funny look. He knew from all their walks in the forest together that she cared little for what flowers were called or good for. "Nope, but I agree with Rose. It is very pretty."

Rose smiled when her big sister agreed with her.

Nathan gave a small laugh. "Well I, too, agree it is a pretty plant. But it is not just pretty. It is a violet brettal bush. If you were to eat its berries you would get very sick. On the other hand, brettal bush leaves can be very useful. I am going to teach you as much as I can about every plant we see while exploring."

Nathan worried about keeping the girls minds busy, distracting them from thinking about all the bad possibilities of what transpired in the village while they fled to the swamps. He would use all the lessons and knowledge his mother passed onto him to fill the days they would stay there.

Rose smiled and lifted her hand like she were in a class room "violet brettal bush, don't eat the berries but keep the leaves. Got it"

Nathan was glad the girls were receptive to this. "Excellent, now let's go explore."

Every day they would walk through the swamp trails, Nathan would explain which plants were edible, which were poisonous and as many uses as he knew for each one. Then he would quiz the girls, occasionally trying to trick them up by miss-identifying a plant. However, the girls were both smart and quickly caught onto his tricks. By the end of a week, the girls knew more about the swamp then most adults.

It was a few days before Nathan and Ava had a real discussion about the attack. Nathan reassured her that it was likely her parents were not even in the village when the attack occurred; she knew this was mostly wishful thinking but left it alone. Instead she mentioned his parents and her fear for their safety.

Nathan wasn't sure what to say, should he be honest as to what his fears were or continue to pretend like thing would all be okay. He decided he should be honest with her, he would try being gentle about it but the truth was going to be hard to deal with now or later. Nathan looked to make sure Rose was out of hearing distance. She was safely out of listening range, chasing butterflies. "Honestly, Ava, I think something happened to my parents. They know where we are and would have come for us by now. Bends knows we are here but really only my mother and father know to look for us here. Everyone else has to wait for us to return." Nathan paused for a moment, having finally said it made it feel more real and he knew it to be true. His parents were gone now. Tears began to flow.

Ava hugged him tight. "It's okay, Nathan. We will get through this."

Nathan tried to compose himself, with a sniffle he wiped the tears away. "I know we will. It's just so hard to accept. You know what one of the last things my father said to me was? For the first time ever he told me something about my family. My full name is Nathan Stoneblood. And that I have birthrights in the north, whatever that means." This was something that confused him. Why had they never told him about his last name. What did it mean? Why was it a secret? he thought while waiting for Ava's reply.

"Stoneblood? That sounds ominous. Well, it always was strange: A northerner marrying a woman from Balta and living in a small village like Elderwood. You had to know they were keeping some secrets from you," replied Ava.

Nathan admitted this was true; this wasn't the first conversation he and Ava have had about the subject. "Well I always knew there was something, sometimes I could see it in their eyes when I would ask about their pasts, they wanted to tell me but something always held them back."

"Well you promised your dad you would keep us out here for a week, let's keep that promise then we can try figure things out." Ava said.

Nathan agreed, they could get through the next few days easy enough. What came after might be a different story though.

On the seventh day since the attacks, they had yet to see another soul. "Rose I have very bad news," said Nathan.

Rose gave him a very stern look. "Pardon me?" she said in a haughty voice.

Nathan had forgotten, ever since he told her they would be a building a castle she had insisted on being called 'Queen Rose' and that he was a lowly servant there to provide for the ladies' entertainment. Ava had further enhanced the game, building her little sister a crown out of vines and flowers. "Forgive me your highness. Queen Rose, I'm afraid that our castle has been bewitched and is no longer safe for your highness to sleep here. I must insist that we go back to the village today."

Rose looked at him and then gave her a sister a big smile. "We are going home now?"

Ava returned her smile and nodded. They were finally going home.

Rose turned back to Nathan "Very well, good sir, by royal decree I declare this castle no longer our home. To the village we go..." she turned to Ava, "Can I keep the crown?"

Ava laughed and replied "Of course you can, your highness, now come on let's go home."

By noon, they made it back to the village. Nathan sat for a few minutes at the edge of the woods and surveyed the situation. He noticed a few homes were completely burnt and there seemed to be no one around. Once he was sure that no soldiers were around, he carefully took the girls into the village, going directly to the Dollan house to check if they still lived.

When he opened the door to the Dollan house, Nathan was full of trepidation. Would old Bends be there? Were the girl's parents alive? He didn't even want to think about his family or the rest of the village yet. He just focused on finding the girl's family. But as soon as he opened the door his questions were answered. Right away he saw Suzie Dollan. As she recognized him she froze with nervous energy "My girls..." she started to ask. Before she could even finish the sentence, Rose and Ava ran past Nathan and into their mother's arms. The trio sobbed with joy, re-united.

As the mother and her children huddle in joyous reunion old Bent came into the room and spoke to Nathan. "Glad to see you son, we began to worry that you wouldn't be coming back." But as cheerful as the words were, Nathan felt the sorrow behind them.

"Bends, my parents are gone aren't they?" Bends, with tears in his eyes, confirmed Nathan's fears.

"I'm sorry son, they both died during the attack. As well as many others…" Bends said as his eyes shifted from Nathan to the girls who had begun looking around for their father.

"Mother, where is father?" asked Rose. She looked around, hoping that he was hiding in a corner and would appear at any second.

Suzie still holding both girls looked down with sadness "Your father is gone. He was very courageous and brave. He tried to help fight the soldiers, but there were too many, and they killed him."

The joy of being home was now lost to the girls as a wave of sadness hit them. Bends took Nathan outside to leave the girls to mourn with their mother. Outside Bent filled in Nathan on what happened during the attack and the week he spent in the swamp. "The king sent a company of men to track down bandits and they followed the tracks of one group to the forest east of here. One of the scouts saw you and your father training. The leader, a duke, decided that the village was full of bandits. At the same time a group of horsemen from the south came up the main road. So this duke thought it prudent to attack the "bandits" before the horsemen could help us."

Nathan interrupted at this point. "But the village has been here for over a hundred years and we trade with Salba all the time. How can they assume we are bandits?" Nathan exclaimed. Anger edged every syllable and sound coming from his mouth. He wanted to sob, to hit, to scream. He wanted ...well he really did not know what he wanted. His worst fears had been realized. His fragile hopes that his parents would be waiting with open arms were dashed.

"This duke was ignorant of our long and peaceful history of trade with Salba. He refused any help from Salba or any council from its leaders. He wanted the glory of defeating the bandits all to himself. Hours after the attack, the horsemen from the south arrived. They helped with the wounded and with burying the dead, then continued on to Salba. The next day, the count's men arrived with supplies and medicine. They took the wounded back to Salba and said anyone who wanted to leave with them would be looked after in Salba. The count made it clear that this duke was the one at fault and that the king felt terribly sorry for the actions of his men and would do whatever he could to help our people."

Nathan listened as Bends explained. He was glad to hear that the count and king were sad and wanted to help but even a king can't bring back the dead.

Bends continued his story. "Only a few families are still here. Some of us older bodies that didn't want to go to

Salba and Suzie who needed to wait for you to bring the girls back. A few of the young ones are still around as well. From over a hundred villagers down to barely a dozen now, Elderwood will never be the same." Bends spoke with regret at the tragic loss of life. "The count left word for you. When you are ready he would like you to come to Salba so he can talk to you." But Nathan wanted nothing to do with anyone from the kingdom at this point. He was too full of hurt and anger over the loss of his parents.

Chapter seventeen

DURING THE WEEK in the swamp, Nathan accepted that his parents were likely dead and had gone through a range of emotions. From being angry at whomever was behind the attack on the village, this duke people were speaking of or the bandits that caused the soldiers to come, to sadness and the grief from the loss of his loved ones. Now he was alone and all he felt was numb. Except for when something reminded him of his parents, then the bouts of anger and sadness came roaring back.

"Bends when I came and got the girls, you said that you and my father had made a plan for if something were to happen. What did you mean by that?"

Bends put a caring hand on his shoulder. "When your parents first came to Elderwood, they were strangers here. They worried that people from their pasts would come looking for them, that your life would be in danger. They made me promise if the day ever came that someone came looking for them, we would hide you. As years passed, this fear faded but was never forgotten. I never did learn what they were worried about but it was always obvious that your mother was a lady, and that your father was a warrior. Definitely not the normal sort of people who would choose to live in a small village, but they made it their home and yours as well. They gave you a good life here."

Nathan took in this. Bends didn't know any more about his parents than he did. He could see that Bends was eager to get back into the house to see his grandchildren. "Go back in, Bends. The girls missed you terribly when we were in the swamp and will need you more than ever." Bends looked grateful to hear this. Bends wanted to do more for the boy who had made sure the girls were safe, but he truly needed to be with the girls right now.

"I can never thank you enough, Nathan. If there is anything you need, come see me," said Bends as he turned back to his grieving family.

Leaving old Bends to be with his family, Nathan walked towards his own home. He came past his father's blacksmith shop on the way to bringing the girls home. It looked intact. He was glad the shop looked to be okay and would inspect inside later but right now he just wanted to go home.

As he walked closer to home, the degree of devastation increased. Many of the homes in the area around his parent's home were burnt to the ground. The Burning Candle, the local Inn run by the widow Noggins, remained intact. Nathan could see signs that the Inn had been cleaned up; hopefully the kind widow was still alive. Not ready to speak to anyone right now Nathan did not go in. While the Inn still stood the next three houses had burned completely to the ground. When Nathan came to his own home he was not surprised by the fact it remained partially standing. It certainly had not escaped the fighting unharmed. Most of the roof was gone, as well as the front door.

His father had built the small cottage himself using cob, a mixture of clay, straw and sand. The cob was not as quick to build with as lumber but retained heat better in the cold months and stayed cooler in the hot months. It obviously was harder to burn down Nathan noted, as he walked into the wreckage that once was his home.

The cob walls had not burned and were probably the only reason there any of the house remained. Once the roof finished burning, along with the interior support beam and the door the fire had obviously died off. This left the house furnishings blackened and partially burnt yet intact. The smell of burnt wood and soot assailed his senses, normally he would enjoy the scents but right now they triggered visions of burning houses, and images of his parents burning filled his mind. He could not be here right now.

It would take a lot of work, but if he chose, Nathan was sure he would be able to rebuild the cottage. At this point he wasn't sure if he wanted to. Right now it seemed all that had made this his home was gone and being in the burnt home reminded him of what he had lost. Nathan decided then, that for at least a while, he would head back to the woods and the solitude of the swamp.

It was only mid-summer now so there were months before it would be too cold to stay out camping in the woods. Nathan went through the house grabbing what supplies he could find: a few changes of clothes, his mother's herb satchel, with a handful of vials, his mother's tools and a large pack of food such as dried meats and small blocks of cheese from the pantry. The forest would provide everything else he would need. Nathan gathered his supply packs and his daggers, took one last look around the house and headed off to say good-bye to Ava.

He headed back to her house and knocked on the door. Bends answered the door. Bends noted right away that Nathan was packed to leave. "Are you sure you want to do that, son? I know you lost your parents but there are still people here that care about you. The girls will be devastated if you leave."

Nathan knew this was true but was feeling overwhelmed by the sadness of losing his parents. He wanted to leave as quickly as possible to get away from the pain. "I just need some time to myself. The house and everything in the village reminds me of mother and father. I think I will be back soon, but I need to say goodbye to Ava. Can you get her for me?"

Bends certainly understood what Nathan was going through. Everyone that remained in the village had lost family or good friends. "I'll get her right now."

When Ava got to the door she looked terrible. The joy of finding her mom and grandfather alive, followed by the pain of learning of her father's death had been hard on her. When she seen Nathan at the door she ran up and gave him a huge hug. "Are you okay, Nathan? Bends told me about your parents."

Nathan held her tight. To leave her right now was so hard to do, but he had to get out of the village. "I'm at a lost. When no one came out to the swamps to get us I knew something bad had happened. So I was somewhat prepared for the news. It wasn't bad 'til I got home. Now everything reminds me of them, it hurts so much."

Ava held him tight before finally letting go. It was then that she noticed his bags. "What is going on? Why are you packed? You can't leave me." Ava started to cry.

Nathan held back his own tears. "I'm sorry Ava. I need to go away for a while. I can't stand being here. The cottage, my father's blacksmith shop every time I look at them I think of my parents, and I am so sad and angry, I think I am going to burst."

Ava thought about how hard it had hit her finding out her father was dead. She could only imagine how it was for Nathan losing all of his family. "Promise me you will come back. Swear it."

Nathan exhaled loudly and took a deep breath. He gently lifted Ava's chin so that he was looking into her eyes. "Ava, I swear I will be back."

Ava held his gaze for a moment longer then leaned in to give him a kiss. The kiss seemed to last forever to Nathan but in reality only seconds passed when their lips parted. "You better come back, Nathan. Don't make me have to come find you."

With that, Nathan released Ava and took up his packs. If he lingered any longer he would lose his nerve and stay. He needed to be away from everything for a while. He turned and headed for the forest.

Nathan knew every inch of the land within a day's walk of the village but, beyond that, found himself in new territory. To the East of the village lay the road towards Salba and the kingdom of Broguth.

To the south about two days walk away was the village of Birchone, a slightly larger village than Elderwood. Nathan and Velaina would visit it once every couple months to sell herbs and medicinal salves at its daily market. From Birchone it was a quicker journey to Salba. During the summer months, most travellers would take the direct route until the few creeks ran dry, making it expedient to take the more northern route pass Elderwood.

To the north lay the swamp lands and then the land started to rise quickly into the mountains. In the west, lay more forests and plains with few villages or roads. Nathan decided he would head north into the familiar swamp lands, which offered plenty of food and shelter. Then, he would start working his way west to explore some new land.

Chapter eighteen

THE NEXT COUPLE weeks went by quickly for Nathan. Every day he would follow roughly the same routine. He continued traveling through the forest and swamp lands, keeping to high ground, until his eye caught sight of a berry bush or swamp pod of value. He would pick the berries, herbs and wild vegetables as he found them. As much as berries and edible roots were abundant enough to help fill his belly, he needed to hunt for meat. Worpon, a small docile variety of wild hog, was an animal easy to hunt and provided a satisfying meal that replenished his energy.

Most curious and fortunate for Nathan was the day he had been stalking a rabbit when from out from nowhere came a fox and quickly snatched the prize. Nathan groaned. In his mind he thought, drop that damned rabbit, I saw it first. He swore out loud. The fox dropped the rabbit. Nathan could not believe his luck. The fox stopped and looked back at Nathan, then at the rabbit, before taking one last look at Nathan and running off into the woods. The incident reminded Nathan of his encounter with the wolf.

By mid-day, he would stop and eat the berries and vegetables he had gathered, along with any leftover meat from the night before, if he had been successful hunting. With hunger almost satisfied, he would spend hours working with the daggers, remembering each move his father had taught him. He would work on each progression of attacks and counter-attacks. When he tired, he would sit for a few minutes and practice controlling his breathing. Many of his father's lessons on fighting had been not only about how to use weapons but also how to control his own body and mind. Losing control of one's emotions or not being able to control one's adrenalin during a fight were as dangerous to a warrior as any enemy's blade. Nathan focused on the breathing techniques his father taught him to bring his heart rate down and calm his mind. He would continue wandering and spend the afternoons looking for more food and herbs, always keeping an eye out for a suitable spot to make camp for the night. Each night before dusk, he would make camp by finding a sheltered spot to sleep and make a fire. If he had a successful hunt it was a cooking fire. If he came up empty-handed or had leftover food, it was a comfort fire.

In the firelight, he would sort his daily pickings. Velaina had taught him well. He knew what to look for while wandering through the forest and swamps. Each day, he would pick wild rose petals, any aromatic flowers petals he came across, wild mint leaves and white cedar to make perfume. Perfume wasn't very useful but it always sold for a good price in the markets. Cattails, marsh mallows and birch sap made a good salve for cuts and bruises, and a liquid version with ginger root and honey was good for indigestion, colds, fever and upset stomach. Nathan knew many other cures and potion formulations but the perfume, salve and ginger root drink would sell quickly anywhere. With his mortar and pestle, he ground up the herbs and made his potions. Many of the herbs that Nathan picked also were edible. Cattail roots made nutritious flour. The flour would have been tastier had he been able to fry it in butter. However no matter how much he wished he could pull out a cow in the middle of nowhere butter was not on the menu. Taste was not the main concern. Survival, food for energy was the main concern. Strawberries, small and tasty, were in season. He ate the berries and saved strawberry leaves. The leaves made a fine tea for treating disteria. Each day, after he was done gathering materials for making potions and salves, he would eat supper sitting by the fire looking up at the stars, wondering if his parents were up there watching him.

Nathan was stretching out after a tasty meal of a particularly fat and juicy quail when he heard a ripping sound. He looked down at his shirt. He had just torn the seams of his tunic. His clothes were getting old, ragged and rather on the small side. Before long he would need to trade or make some new clothes or end up walking around the forest naked. I really do need new clothes Nathan thought to himself. While he enjoyed the solitude and peaceful surrounding of the forest and swamps, he was starting to miss the sound of other people, not to mention Ava. While not ready to return to Elderwood, he was ready to socialize with the world once more.

Deciding to leave the swamplands, he started heading south. He was already several days walk west of Elderwood. Heading south now, it would take only him a few days to reach Birchone, even with his heavy sack filled with nature's bounty. At Birchone, he planned on selling goods at the market, staying in an inn for a few nights and eating someone else's cooking.

As he walked south, the land changed. The damp wet—lands filled with cattails, birch and bushes full of berries—dried. The trees became taller, growing pines and cedars. Even the scent of the forest changed. The lighter woodsy smells of cedar, and combinations of wild flowers, started replacing the musky pungent odors of the swamp. Nathan enjoyed the walk. As much as the northern swamplands were filled with valuable herbs and plentiful amounts of food, they were not the prettiest or most inviting lands.

The woodlands to the south presented a much more appeasing landscape. After three days of walking south, Nathan started to recognize some of the land. He was back in familiar territory and only a day's walk from Birchone.

Following a meandering brook, Nathan stopped at a small water pool for the day. First he built a fire, then started collecting a few items from his packs and started making some soap. It wouldn't help his sales to come into the village smelling like he had been camping in the woods for over months.

He crushed up some wood ash to made lye. This he combined with aloe and sunflower oil, mint leaf and lavender. Nathan heated the mixture then carved out a chunk of bark to create a mold for the soap. He poured the soap mixture into the bark mold and let it cool. The lye combined with sunflower oil turning the oil into a harder, more solid bar of soap.

Nathan stripped down and jumped into the pool of water, finding it cool and refreshing. He quickly scrubbed himself down with the soap and then gave his clothes a quick scrub as well. As his clothing dried in the afternoon sun, he took one of his daggers and used the reflection of the pond to give his hair a trim. He had been getting rather shaggy.

Looking into the pond he was almost startled by his reflection. He had grown in the last months. Taller and leaner, his skin was bronzed by the daily sun. His dark hair and brown skin make his bright blue eyes stand out even more. He had not gotten his dark hair from his mother, but he certainly had gotten his bright light-blue eyes from her. While he was lean from constant walking, he was wider in the shoulders now. Tall and strong with narrow hips and wide shoulders, standing over six feet tall now. He would look most men in the eyes or down on them. Nathan was quickly becoming a young man.

Birchone, while by no means a city, was a much busier place than Elderwood. Being on the main trade route from the south to the east, it drew a fairly steady stream of travelers, most on route to the large cities of Progoh and Venecia. The village of Birchone had many farms in the surrounding area. They would bring their grains, vegetables and livestock to sell to the traders, who would take those goods into the larger markets to resell. Nathan had always enjoyed coming to Birchone with his mother to sell their goods.

The markets were always full of interesting things, as the profession traders were always willing to exchange goods instead of coins. Every time they sold a good in Birchone, it gave them more space to take on new goods to sell in the cities.

Besides the trading markets, Birchone was home to several businesses that catered to travelers, such as blacksmith shops, a livery, and several inns and pubs.

The Winking Mule was Nathan's first order of business on entering the village. It was his favorite place to stay when in Birchone. The inn was a two-story building, with individual rooms upstairs and a large common room on the main floor. They served excellent meals and made rather tasty honey mead.

Nathan walked into the building and looked around, behind the bar stood its proprietor, the man known as Big Willy. Hearing his name, one might conjure an image of a large burly man with an oversized belly, but Big Willy was nothing like that. Big Willy, or William Biggs, was a small slender man in his later years. His stature may have been small but Big Willy had a large smile and was always friendly with Nathan and Velaina when they traveled to Birchone.

As Nathan walked up the bar Big Willy gave him a thoughtful look before breaking into a smile "Why hello there lad, I hardly recognized you. You have grown some since the last time I saw you." Big Willy chuckled. "But your clothes haven't. It looks like you are going to have to spend a coin or two at the market and get some new ones."

Nathan looked down. He had managed to do a good job cleaning his clothes the day before. But no amount of cleaning could hide the fact that his shirt and trousers were a couple inches short. "Clothes and some good shoes for sure, but first a room and meal," said Nathan with a sheepish smile.

"Certainly, I'll bring a bowl of stew and some fresh bread out for you in a few minutes with a mug of mead. Take the first room on the left; you will be able to see the traders set up for market in the morning through your window. You can get a peek at who has some decent clothes."

Nathan placed two silver coins and a copper on the bar. "I'll want the room for at least a few nights; this should cover it and my meals."

Big Willy took the coins and laughed. "Well, I don't know about that. It will cover the room for sure but, from the size of you, I would say you're going to eat enough to drive me into the poor house at that rate" with a wink he slapped Nathan on the arm. "Take a seat and let me go get you some food."

Big Willy headed back to the kitchen while Nathan took a moment to survey the room. Besides the large bar and hearth the inn's common room was filled with an assortment of large and small tables. Most were filled with patrons finishing off their dinner while enjoy a pitcher of mead or wine. In the corner Nathan found a small empty table at which to take a seat.

Soon, Big Willy came back out with a large bowl of steaming stew and a half a loaf of fresh bread. The aroma of the fresh baked bread made Nathan's mouth water. He took a mouthful of the savory meal and sighed contently. He enjoyed eating someone else's cooking, especially a nice hot stew like this, full of chunks of beef and garden vegetables. A nice change from the mostly wild fruits, game and plants his meals had consisted of during his stay in the swamps and woodlands.

After enjoying the stew and fresh bread, Nathan headed up to his room. A proper bed was a winning proposition on all accounts. As Nathan got to the stairs leading up to his room Big Willy stopped him for a brief moment. "We heard what happened in Elderwood. I am sorry for your loss. Both your parents were fine people and always treated me well. They will be missed," spoke Big Willy solemnly. Nathan thanked him and headed up to his room. The room was sparse but clean. Nathan sat down on the bed, his lanky frame filled it. This was so much better than sleeping on the ground, he thought to himself as he fell into a restful slumber.

The next morning, Nathan woke refreshed and full of energy. The quality sleep and prospect of new proper-fitting clothes did wonders for his mood. As he exited the inn, Big Willy gave him a heads up that several traders had set up in the market this morning and that he should visit the tall balding man at the north end of the street. Big Willy explained that his clothes were more expensive but they were high quality and he was the most likely to give Nathan fair value for his perfumes. Big Willy had already spoken to the man and let him know that Nathan's family always produced goods that fetched top dollar among the royal families.

"Thank you, Big Willy, that sounds perfect. I will go right now." Nathan was feeling sheepish about his clothing, or lack thereof. It was time to remedy the situation.

The tall balding trader was expecting him when Nathan arrived. He quickly sized up Nathan's build and picked out several garments for Nathan to look over. Many of the tunics and pants were obviously meant for richer city folk, bright colors and intricate designs were a common theme. But the clothing was all high quality thick Morthon cotton with silk threading. Hester, the tall bald trader, had evidently been trading clothing for a while. His experience showed when the garments he had chosen for Nathan all fit perfectly.

After Nathan picked out a few that he might like, he opened his satchel to show Hester his own goods. His mother had been known for her high-quality perfumes despite the fact she did not often make them. She had preferred to spend most of her efforts on healing salves and potions, but she always got excellent value in trade for them. Hester examined a few of Nathan's vials looking to see how clear the oils were. Cloudy oils would indicate a low quality perfume not properly mixed. Satisfied that they were all very clear and of a good consistency, he opened one of the vials to give it a sniff.

Hester could tell right away that he would get excellent coin for the perfume. The combination of rose petals, jasmine and a hint of lavender were the notes that Hester could detect. After a short bit of haggling, Nathan traded six vials of perfume and two small pouches filled with a healing salve. He received two pairs of pants three tunics and two pair of shoes.

Once Nathan was done trading with Hester, he spent the next hour wandering the market and making small trades. He found a glass trader and replenished his supply of vials for future potions and traded several pouches of salves for a large sack of food, the cured ham, cheeses, bread and fresh fruit were a welcomed change from his previous road meals.

He sold his last vials of perfume for twenty copper coins. He probably could have received better value trading for merchandise, but having the coins would allow him to eat and sleep at the Winking Mule for as long as he wanted.

Taking all his new clothing and supplies back to his room Nathan went back down to the common room for a midday meal. Sitting at the same small table as the night before, Nathan looked around the room observing the different people talking and eating at their tables. At the table next to Nathan sat three traders exchanging tales of their journeys.

Nathan was not eavesdropping, but when he heard one of the men at the next table mention Elderwood that he started paying attention. "Hardly worth even stopping in Elderwood anymore, only a dozen or so villagers left. All they have now is Elderberry wine. Which is fine but hardly profitable enough to justify worrying about all the bandits that have moved into the area," a portly gentleman spoke.

Nathan looked him over, he remembered him. The portly man was one of the many traders that would find cheap goods in the small villages, to sell in the next village or sell something from the previous village. He would dicker and deal, trade his way south or east until he got enough goods to make a profit in one of the capital cities. If traders like him were avoiding Elderwood, the village would be in trouble. Even before the devastating attack, most of food supplies for the village came from trading. Now even more than before, a higher percentage of the villagers would be relying on these traders. Nathan felt a pang of regret that he had been gone from the village this whole time. He wondered how he could help the villagers, his friends. An idea formed. He could help the remaining villagers recover from the tragedy they all had suffered.

Nathan stood and took a step over towards the men's table. "Excuse me sir, I couldn't help but over hearing and I just wanted to tell you that on your next trip it would be wise to stop in Elderwood."

The three men looked at Nathan. At first glance he could be mistaken for an adult due to his tall wide frame but his boyish face and soft voice gave strong evidence of his true age. Nedd, the man who had been speaking earlier, recognized Nathan. "Ah! Hello there lad, I have not seen you in a while. You have grown. Since your parents' deaths and the burning of the mill, Elderwood hasn't been the same."

Nathan relaxed, the fact that the trader recognized him would make getting him to come back to the village easier. "I've been gone from the village since it happened. But I am on my way back now and will be selling a lot of the same perfumes and medicines that you got from my mother."

At this, all three traders perked up. Elderberry wine was okay but perfume and medicines had much higher profit margins in the cities. "Alright, lad, if you can promise that, all three of us will make sure we come through Elderwood. "Are you looking for coin or goods?"

Nathan thought about it for a moment and decided that the best thing would be as much food as possible, and supplies such as vials and small pouches. Once the village was reestablished as a good trading post he would ask for coins. "Supplies mostly. Once we have re-established good trade. I would like more coin but to start I will need goods."

The traders had no problem with this. Glass, leather and food were not exotic items so they would not have to make any special preparations before visiting Elderwood again. "Well, I am still not fond of the idea of taking the northern roads into Salma with all the bandit problems of late, but good perfume gives me a better paying clientele in the cities. I will come to Elderwood for that," spoke up the other trader Nathan had overheard. The trader and his traveling companion were taking their wares south to Valencia and would be back in about six weeks. Nedd had business to attend to in Progoh and would visit Elderwood in about three weeks. Nathan was satisfied with his efforts. He would have plenty of time to organize and make potions to trade. The men had treated him as man, not a child. Indeed, he was surprised and satisfied all at the same time. He was not used to being treated as an adult. His size was deceptive. His maturity and mannerisms added to the deception. Nathan had changed greatly.

Having made the decision to return to Elderwood, Nathan returned to the market and traded the remainder of his salves and potions for additional food and more empty vials. His pack was now completely full and he had a second smaller pack of supplies. His walk back to the village would take longer with the heavy packs but would be well worth it in the long run.

With clean new clothes that fit, two full packs of supplies and a new found purpose, Nathan was ready to return to Elderwood. With eager anticipation of his return home, he quickly packed his gear, gave his room a tidying and headed back down the stairs to say farewell to Big Willy. "Once again, your hospitality has been delightful Big Willy. I believe I have gained five pounds eating here these last few days, but I am off to Elderwood now."

Big Willy smiled; he took pleasure in having the best food in the village. "You take care, boy, I am glad you found some clothes that fit; you look like a young prince now instead of a vagabond. Be wary of strangers. The roads are a dangerous place these days."

Chapter nineteen

NATHAN LEFT BIRCHONE with a spring in his step. A lovely day to travel, he mused to himself as he adopted a ground eating pace. The journey home on the main path would be much shorter than the winding meandering walks of the last few weeks. Eventually, the heavy packs would make the journey a very tiresome endeavor but for now he strode with purpose. With good weather and lightly burdened, the trek from Birchone to Elderwood was normally about two days, but with the heavy packs, he would not be able to keep to that timetable.

As Nathan walked, he breathed in the clear crisp woodsy air and smiled to himself as the familiar scents triggered memories of walking through the forests with Ava. By the gods, I do miss her so, he thought to himself. It seemed like forever since they last walked through the forest to sit at the pond, able to enjoy each other's company without a care in the world, before their innocence had been prematurely stolen by the tragic events. Vivid flashbacks invaded Nathan's mind as he walked. Memories of her infectious laugh, the gentle caresses followed by swift punches, the way her lips felt on his skin... He knew the decision to go off and be alone was the right one. He felt much more at peace with himself having had the time and space to properly mourn the loss of his parents. Yet the whole time he was away, he never stopped thinking about Ava. He wondered how she felt about him and how they would interact when he returned to the village.

With his thoughts bouncing from scenario to scenario, the miles and hours moved quickly. That first day he covered a great distance before the heavy weight of his packs and the nonstop jaunt took its toll. Finally, he gave in to the desire to rest for the evening. He ate a quick meal and slept the night away dreaming of a certain girl. The next day Nathan continued his stroll towards home. The journey was uneventful; with the roads being mostly deserted, he encountered no travelers. But nightfall would reach the land before Nathan could make it all the way back to the village. He would need to spend one more night on the road before reaching his destination. Nathan remembered a nice camping spot a short ways up the road that would make an excellent place to sleep for the night. It was a spot where the creek came close to the road, fresh water would let him clean up a bit before completing his journey.

Not much later, he found the spot from his memory. From where the creek lie, it was only five miles to

Elderwood. He would be home the next morning. Grateful that his journey was almost complete, Nathan set up his camp, making a fire and washing up at the creek. Later that night, while Nathan sat beside his fire, staring up into the stars, musing his upcoming return to Elderwood, he heard a twig crack; someone or something was coming from the road towards his fire. It was not unheard of for travelers to be on the main path this late at night since Elderwood was a couple hours away. But the custom of the road was always to yell a greeting before walking up to a stranger's fire. Whatever or whoever was out there was not friendly.

Nathan was sitting on the creek side of the fire opposite of road so who or whatever lurking out there would look into the fire to try seeing him. Nathan slowly and as quietly as possible grabbed his daggers. He slipped away from the fire into the darkness of the trees besides the creek. There he crouched and waited. Dark forms made their way towards the fire. Two armed men were standing beside his fire: bandits!

"Come on out, boy. We saw you walking up the road. No point hiding. We know how heavy your bags are, and we just here to help you out. We will be taking those bags for you, along with any money you have," said the tall bandit beside the fire. His rough voice left no doubt, that while his words were almost pleasant, this was a robbery. Nathan calmly thought about the situation. Many of his father's lessons about combating multiple enemies came to his mind. He readied himself for what was to come.

As the first bandit moved closer Nathan analyzed his opponent. Against the light of the fire, Nathan saw his rough leather clothing and iron sword, at least this one was not well armed. Nathan took another step back into the trees. His body disappeared into its shadows. As he waited beside the tree, he watched the second bandit circle the fire. Once the bandit was outlined by the fire, Nathan spied a double-sided ax and a large dagger on his belt. Well put together and soft moving, this one was the danger.

Nathan now had a good assessment of his enemies so he stepped out of the shadows and spoke. "You're welcome to sit by my fire. I will charge you only five coppers a piece, but I'm afraid my bags stay with me." He was not nearly as confident as he sounded, but his father had taught him well. He would not dishonor his father by cowering from the likes of these men.

The bandits laughed. It amused them that a young boy, albeit a large one, armed with only two large daggers would be so cocky. They would soon show him that he should have been much more afraid. In unison, the two bandits attacked without a further word. The talkative one came from the right with an overhand swing of his sword. While the other came from the left taking a low swing towards Nathan's knees. It was obvious that these two had worked together before by the well-timed and co-ordinated attack. Nathan quickly jumped towards his left to get out of reach of the ax swinging towards his knees. The sword that had been coming down from the side was now directly overhead. He easily blocked this attack with his left dagger while bring his right dagger up to slice across the body of the sword wielding bandit. The sharp northern steel sliced through the man's breeches and quickly drew blood. The sharp intake of breathe gave evidence of stinging pain. The bandit growled deep in his throat.

Nathan circled farther to his left, bringing the now-wounded bandit between himself and the ax man who was readying himself for another swing. Enraged by the sting of his wound, the first bandit swung his sword wildly around. He just missed the second bandit on his backswing, before slicing through the air toward Nathan's chest. Again Nathan easily blocked the blow, this time with his right dagger. Pushing back against the attacking sword he forced its blade up against the hilt of Nathan's dagger where it caught in the grooves above the hilt. Nathan gave a hard twist of his wrist catching the bandit off guard and removing the sword from his hand. At the same time, his left dagger sliced across the bandit's face opening up his cheek and carving a small chunk out of his ear.

The now swordless bandit lifted both hands toward his face instinctively covering the cut across his cheek. The second bandit was still behind the first. So Nathan had time to place a hard kick into the man's now defenseless chest, sending the wounded and defeated bandit backwards into the fire. Now that the bumbling would-be swordsman was out of his way, the second bandit swiftly resumed his attack. From the calculated and smooth way the bandit moved, Nathan could tell he was a dangerous adversary, unlike the one crying and desperately rolling to put out the flames on his clothing.

The bandit swung his ax in quick short swings, not allowing his momentum to carry the ax past a point where it would not swing back to block any attacks from Nathan. They fought by the fire for several minutes. Nathan blocking the ax attacks with his daggers but unable to gain any advantage over his opponent. Finally, the bandit made a near-fatal error. He brought his left foot back around him, to take a larger swing at Nathan. This larger backswing gave Nathan the opening he needed to get close enough to the bandit to strike. Nathan quickly stepped up towards the bandit stabbing into the man's right leg with one dagger while the second dagger sliced out across the bandit's chest from the right. The dagger coming towards his chest forced the bandit to stop his swing and turn his momentum backward in an attempt to avoid the incoming blade.

The bandit now stood on his good leg and warily watched Nathan who had quit advancing. Nathan sensed that his combatants' desire for combat had been dampened; he wondered if they would leave now if given the chance. "If I were you two I would take this opportunity and leave. Before you both end up as crows' bait." Nathan's words no longer sounded as those of a boasting child to the bandits. They now sounded like a trained fighter giving a beaten opponent a merciful opportunity to retreat. The ax man wisely took the opportunity to gather up his accomplice and hobble back to the road.

Nathan's heart was pounding as he carefully watched and listened as the two enemy combatants retreated into the night. Remembering one of his father's lessons on combat he started controlling his breathing by taking deep breaths. Holding them in for a ten count and then slowly exhaling. As he did this he closed his eyes and replayed the battle in his mind.

He found fault in several things, starting with sleeping too close to the fire. He had been lucky the bandits had come directly from the road and made too much noise. If he had not had the opportunity to retreat into the shadows, he could have been attacked while on the ground, which could have been deadly.

Next, he went through the battle, retracing his footsteps and moves. He had scored blows against both opponents but none had been fatal. Against two more-skilled warriors, he would need to have more accurate strikes to vital areas of the body. A man will fight through a sliced thigh but a sliced groin is another story. Overall he had to be happy he had survived his first real combat without injury. He also had to concede that luck and poor opponents were the main causes of victory. Nathan would not make the same mistakes again.

Chapter twenty

WHEN NATHAN AWOKE, the sun had not yet begun to show itself over the eastern horizon, but it was fast coming and the dreary pre-dawn light was enough to see the creek. Stripping down, Nathan tiptoed his way into the cold water. Crisp and invigorating, the water quickly removed any mental fog. Nathan was now wide awake. He wasted little time cleaning himself; with a final dunk of his head into the water, he flipped his head back to remove some of the excess water from his hair.

After exiting the water Nathan did some light stretching while stark naked, mostly to remove the water but also to insure he didn't have any tight muscles from the long walk or the brief yet intense action of the previous night's fight. Dry and feeling the blood flowing nicely from the stretches, he donned his second set of clothing. It felt good to return to town wearing his new clothes. If he was being honest, he would to confess that he wanted Ava to see him at his best. As he finished dressing, the sun finally started to push its way into the horizon. The gentle first rays of morning felt good on his face. Able to clearly see the path ahead now, he began the last leg of the journey home.

It was a bright and clear sunny morning as Nathan walked up the road and into the village. He could see signs of rebuilding on a few of the homes and buildings but for the most part there was still a lot of damage from the attack. As Nathan approached his own family's house, he was surprised by signs of work.

Someone had started replacing the roof timbers. Nathan did not know what to think. Why would anyone squat in a damaged house when there were several empty houses? Many had been abandoned or left empty when the families living in them died during the attack. As he pondered this he carefully walked up to the building, hand resting on the handle of one of his daggers just in case some squatter wanted trouble over him retaking his family's home.

As Nathan entered the front entrance, still missing a door, he looked around. The room was clean and tidy; someone had done a lot of work here. As he looked for evidence of the mysterious and industrious guest, he heard a voice from above.

"Well, are you going to just stand there, or are you going to pass me that timber leaning against the wall?" spoke out a mysterious voice.

A slender blonde-haired man with delicate facial features sat on one of the main support beams for the roof, notching in a side beam. He looked to be middle aged and in good health, not someone he would assume to be a squatter. The friendly tone of his voice made Nathan relax the grip on his dagger. Nathan grabbed the timber from the wall and handled it up to the stranger.

"What is it that you are doing here?" Nathan asked as he watched the man put the timber into place.

"I am fixing the roof. What does it look like?" said the stranger with a smile.

Nathan chuckled, if nothing else this man had a sense of humor. "I can see that, but why are you fixing my roof?"

The stranger laughed. "Well, I hear it tends to rain around these parts. A roof will keep the water out of the house."

Nathan was beginning to think this man was a little crazy. "Okay, that make sense, but I am still not sure why YOU are doing it." The man stopped working on the roof for a moment and studied Nathan. "You surely look like your father but you have your mother's eyes. I am Verin Albet and I am your uncle."

Nathan was surprised to hear this. Neither of his parents ever spoke much about their pasts. Nor had they ever mentioned any family. But it was rather possible that this Verin could be his mother's brother. His blonde hair and blue eyes were a match and the delicate facial features very much resembled his mother. It struck Nathan that this was the second time he had learned a family name under weird circumstances. This was the first time hearing his mother's maiden name.

Taking a second look at the man, he compared his memory of her to the face of the man in the roof. He could only wonder why he hadn't noticed it earlier. This man Verin was obviously his mother's brother. "You will have to forgive me; I did not know I had an uncle."

This did not surprise Verin. Velaina and Soron had wanted to live a simple life together and had come to this small village far away from the intrigue of either of their native homes. "Your parents had good reason to keep their pasts quiet. I am sure as you got older they would have filled you in on who you are and why they were so secretive." Verin paused for a moment then sighed. "Let me come down. We will eat a bit of an early lunch, then I will tell you all about Velaina Stoneblood."

Verin swung down so he was hanging head down from the timber. Then with a twist, he pulled his feet back so he would drop to the floor, did a half summersault and deftly landed on his feet. Verin pulled out some bread and elderberry jam from one of the newly restocked pantry shelves while Nathan grabbed some dried meats from his supplies. They ate in silence, both wanting a few moments to collect their thoughts before getting into the story of Nathan's mother.

147

Finishing his meal, Verin told Nathan about his mother Velaina Stoneblood, or Velaina Albet as she had been before marrying Soron Stoneblood. Verin began his story by giving him some basic family background. Velaina Albet was the third of five children of then ruler King Vellin Albet of the kingdom of Balta. Velaina's mother Muriel came from a family of healers and it was said that King Verbon met her after a great battle in which he had been wounded; Muriel had helped heal the king who became infatuated with her.

As a young girl, Velaina learned the healing arts from her mother. When she was of a marrying age, King Vellin sent her to live in the courts of Venecia to be properly courted by nobles from the city and surrounding lands. Velaina, while a beautiful young woman, was also a practical one. Despite being of noble birth, she enjoyed going out and picking herbs and plants for making medicine. It was on one of her journeys into the countryside of Venecia where she first met Soron.

She was walking her horse through the forest when she came upon a small meadow filled with wildflowers. She stopped, dismounted and was gathering flowers when a small group of men entered the meadow.

Velaina greeted the men with confidence. A smart woman, she noted the high quality clothing of the men and way they were following a deer path through the forest. Nobles out on a hunt, she quickly surmised. The men seeing how beautiful she was gave up the search for deer and came up to Velaina. While the men were dressed like nobles, Velaina had warning signs going off in her head.

She wanted to step back and create some distance herself and the approaching men but could not see a way of doing so without appearing rude. So far, the men were acting nice and were friendly as they talked to her about the forest and any signs of deer she may have noticed. One of them, a shifty-eyed scarecrow looking fellow, smiled and commented about the fine form of her horse. His eyes however were not fixed on the horse. She grew nervous. When he asked where her companions were, she recognized danger and her fear showed in her eyes. She had read his emotions changing and they were ugly.

While she spoke, one of the men came to look at her horse. Suddenly the man was right beside her with his hands firmly around her horse's reins. The shifty eyed man who had smiled while talking to her was now smirking. A rather sinister tone to his voice had Velaina preparing to jerk away and flee. "Relax princess, you are not going anywhere."

Velaina was getting ready to make a run into the forest when a voice responded from behind her, "Why would she be going anywhere? It is a beautiful day and there are still many flowers to be picked."

...

Verin stopped his story to take a sip of elderberry wine.

Nathan had been hanging on every word. His impatience at the break in the story telling showed on his face. Nathan was just picturing his young and beautiful mother on a horse surrounded by hunters on foot when Verin upped the suspense with silence. "That is a terrible place to take a break. Please keep telling the story," spoke Nathan in protest of the dramatic pause.

Verin gave a small chuckle before quickly continuing with the retelling of the romantic meeting of his sister with the handsome stranger who would rescue her. Watching the face of his nephew, he saw reflections of his beloved sister Velaina. Finding her son was a blessing of the gods.

Verin began artfully retelling how the men quickly turned to see who joined them in the meadow.

...

Velaina had never seen four faces turn so white and fearful so fast before; the man behind her terrified these men. They began backing away, the one who had been holding on to the reins hastily let go to rejoin his companions as they continued to back away from her.

The sinister sounding one now took a contrite and fearful tone as he mumbled, "You're absolutely right.

But picking flowers won't catch us that deer, so we will be leaving now." The men almost tripped over each other as they turned and ran into the forest.

Velaina watched with amazement as the men ran off. Finally she turned to see who had inspired such fear. Velaina was looking at an incredibly tall and strong looking stranger with long dark hair and a clean-shaven face.

Besides his great size, Velaina could only wonder what terrified the men so much. The big man did not appear to have a weapon on him. "They sure ran off fast. You must be one dangerous man to scare them so."

The giant man smiled, "Maybe to scoundrels like them, a lady such as yourself has nothing to fear from me. Those spineless cretins are sons of noblemen who flaunt the law as if they are above it. There used to be ten in their little group of rapist bastards."

Velaina was shocked to hear that she had so narrowly avoided a dreadful outcome, but she kept her calm. This tall dark stranger made her feel safe. She smiled. "Used to be ten?" she quizzed.

The big man shrugged his shoulders. "Things happen."

She could imagine what things he had done and it explained the fear the men had shown at his arrival. She suspected his arrival was no more a coincidence than the deer hunter accidently finding her in the meadow. This big man had been stalking her stalkers. Before she could even thank him, he gave her a brief farewell telling her she would have no more problems on her journey today and disappeared back into the forest. She regretted that he had not given her his name. He was foreign. He was intriguing. And she suspected he was the sort she had been warned to stay away from.

Later that week, she sat at a royal dinner when in walked in her mysterious and handsome rescuer. He was sitting at a table of visiting emissaries from around the world. Wanting to find out more about the man before he had the chance to disappear again, she walked over to his table and smiled "You turn up in the most interesting places, sir. Are you going to at least introduce yourself tonight? "

The tall northerner smiled. "My name is Soron Stoneblood."

...

Verin stopped his story for a moment. "Your mother told me all about how she met your father when she came home to announce she was would marry a northerner and be staying in Venecia. Your mother was always a strong and independent woman. Where others feared your father for his sheer size and ferociousness in battle, your mother saw a shy loving man with no love for killing. At times it was hard to tell who courted whom. Your mother would show up at functions where Soron was acting as an emissary for the northern tribes and would wait outside for him to walk her home.

Nathan was enthralled by the story of his parents meeting. Excited to learn more, he peppered Verin with more questions. "What about my father? What can you tell me about him?"

Verin gave it some thought before beginning "Soron Stoneblood, son of Theron Stoneblood, Theron is the leader of the northern tribes a fierce collection of warriors and hunters. Soron and most of the northerners, or Pellians, are decedents of giants. Although very few giants still live in the north their blood lines run strong. Many of you northern blooded men are big and strong beyond comparison. "

Nathan was surprised, so there actually was something to the children's stories of Giants and other mysterious creatures roaming the north. Being the descendent of a giant was a shocking yet very intriguing idea he thought to himself as Verin continued his explanation of the northern people.

"The northern tribes are often nomadic moving from hunting area to hunting area. Others are raiders living off the wealth they accumulate attacking other northern village and tribes. Along the northeastern coast, there are seamen who raid along the entire continents eastern shore line. Theron Stoneblood was a fierce warrior in his younger days, defeating all those who would try invading Stoneblood lands. Your father's tribes control the northern slopes of the Applomean Mountains and the valleys below. They are rich with minerals and the produce some of the best steel known to man."

Nathan knew a little about this, his father may have avoided telling him about his past but he had passed along his knowledge of metal work. Nathan knew all about northern steel and Verin's explanation about it was not necessary but he said nothing, glad to just hear any talk of his father.

"Northern steel is harder and less brittle than any other steel produced today. Looking at your daggers, I can see your father taught you some of the Stoneblood blacksmith secrets. Stoneblood weapons are still even harder than northern steel and are some of the finest weapons ever produced. When your father was a young man, barely older than yourself, his father sent him to learn how to forge the steel and to help protect the mines. Such valuable steel producing mines were often the target of other clans trying to steal any weapons or minerals they could. Your father had countless battles before his sixteenth birthday. "

"By the time your father turned twenty he was a grizzled war vet tired of the bloodshed. He spoke to your grandfather about his dislike for the violent nature of the north, he ended up helping a caravan make its way from Salma to Venecia. It was there that Soron met Velaina.

After your father met Velaina, he returned to the north. He told his father that he had met a woman in the southern lands and would be returning to her. Theron became furious and told Soron to never let him see him again. Later Theron would realize his mistake and try to make amends with your father, but Soron was in love with no intentions of returning to the north. Your parents lived in Venecia for a year, but when they found out she was pregnant with you they moved here to this small village. In Venecia Soron and Velaina were always in danger because of their bloodlines. They did not want you to live like that so they moved here, stopped using their full names and became simple tradespeople, a blacksmith and a maker of potions."

Suddenly it all made sense to Nathan, that was the big mystery and why they kept so many secrets. His parents had chosen to raise him in a simple village but in order for that to work no one could know of their true pasts, not even their own son.

"How did you come to be in Elderwood Verin?" Nathan was happy to learn more about his parents and their pasts. But he was also curious as to his own future, and what role Verin planned on playing in it. "When word that Duke Evollan attacked the village and that your parents were among the dead, Count Mavane, one of the few people in the continent with knowledge of both your parent's identities, sent word to both families.

He explained how the duke had been sent to deal with the bandit issue. That through bad timing and poor decision making the duke came to think the village was full of bandits. And a group of southern horsemen were racing towards the village to join in an attack on him and his men. Instead of using logic or common sense the duke decided to attack the village before the horsemen would arrive. The duke gave his men orders to attack everyone, woman included, as a way of punishing bandits.

A vile man that duke Nathan thought to himself. Nathan knew that the king's army had been involved in the attack on the village but he had never understood what really had happened until now. "And what happened to the duke?"

"When the count told him how badly he had screwed up, killing innocent villagers, and two members of royal families from other kingdoms, he understood that the king would have no choice but to imprison him and have a trial. The honorable thing to do would have been to submit himself to the kings mercy, explain the circumstances of the situation and hope that the king would be able to avoid war with Balta or the north. Instead the duke went into hiding and is now a wanted man. No better than the bandits he was sent to find," said Verin.

Nathan was startled by this "Why would a war start?" Nathan was a bit confused by this idea.

"Your parents may be a simple blacksmith and a healer in Elderwood. But in Balta and the north they are still a prince and a princess slain by a king's army. Wars have started for much less. If my father had still been king then yes war surely would have started. But father has been unwell for a few years now and my older brother Verbon is now king. It was Verbon who sent me here to find out the truth of what happened and to find out if you were alive or not. "

Nathan had much to digest. He remained silent. His father was a prince and his mother a princess. He suddenly remembered the funny smile his father had given him when he said his arm bracelet gift was fit for a queen. He sighed. So much he did not know. Verin appeared to believe it was the infamous duke that blame and retribution needed to be heaped upon. Nathan listened as Verin explained his perception of what the truth was.

Verin had been in Elderwood over a week and spent that time talking to the remaining villagers and a few scouts that Count Mavane sent to the village to check on them. Verin believed that it truly was the duke at fault and that war between Balta and Progoh could be avoided. Verin was not so sure about the prospects of war with the north being averted. Northerners were a proud people and the death of a prince was something not likely to go unanswered.

Nathan was not sure what to think, he wanted retribution for the atrocities committed but war sounded like a terrible idea. "And now that you know I am alive what is your plan?" asked Nathan.

"Well that's up to you Nathan, if you like I can take you back to Balta or stay here with you for a while. I'll show you a bit of the world if you like, and there are many things I am sure your mother did not teach you that you should know," said Verin.

He thought about this for a few moments. He had just gotten back to Elderwood and wasn't ready to leave yet but the idea that he had more family in Balta was intriguing. "I would like to see Balta but before I leave Elderwood I would like to help the village. The ones that have chosen to stay need some help. Without the mill that burnt down during the attacks the main income is elderberry wine. Elderberry wine is not enough by itself to bring traders north during the wet season when they can travel straight from Birchone to Salma and on towards the capital. They need to do something different."

Verin took pride in his nephew's words. Often the children of royal lines were raised to believe they were better than their fellow man and grew into selfish uncaring adults. His sister raising Nathan in a small village had been a good thing despite her tragic end. "Okay and how do you intend to help the village then Nathan, son of Soron?"

"I have a plan."

Verin laughed, "That may be so, but first there is a certain girl that has been coming here every day to check if you were back yet. If I were you I would go talk to her, then we can discuss plans."

Chapter twenty one

LEAVING VERIN, NATHAN went to the Dollan house to find Ava. With trepidation and excitement, he looked forward to seeing her again. When he knocked on the door, Bends answered, letting him in.

"Nathan, it good to see you, boy." Bends paused for a moment, taking a good look at Nathan. "I might need to stop calling you 'boy' if you keep growing like this."

Nathan smiled. It was good to be around a familiar face again, even if it was ol' Bends teasing him about growing. "Hello Bends. It's good to see you again too. How are things here?"

Bends gave a half-hearted smile, "Things are a little slow. Not many villagers are left and hardly any traders come through the village any more. But we are getting by."

Nathan suspected that they were not getting by as well as he made it sound. But he didn't want to put a damper on the friendly reunion by questioning him further. "You wouldn't happen to know where Ava is? I would like to say hello."

Bends chortled. "I was wondering how long it would take for you to get around to asking me that. I should say you better go find her to say hello. If she walked in here and found you just chatting up this old man, she would probably come unhinged and kill you. "Bends rubbed his chin, pretending to ponder this for a moment. "Say, that might be worth watching. Stick around, she will be back eventually."

Nathan laughed, he could picture it happening that way. "I would rather not die today if it is okay with you."

With a wink, Bends told Nathan where to find Ava. "She's with her mother and sister, picking elderberries. At this time of day, you will likely find them at the creek washing the berries off."

Grateful for the warm welcome, Nathan said goodbye. "Thank you, Bends. If you will excuse me, I am going to avoid the grim reaper by finding her now."

Bends waved him off. "Get out of here. Welcome home, Nathan."

The creek was only a short walk from the house and took less than a few minutes to get there. Immediately Nathan spotted the women working and waved to them, "Hey, everybody."

Ava's and Rose's heads popped up at the sound of Nathan's voice. Within seconds, Nathan found himself crashing to the ground enveloped in a bear hug with both of the girls. "Hey, you are getting my new clothes dirty," Nathan protested.

But the girls were having nothing to do with it. They kept hugging him. "We missed you, you big bung beetle. I thought you were never coming back," said Ava.

Finally, the girls let Nathan up. "Hello, Nathan. It is good to see you again," said Suzie, the girl's mother. "You seem different. You have grown, and those new clothes suit you well."

Nathan dusted off his dark green tunic and new pants. "They are a bit fancy but my old ones didn't fit any more so these will have to do."

Ava agreed with her mother. "You look very nice, Nathan, and you certainly have grown."

All of a sudden, Nathan felt a strong kick to his shins. Rose had wound up and given him a hard kick. Before she could think of doing it again he stepped back "Oww. What was that for, Rose?"

The younger girl was frowning and giving Nathan a stern glance. "That is for leaving." She stepped closer and delivered another swift kick to Nathan's shin, "And that is for not saying goodbye." With tears in her eyes, Nathan could see how hurt she was.

Nathan squatted down so he was eye level with the girl, took both her hands in his and spoke softly. "Rose, I am so sorry. Can you ever forgive me?"

She choked back a few tears, gave him a big hug then stepped back, breaking into a big smile "Okay, but don't let it happen again." Rose shook a berry-stained finger at him for good measure.

Nathan was grateful with how quickly the young girls mood cleared up, leaving the past behind them. Wanting to spend some time with Ava, Nathan helped the girls finish up with the elderberries. When they were done, he took Ava for a walk into the woods. They naturally headed for their favorite spot: the pond. They said little on the way, just content to be in each other's company once again.

When they arrived, Ava finally spoke, rapidly asking a series of questions. "How are you, Nathan? Have you been home? There is a man there that says he is your uncle, and he does remind me of your mother, is he?"

Nathan laughed. The quick series of questions was a thing Ava used to do when excited, some things never change. "Yes, I was home. Verin is my uncle. He has already told me so much that I never knew about my mother and father. It is nice to be around family again." Nathan looked very thoughtful. He wondered what else he didn't know about his extended family. When he had asked his parents about family, the topic was changed, re-directed and sometimes the reply was they were a part of a sad past and that the future was what counted. As a young boy, the answers had satisfied him. He was a child no more and the simple answers no longer satisfied.

Ava nudged his elbow. She prompted him, "and...."

Nathan continued filling in Ava about his travels through the swamp and how he ended up in Birchone. He talked about the bandits on the way home and about meeting Verin.

Ava smiled at his tales. "You have been busy. I am glad you have grieved losing your parents enough to come back. It has not been the same here since the attack." Ava grabbed a hold of Nathan, held him tight and whispered, "I really missed you." She took his hand, squeezing it tight.

Nathan was awash with emotions and simply replied, "I missed you, too," while gently squeezing her fingers back.

Chapter twenty two

AFTER NATHAN RETURNED from spending time with Ava, he found Verin preparing a stew for supper. "Have a seat, Nathan. Dinner will be ready in an hour or so—plenty of time for us to talk about this plan of yours."

Nathan's plan was simple. Of the remaining villagers, the majority were elderberry pickers. Only a few others like Haren Frinkle, the only remaining elderberry wine maker, and the widow Noggen, who ran the village's single Inn, remained. If enough traders purchase Haren Frinkle's wine then he would keep buying elderberries and the rest of the village would have work. If the elderberry trade died off, then the village would die off.

Since his visit to Birchone, Nathan understood that if he stayed and made salves and perfumes that traders would come. Nedd, Balvin and Verto, the three traders he had met in Birchone already intended to come to Elderwood. More would follow if Nathan stayed. The problem was he wasn't sure he would stay. He wanted to stay out of loyalty, to rebuild...but he wanted to go. Nathan looked forward to travelling with his uncle. He wanted to learn more about his parent's past and the world beyond that which he knew. To keep the village going, Nathan knew someone other than himself would have to produce the medicines and perfumes that would entice traders to keep coming back to Elderwood. Nathan was torn by this; his mother had taught him many secrets that could be dangerous in the wrong hands. He decided he would not have to share all the secrets, just those safe and innocent enough to produce desirable salves and perfumes. As much as his mother had taught him, he did not see himself as a healer in the future. Passing those skills onto others would be a way of honoring her memory.

The solution to this problem was simple. When the attacks had happened, Nathan took Ava and Rose into the swamp for a week, he had spent a large portion of the time teaching the girls about the plants and flowers and what they were good for. Since they already knew which plants to gather, it would not take long to teach them how to make the perfumes and enough medicinal salves to sell. When Nedd came in a few weeks he would be bringing the supplies that Nathan had requested. Suzie Dollan and the girls would be able to use those supplies to make potions for Balvin and Verto when they came in a few months.

While Nathan explained his plan with Verin he told him about his trip to Birchone and how he was attacked on the road. Nathan gave an honest retelling of his battle with the two bandits, to which Verin commented, "Your plan to teach the Dollans basic potion making is solid. But it won't help them if you don't solve the bigger issue."

Nathan was not quite sure what his uncle meant by this. "What is the bigger issue?"

Verin walked over to where Nathan was sitting and, after asking permission, took one of Nathan's daggers. As he inspected the weapon, he continued to talk, "The big problem is bandits. Bandits started this whole mess and as long as there are bandits roaming free in the woods along the roads to Elderwood, then Elderwood will struggle. Those bandits you fought will still be in the area and likely belong to a large group."

Nathan understood his uncle's logic but was not sure how they could solve that issue. "But we aren't in the kingdom, and after the duke's attack, the king's army will not leave the kingdom. They don't want the outlying villages and cities fearing an expansion. Nobody wants war."

Verin flipped the large dagger, catching it by the tip, and then flipping it again. "Bandits may be the king's problem, but once you made the village's survival your problem, then the bandits became your problem. Are you going to wait for someone to take care of your problems for you or are you going to take care of them yourself?"

Nathan watched his uncle play with the dagger. He was obviously familiar with his weapons and had excellent hand-eye coordination to handle the weapons so easily. He pondered the question of the bandits for a moment. He had not thought of hunting the bandits down. He was no warrior yet, but he was not afraid. "So, how do I do that?"

Verin smiled and pointed the large dagger in his hand at Nathan. Flicking his wrist he flipped the knife around so that the blade was in his hand and threw it towards Nathan. It sunk deep into the timber beside his head.

Wide-eyed, Nathan looked at his uncle as he calculated how easily he could have died.

"While you train Suzie and the girls how to make potions, I will train you to become a ranger," said Verin.

Nathan nodded thoughtfully and smiled. If all rangers could throw knives with accuracy like his uncle demonstrated, he wanted to become a ranger. "I will be your pupil," he said to his uncle. "When can we start?"

Verin chuckled. "Finish your stew first, and then go talk to your friends. Tomorrow will be soon enough." Verin was beginning to really like his sister's son. Nathan had shown loyalty and courage, and was eager to learn. Perhaps Velaina had been wise to raise her son away from pampered courtyards where entitlement ruined many a royal prospect.

...

When Nathan approached the Dollan family about his plan, they were very excited, especially Ava and Rose. Ava clasped Nathan's arm and turned to her mother. "We can do this mother. Nathan showed Rose and me all sorts of plants and what to make with them. We really do know what to pick."

Even Rose chimed in proudly, "Yep, we experts mother."

Suzie laughed and smiled at her confident daughters. The truth was she had been anxious about the future and Nathan's plan sounded better than anything she had come up with. "Okay, Nathan. The girls know what plants to collect. But we don't have the tools or the ability to turn them into potions."

Nathan just smiled. "Not yet."

The next morning Verin took Nathan into the small meadow where he had trained with his father. "Judging by your sword breakers and the account of your battle with the bandits, your father has obviously given you some training. Before I can train you further, we will have to see what skills you have. Once that is done, we can start adding to them. Defend yourself." The second he said defend yourself Verin drew his sword and in one quick motion was attacking.

Nathan barely got his daggers out in time to block the attack. Verin moved quickly. Not only were his sword attacks fast but he also moved incredibly fast laterally, attacking Nathan from one side then instantly attacking from the other. It was all Nathan could do to keep blocking the attacks and reposition his body to try and counter Verin's quick movements. This differed greatly from the style of attack his father used against him, but Nathan's training showed. He was able to successfully block all of Verin's attacks. After five minutes of the fast-paced swords play Verin stopped.

Nathan was sweating and he already could feel his heart starting to pound faster. He took the opportunity to take some deep breathes and control his body. Verin watched as he did this. "Good, your father taught you well. The sword-breaker style daggers are not conventional but with your strength, speed and hand-eye co-ordination you defended perfectly. I can see now why he chose those weapons for you. The fact that you understand the value of controlling your breathing and heart rate is also good. One less thing to teach you, but eventually you are going to have to learn to do the breathing techniques while fighting and not just after. Controlling your heart rate and breathing is vital. If we had stayed fighting at that pace, you would have slowed down and been susceptible to quick attacks.

As he worked to get his breathing under control, Nathan thought about what his uncle had said. It was similar to the things he was working on with his father before he died. Nathan could almost hear his father saying the same things.

"Now, close your eyes," Verin commanded. He waited a full two minutes before continuing, "In detail, describe to me your surroundings."

Nathan did as he was told. He used his memory to describe the meadow, where Verin was standing, how far they were from the edge of the forest, every detail he remembered.

"Not bad. But what about the wind? What direction was it coming from? From what angle is the sun coming down. Are there any clouds in the sky that will change how much sun and shadow there is? Is the ground a clay or rocky under the grass? From what spots in the tree line would be most likely to find an archer waiting to attack? You must learn to be completely aware of your surroundings: what can be used against you and what can also be used to your advantage." Verin smiled. "You have a good base of skills to start with. It won't take too long to get you up to being a respectable ranger." Verin paused then signaled the end of the lessons for the day. "Go teach the girls potions. Tomorrow, we will continue your lessons."

Nathan smiled. He was proud that his uncle thought he was worthy of becoming a ranger. He was also proud that his father's training was showing. Content with the lessons, Nathan headed towards the Dollan house.

When Nathan had talked to Suzie Dollan and the girls about learning to make potions, he had given them instructions to go into the swamp and look for several plants. That next day they had gone to the swamp. The girls taught their mother which plants Nathan was talking about, they also took Bert one of the single men left in the Village for protection. Armund had been helping the Dollans, and although he was not being pushy about it, it was easy to see he fancied Suzie Dollan. Nathan had given the girls only a small list of plants to harvest: skunk cabbage, white birch bark, black currents, cedar sap and lavender. Today, he would teach them a simple salve with those ingredients.

He stood at the table of the Dollan house with the woman and old Bends on the other end watching him. It felt a little bit intimidating to be teaching adults and he told them so.

Suzy said, "Don't worry. If you get too bossy and cocky and I'll let you know," she laughed, putting him at ease. And on that note, the lessons began.

"First thing to remember, always have a clean workspace. Wipe the table and all your tools with lemon water before you start." Nathan paused and waited while they followed his instructions. "Second get a pot of water and put it over the fire. You want it to be hot but not yet boiling. While the water is getting hot start crushing the plants. Suzie and Bends probably know what I am talking about but I will explain everything so Ava and Rose know for sure," said Nathan.

Ava smiled at Nathan. She was grateful that he was teaching Rose and herself in the same way as the adults.

"The mortar and pestle are the basic tools used for crushing plants. The mortar is a clay or hard wood bowl and the pestle is a little club shaped piece of wood. I brought four sets from my mother's supplies for you to use. Today we will make a salve for cuts. It's a simple one and the ingredients are easy to find in the swamp. It sells well with healers from the cities, so traders will always buy a few bundles when they come through."

"First, crush and grind the plants and flowers—lavender, white birch bark, black currents." As Nathan talked them through the lesson, they eagerly got to work using the mortar and pestles to crush and grind the plants. The combined scents of the plants filled the room. "Next, add the ground plants to the hot water. Make sure you use the right amount of water or you will waste time waiting for more water to heat, or for too much water to boil off. As you do more potions you will get a feel for how much water to use, depending on the amount of dry ingredients you are using. Add the cedar sap into the water. Now, lower the pot so the water boils. Keep stirring the mixture. As the water boils off, you will have a thick oily paste. Let it cool and scoop the salve into the skunk cabbage leaves. Only put a small hand-sized scoop onto each leaf so the leaf can wrap several times around it. If you can't find skunk cabbage, swamp lily also works," said Nathan.

Nathan watched as they worked on their potions. Everyone seemed to understand his lessons. He had worried that he wouldn't be nearly as good a teacher as his mother had been. "Tomorrow, you will go back to the swamp and get more ingredients. I will teach you another potion, but the basics will be the same as today. Good job ladies."

Everyone enjoyed the lessons, particularly Ava and Rose, who appreciated the fact that Nathan was a patient and thorough teacher.

Ava smiled and flirted with Nathan. "Now that our lesson is done, can we go to the pond and I will teach you how to play splash."

Nathan laughed. "Ha! We shall see who teaches whom."

...

Verin, too, was a patient and thorough teacher. Early the next morn, back in the meadow, he told Nathan, "Your black steel daggers are excellent weapons up close, but not all battles are fought up close. The bow is a valuable weapon for a ranger and is the main tool of a hunter. So today we are going to start your bow work."

Verin held up two different style bows, "A long bow and a recurve bow," he explained, while showing Nathan the two weapons. The long bow was exactly as it sounded: a sturdy-looking bow almost as tall Nathan, with a slow gentle curve. The recurve bow was a little smaller in length and when Nathan held it, the ends were bending back away from him.

Verin continued, "Long bows are easy to make quickly, are a perfectly fine weapon, and are the most common in this part of the world because of that. The recurve bow is harder to make and is harder to pull, which is a negative for some. But it also gives more energy back, so a smaller recurve bow can fire as far as a bigger long bow. Because you are such a strong lad and are only going to get stronger, we are going to build a bigger recurved bow."

Nathan liked this idea. He was proud of inheriting his father's strength. If building a bigger bow would take advantage of it, he would certainly do so.

"At first, it will be difficult to pull but, once you get the hang of it, it will give you range beyond any normal bowman. Northerners are not known for being fond of the bow, yet those who do have great range. However, range without accuracy is useless. We shall practice with both bows while you learn. Once we get a good piece of wood, we will build you a proper bow that takes full advantage of your strength."

Verin set up several targets at different distances in the meadow. Each large chuck of wood had targets painted on with three rings. A ring about foot in size, a smaller second ring half that size inside it, and finally a small bull's-eye the size of a coin in the middle. Verin took the long bow and quickly, with a smooth singular motion, pulled the arrow back and released at the first target. While the first arrow was still in the air, Verin launched the second arrow, and again the third arrow with speed and precision.

Nathan retrieved all three arrows from the targets. All were in the bull's-eye.

Verin was an excellent marksman to no surprise. Verin handed Nathan the long bow and an arrow. He held the grip with his left hand, cocked the arrow into the nocking point with his right and then pulled back until the string was touching his cheek. He looked down the arrow at his target and adjusted his left arm to bring the arrow into line with the target. Slowly exhaling, he released. His arrow flew true and hit the target with a thud. He had hit the edge of the second ring.

Verin approved of his first attempt. "Good. Exhale slower as you shoot. You want to be as steady as possible when you release the arrow, but once you have fired, give it just long enough to clear your bow then begin notching your next arrow. Watching your arrow is not going to help at this shorter distance. Work on precision, then speed."

After a few hours of working with the bows, they stopped and went on the next lesson. Hunting, whether for game or enemies, involved learning to read the signs on the ground. Broken branches, bent grass, depressions in wet ground, all help to show a path where someone had traveled. A skilled hunter reads the signs like a book. A lot of this was already known to Nathan because his mother had taught him so much about the forest and how to read the scat and trails of forest animals. But Verin's lessons were much more focused on the small details. Nathan learned how to recognize each animal's prints, how shod horses had unique markings and how to recognize individual horses and how they moved. Nathan's days alternated back and forth between working with Verin and teaching the Dollans. The days were long but fulfilling.

...

"Perfume is going to be your best seller. My mother, Velaina, had an excellent reputation for the quality of her perfume, even though she tended not to make a lot of them. She preferred to make more useful things like salves. But for you, I would make more perfume. It will keep traders like Nedd coming back," said Nathan.

As he passed his students a vial to examine, he continued the lesson. "Perfume ingredients are basic and it is easy to make. The trick is getting the ratios right and blending it well."

For a week, Nathan had been teaching the Dollans mostly about medicines and remedies that would be useful to them as well as be something to trade. Today, he was going to start with perfume. Good perfume was hard to find in the cities despite how easy it was to make. Few had the inclination or knowledge of plants to make it and even fewer were willing to go into the swamp lands and forests to gather the necessary ingredients. Most importantly, being able to make a pleasant long lasting scent was a bit of an art form., Nathan had learned from Verin, that even at a young age, his mother had an excellent nose of the art and made her own perfumes. It was only when she and Soron moved to Elderwood that she began selling them.

"All perfumes we make will be mostly a combination of almond oil and sunflower oil. These are the carrier oils that are good for the skin. The extra oils are added to the carrier oils to change the scent. Different oils not only smell different but also have different potency and longevity. Lemon oil is light and easy to notice, but it also doesn't last very long. Cedar oil is not as strong smelling but lasts for a long time. Lavender and jasmine are in the middle. The perfume we are making today is mostly scents of rose, lavender and jasmine with a little bit of lemon and cedar."

As he spoke, he carefully added small drops of oil to a vial. Five drops rose oil, eight drops jasmine, eight drops lavender, three drops lemon oil and three of cedar oil. This filled the vial about a fifth of the way up. The rest of the vial he filled with half sunflower and half almond oil.

Rose wrinkled her little nose as if exercising it for the perfume testing. Old Bends laughed. Rose did the wrinkle thing with her nose again, and they all laughed.

Putting a piece of cork in the vial, Nathan started shaking it. "It takes a few days for the oils to blend properly, so make sure to not sell blends you just made. Quality control is vital to making a reputation of being a seller of good perfume. For each perfume vial, shake it daily and remember to keep it out of the sun. Mother had three different perfumes that seemed to sell really well in Progoh and two that sold really well in Venecia. This is one for Progoh and Salma," explained Nathan.

For several weeks, the routine stayed the same. Nathan would spend most of his time with Verin sparing, practicing with the bow and then going out into the forest hunting and learning to track. When Nedd, the first trader, arrived in town they had plenty of goods for him to buy. Nathan explained to Nedd that Suzie and the Dollans made most of the potions and would continue to do so in the future. Nedd, seeing that the quality of the goods was still very high was more than pleased to agree to keep returning to Elderwood. During the weeks while Nathan and Verin were out hunting and working on Nathan's woods-craft skills, they were also keeping tabs on all the human tracks they encountered. They now had a pretty good idea of where the bandits were coming from.

When Nedd arrived in the village, he was greeted warmly by the remaining citizens of Elderwood. His supplies were a welcome sight. Nedd seemed quite pleased by the quality and quantity of perfumes and salves the girls made under Nathan's supervision. He promised to return for more.

When Nedd traded his goods with them, he also gave them information on the bandit situation. Often the bandits traveled in smaller numbers, like those who had attacked Nathan on his return trip from Birchone, and seemed to have one main camp in the mountains, which was the base of operations. From Nedd, they had learned that the bandits had been becoming increasingly dangerous and brazen in their attacks. Besides Nedd, who had been willing to risk the trip for he had given his word and had customers lined up for a very healthy profit, very few were willing to risk traveling in the area. The time had come to deal with this problem.

During their suppers and before sleep, Verin would often talk to Nathan about Balta, or the southern cities, teaching him about how the politics in the cities worked and how he should behave as a young member of royal bloodlines. Sometimes they would discuss the bandits and what would be the repercussions of Verin and Nathan attacking them. While Nathan had previously had combat with bandits, he had never been in a battle like the one that was to come and he had never had to kill anyone. It was a depressing topic but Nedd's recalling of the harm the bandits had been doing lately solidified the idea in Nathan's mind. They must stop the bandits and that would mean killing them.

...

It was Sunday. No lessons from Verin, no teaching potions to Ava and the rest of her family. Today Nathan and Ava were back at the pond in the forest having a lazy day to themselves.

Nathan didn't want to admit it but the lessons were coming along well and soon he would be out of things to teach them. Soon it would be time to leave. As excited as Nathan was about the prospects of going to Balta, he dreaded the idea of leaving Ava behind. As they sat in the meadow grass looking up through the trees into the sparsely clouded sky, Nathan looked over at Ava. She was picking dandelion heads and blowing them into the sky and then letting them fall onto her face. She would wrinkle her freckled nose, puff a breath of air up to blow the particles from her face then repeat the process.

Ava turned and threw a handful of the dandelion heads at Nathan. "All right, spit it out."

Nathan had been trying to figure out how to broach the subject of his coming departure; obviously Ava had sensed something was up. "What? I said nothing," exclaimed Nathan.

Ava sighed. "Exactly, you haven't said a word in the last hour. Even for you, that is way too long. Something is bothering you, so spit it out." Ava had known Nathan long enough to know all his moods; it was obvious Nathan had something to say.

"Well, I guess you are right. I just don't know what to say." Nathan was unsure how to proceed.

Ava, frustrated by the way the conversation was, going blurted out, "You've been thinking about it for over an hour and that is the best you can come up with? Why not start with the fact you have been practically teaching the same lesson for the last three days, or fact that you are going to leave with your uncle soon? Why can't you just admit you are stalling because you don't want to leave and you are going to miss me?"

Nathan was floored; everything he had been struggling with trying to find the words to say, Ava had just covered in one mouthful. "If you knew what I was thinking, why did you let me sit here and struggle with it?"

"Because you were supposed to say it, you big dummy. If I mean so much to you that you are delaying leaving, the least you could do is say it." Ava leaned over and wacked him on the arm, emphasizing her point.

"I'm sorry Ava. This is hard for me. I still miss mother and father a lot and being around uncle Verin has really been nice. I want to go meet the rest of my mother's family, but I also am not looking forward to leaving you. You are my best friend and I don't know what I will do without you."

Ava moved over so that their bodies were touching. She grabbed his arm and pulled it around her, forcing him into a warm cuddle. "I understand your wanting to be with family, I just don't want to lose you. I'm afraid that when you get to Balta, you will never come back."

Nathan couldn't imagine never seeing Ava again; the idea hurt him just to think about it. "Ava, I promise when I go to Balta I will come back."

Ava turned so that she was looking Nathan in the eyes "Say it again."

Nathan locked eyes with her and slowly said, "I promise to come back."

Ava reached over and grabbed the back of Nathan's head pulling him in even closer. "You better come back or you'll never get another of these," she stated before passionately kissing him.

Chapter twenty three

"HAVE YOU SAID GOODBYE to her yet?" asked Verin. He had watched the telltale frequent looks between Ava and Nathan. As much as they said they were just very good friends, their friendship had all the signs of a romance. Verin remembered his first love and wished Nathan better luck in love than he had. Being a warrior was easy compared to figuring out females. It had taken him years to figure out a fine figure and face did not mean a fine and true heart. He remembered his dalliances as a spoiled prince, and the lessons he had learned.

"No not yet." He wished he could put it off longer, but the time had come. Nathan knew that before he left Elderwood to begin hunting down the bandits, he would have to say goodbye to Ava. He and Verin were all prepared to begin the task; the only thing left to do was say his goodbyes. This is going to be difficult, he thought to himself before answering his uncle. "I'm headed there now—just preparing myself."

Verin smiled with sympathy for the boy. Leaving loved ones before a battle or dangerous trek was tough even among veterans. "Be honest with her and respect that this is just as hard for her as it is you."

Nathan nodded. "Okay, I am going now." With his uncle's advice in mind, he headed out to meet Ava. Earlier, he had left word at her house to meet him at the pond for dinner.

He placed the basket down beside the blanket. Nathan had put together a simple meal of meats, cheeses and fresh bread, hoping a meal would make the dreaded conversation go better. He even had Miss Noggins bake him an apple pie for desert. Not long after he laid the meal out on the blanket, Ava arrived.

She smiled at the arrangement of foods. The smile was a bit forced, as if she wasn't really happy to see it. It wasn't the first time Nathan used food to soften her up or appease her. Something was up. "Eat and then talk?" she queried.

Nathan was more than happy to simply sit and eat together. He readily agreed. Perhaps this wasn't going to be so bad after all. But as they ate, the silence became like a cloud over the meal. Normally silence between them was accepted and natural; this one felt like a brewing storm. As they nibbled on the pie, Nathan broke the silence. "I am leaving with Verin tomorrow."

Ava looked at Nathan for a while. She stared into his eyes before asking, "Are you going to Balta now?"

Nathan looked down, unable to hold her fierce gaze. "No, we are going to go look for bandits. I will be back before I leave for Balta." Nathan understood that she didn't want him to leave. What Nathan did not understand was that Ava was as frustrated with him for going hunting bandits as she was for him wanting to take the trip to Balta.

"This whole hunting bandits idea is so stupid. Why can't you just leave it to the king's men?" Ava was angry and it showed. "You are just a boy and will get yourself killed." Nathan took exception to these comments. "Do you not remember the last time the king's men came hunting bandits? And this won't be my first altercation with outlaws."

Ava could not accept the idea of Nathan being a warrior. She saw only the gentle friend who never minded when she hit or tripped him. She saw the boy but not the fire inside him. Raising her voice she took a hard stance. "Fine, go get yourself killed. See if I care. And while you are at it, you might as well just head to Balta when you are done getting killed. Obviously there nothing important here in Elderwood for you." Ava had tears in her eyes but was not backing down.

"I am going after the bandits because there is something important in Elderwood for me: you. And Balta is not forever, I just want to see my family and learn who I am. Mother and father kept so many secrets from me."

"Just go," said Ava as she walked away.

Nathan watched as she left him, not looking back. Tears ran down his face. He did not know what he could say to her to make it different. He was going no matter how much it hurt. As much as it hurt him to leave her, the idea of leaving for Balta before making the area safe was crazy. He would not be able to live with himself if something happened to her while he was in Balta. No, Nathan thought to himself, his resolve strengthening, I have to do this. Wiping away his tears he picked up the basket and blanket, and headed back to the village to say his goodbyes to the others, especially Rose. She was upset but not nearly as much as Ava. Rose thought killing bandit sounded exciting and wanted to tag along.

When it was time to go after the bandits, Verin let Nathan lead the way. While he was the more experienced tracker and had years of combat behind him he felt that the best way for Nathan to learn, was to do. And since Nathan had made helping the village his mission it was he who needed to find the bandits and determine how to defeat them.

Verin would help as much as necessary, but the burden of responsibility lay on Nathan's shoulders. Nathan was more than willing to accept this role. He appreciated everything that Verin was doing for him, but he needed to do this and would face this danger head on. Moreover, he was ready for this. Between his father's training and that of his uncle Nathan had gained an incredible knowledge of fighting skills. So similar and yet so different, he mused to himself. His father had focused on defensive skills using his weapons and strategy to stay safe, fending off any number of attackers. Verin's lessons were much more offensive, using weapons and strategy to defeat the enemies as they were found. Both styles had merit and when combined gave Nathan a well-balanced approach to battle. One he would need as they tracked and hunted down the bandits who terrorized the lands surrounding Elderwood.

The bandits' trails, from their mountain stronghold, led a couple hours north and to the east of Elderwood. Despite finding these trails several times, they had not ventured too close at any time. They had not wanted to run into any bandits before they were ready to make an attack. Now that they were prepared to do so, they carefully followed one of the trails into the mountain. It was an older trail and whoever had come this way had made an effort to hide his tracks. But Verin was an excellent teacher and Nathan had learned more than enough to pick up the traces left by the bandit. They climbed at a rapid pace into the mountains. Still in the thickly wooded forestlands, the terrain was now becoming steep and rocky. The trail that they followed soon joined a set of tracks from another well-used trail, and within minutes a third trail, they were getting close.

The trail was leading up a shallow ravine that was sloping off to the left. It widened and flattened out into a small meadow high in the mountain. Knowing the general direction of the paths all lead this way, Nathan decided to leave the trail and veer off to the right, further up the slope circling high above the meadow. As they got higher, they saw the entire meadow. At the north end of the mountain meadow, they found the bandit encampment.

Nestled into a corner, where two steep slopes of the mountain met the meadow floor, the bandits had built a large wall across the V formed by the two slopes. Any large force attacking the bandits would have to break through the thick and sturdy-looking gate centered on the wall. At the far end of the encampment was a narrow and steep trail that went further up the mountain. It looked like it would eventually lead over the mountain into the northern lands. The bandits had turned a mountain pass into a veritable fortress easy to defend and with a built-in escape route. Impressive, thought Nathan, while he looked for opportunities, weaknesses.

Continuing up the mountain Nathan and Verin were able to get across the side of the mountain through the trees and onto the path. They carefully walked up the path until they were almost at the top of the mountain range. They were almost a mile above the bandit's camp. High enough for them to see that the path did lead across and down onto the northern side of the mountain range. If they attacked the encampment from below the bandits would easily slip up this trail over the mountain and be free to return and harass the lands whenever they chose. They backtracked down the path towards the encampment.

As they walked down the mountain, Nathan began to formulate a plan. He knew Verin would give him advice now if he asked, but would leave the decision up to Nathan unless his plan was so terrible it could lead only to their deaths. Before they got too close to the encampment, Nathan stopped and explained his plan.

"The encampment is well built and would withstand an attack from any of the king's army for days. Or, if they wanted, they could slip out this way and into the north. We can't allow that. But maybe what makes it a strong camp against a large force would be a weakness against a small one. The path up the mountain is step and narrow, hard to move fast on. Up here an archer could pin the bandits in so they have to stay in the encampment or go out the front gate. The front gate is heavy timbers, lifted by pulleys and ropes. Difficult to breach from the outside but if those ropes were cut then the gate would be locked shut, and the only way out would be up the mountain," said Nathan.

Verin could see Nathan had thought the plan through, well before mentioning it. It was risky and meant they would have to split up, but two men attacking almost twenty always would be. "You want to me sneak in cut the rope and cause havoc while you pick them off from the road. It is dangerous but it could work."

Nathan was not willing to let his uncle take the hard job; it was he who made the decision to help the village so it was up to him to take the point on this attack. "No, uncle. You are the better archer and inside the encampment are lots of narrow spaces where one man with daggers can attack and defend against many. A sword would be harder to use and less effective in that close range. I sneak in while you attack from the high ground. We wait 'til tomorrow's first light. I can sneak down the mountainside during the night and get into the encampment. The sentries will be tired and the rest will be still sleeping. We can narrow the odds down drastically before they know what hit them," said Nathan.

Verin nodded impressed with Nathan's willingness to take the lion's share of the risk. He was also impressed with the fact the plan seemed logical and had a good chance of success. Verin would be almost impossible for the bandits to get to and would be able to provide cover for Nathan. He would pick off any bandits who snuck behind him unnoticed. It was almost dusk now, so while the shadows of night would be useful, waiting for the enemy to be tired and asleep was the prudent plan.

Nathan and Verin slipped back into the trees further away from the trail down into the encampment. They ate a dry supper, not risking a fire, and sat hidden in the trees. They needed some sleep before the attack. It was still dark out when Nathan woke. He knew about an hour remained before the sun would come over the mountain and bring with it dawn. Verin was already awake and just waiting for him to make the call. Nathan was ready. He would sneak into the encampment very slowly and very carefully. Moving around in the dark was risky business when trying to be quiet.

They made their way back down the slope to a point on the path where almost the entire encampment was in view. They were still about two hundred yards from the encampment, close enough to be within bow range, but far enough that shooting required a high degree of skill. Nathan turned to Verin. "I'll take the two on the wall. When I kill the first sentry, shoot the two sentries walking around on the ground. After that it will be pretty chaotic... once someone wakes up and starts yelling, hit anything that moves."

Before Nathan started down the mountain Verin clasped his arm and wished him luck.

Chapter twenty four

SLOWLY NATHAN CREPT down the path until he was almost to the bottom. The first twenty feet, where the trail hit the meadow, was very steep and the trail zig-zagged. Nathan wanted to avoid this section, as it was easy to see and, even in the dark, would be dangerous. He crawled along the slope, winding his way down the mountain, using trees and rocks to lower himself into the meadow and the flat ground of the encampment. Inside sat two log cabins, a large half-shelter that looked like it was mostly for livestock and a couple of small buildings that might have contained supplies or stolen loot. Waiting until he could place the sentries' locations, he sat frozen in place, eyes down and just listening for the sentries' movements. Once he had the basic pattern of the sentries' movements, he started working his way behind them towards the front wall.

The sentries on the wall were looking out into the meadow watching for any movement coming from the south. As long as he was silent, the only worry would be the sentries on the ground. When Nathan got to the wall he found a spot where he could see both wall sentries. If they didn't move this was where he would fire the first shot. Taking his bow off its sling, he removed it from his back and sat his quiver of arrows down in front of him. From this position, he could fire at both sentries with a good line of vision towards the door of one of the cabins.

Nathan could find no spot where he could see both doors and the sentries but this was as good a location as he could find. This is the spot, he thought to himself. He silently waited against the wall. The first light of dawn would be coming any minute. As he sat there in a camp full of bandits, waiting for the combat to come, Nathan focused on his breathing. Deep breathes in, hold and then slowly release. He repeated this until he could feel his heart rate slow. The sky had begun to grow light and Nathan could see the forms of the men walking on the ground. Against the wall, he was still hidden in shadow but in a few moments that would change. Nathan drew back his first arrow and lined up the bandit on the far side of the wall.

Just breathe, he thought to himself. Nathan fired his first arrow. As soon as he shot it, he knew it would be a solid hit. He quickly turned his attention to the second sentry. He was closer, only twenty feet away. Nathan could not afford a miss. As the first sentry slumped against the wall, he slid off the narrow walkway along the top of the wall and fell to ground with a loud thud. As his body hit the ground Nathan had his second arrow ready and was taking aim. The sentry barely registered his companion falling before an arrow pierced his chest.

Verin had not been able to see Nathan moving through the camp in the dark. He did not try. Instead, he focused on the dark forms of the sentries walking around on the ground. When Nathan took the first sentry on the wall down, he would begin firing his arrows. The light of morning was just cresting the mountain when he saw the first body slump. He let fly the cocked arrow. As quickly as possible he located the second sentry and dropped him with another deadly shot. All four sentries had died within five seconds and with almost no noise. Things were going according to plan.

Once all the sentries were down, Nathan quickly made his way to the front gate. The top of the gate was attached to two ropes on pulleys that came down to one long double-handled winch. Using one of his daggers, he quickly jumped and cut the ropes as high up as possible. Since the gate was already in the down position the task was done without any noise. While Nathan was focused on cutting the ropes, Verin had been firing into the sleeping bodies of the second group of sentries sleeping along the wall. The first two shots had found their targets but for some strange reason the third bandit was sleeping backwards and the arrow intended for his chest caught him in the leg. Awaking with a scream, the bandit jumped out of bed, despite the arrow in his leg, and yelled out the alarm.

Verin's second arrow cut him down but the damage was done. The entire encampment had heard the scream and was waking up. Nathan, having cut down the ropes, returned to his previous spot. He reclaimed his bow and was reaching for an arrow when the first cabin door burst open. A panic filled bandit burst out the door. The bandit looked towards the wall to see if the gate had been breached.

Before he could notice that the gate was closed but unusable, Nathan's arrow brought him down. Two more bandits quickly exited behind the first. As their companion fell, they noticed the movement of Nathan releasing his arrow. "Archer inside the wall," they yelled back into the cabin before attacking Nathan.

While the two men came at Nathan, the door to the second cabin tucked behind the first came open and three more bandits entered the yard. Verin waited for the three to get a few more steps away from the door before unleashing his attack. The first bandit dropped dead from a shot to the chest. The second bandit was more fortunate, having turned at the last second; he caught the arrow in his arm instead of a more deadly blow to the body. He did not see Verin but knew the arrow had come from up the mountain. He turned the corner to get around the end of the cabin and out of Verin's line of sight. The bandit yelled to his companions, "Archer to the north. He is up the back trail."

As the two bandits ran at Nathan, he could see more pouring out the door behind them. Nathan fired one last arrow into the closest attacker and dropped the bow. Pulling out his daggers he met the charge of the second attacker. This bandit had expected Nathan to continue using his bow and had been running as hard as he could, trying to get to Nathan before that could happen. When Nathan dropped the bow, the man did not slow down. This brought him within striking distance of Nathan. The charging man had been so focused on closing the gap, he had failed to bring his sword into a ready position. As he raised his sword to take a swing, Nathan's blade was already penetrating his chest.

Pulling out his dagger, Nathan let the man fall. He surged forward to meet the second wave of attackers who came out the door behind the two fallen bandits. These bandits had moved a little slower and were in a battle-ready position when Nathan came to meet them.

As one, two of the men swung their swords to strike Nathan. He quickly deflected these blows and countered with an attack of his own. An arrow from Verin caught the one on the left in the chest and dropped him. The one on the right made the mistake of looking up to see where the attack came from. His glance upward gave Nathan all the time he needed to sidestep to the right and bring his dagger around into his side, unblocked. Metal met bone with a sickening crunch.

While Nathan turned to meet the third and final attacker in this group, Verin turned his attention back to the two men coming out of the second cabin, attempting to sneak closer to his position on the mountain.

One stood at the corner of the cabin with only a foot showing while the other was behind a wagon readying an arrow. With deadly precision Verin fired an arrow into the exposed foot. The man stumbled forward in pain, exposing the rest of his body. Verin's second arrow relieved the agony of his foot. The man dropped dead to the ground.

The bandit behind the wagon fired a shot up the mountain, toward Verin, but his arrow came well short of hitting him. Verin could not see the bandit behind the wagon so he raised his bow up and fired a high lobbing shot over the wagon and into the man. He scored another hit.

The warrior attacking Nathan was skilled with his sword. But he was slow and unprepared when Nathan blocked his attack with both daggers. Nathan pushed hard on the right dagger, causing it to hit the sword against its cross-hilt. With a jerk of his arm, he snapped the bandit's sword. His left dagger sliced through the shocked man's neck.

Ungar, chief of the bandits, watched the battle unfold before him. He recognized the boy killing off his men from the description Bareth and Merla had given him. He had scoffed at their tail of a boy that whipped their asses. He had thought they had been drunk and stupid. Perhaps they were not stupid liars after all. The boy, whoever he was, was accompanied by a deadly archer, raining down death with unnerving precision from high on the mountain. As far as he could tell, this archer and the boy had complexly decimated his forces. . It was pathetic, unthinkable.

Two men, one of which was only boy, had wrecked all his plans. Ungar felt the rage building inside. He would kill the boy himself then deal with the mysterious archer. He would do what his men had failed to do. Ungar, an outcast warrior from the north had found this hidden pass through the mountains and built it into a bandit safe haven. He would have been rich within another year just from the raids his men did around Salma and the northern roads around Elderwood. He would not let it end like this.

While Ungar's men had rushed out to meet their doom, Ungar slowly and methodically put his armor on. He then took his time at the door studying his opponent as Nathan slew his men. Finally, once everyone else was dead, Ungar lifted his shield and exited the cabin. He felt no remorse for his men. They deserved to die if they were so pathetic that they could not defend themselves from an army of two. Using the shield as protection from the archer, Ungar slowly walked out of the cabin to the side of the cabin hidden from the archer's line of sight. If the archer wanted to help this boy, he was going to have to come down to where Ungar was.

Verin watched as the giant man in full armor exited the house slowly with his shield raised high. While Verin's arrows would kill a man at this range, they would do little against this man's armor. Nathan would be on his own for the next few minutes. Verin started down the mountain, moving as fast as he could. Nathan faced a battle-hardened northerner warrior, Verin could only hope the training Nathan had was enough to overcome this difficult adversary. He rushed to gain a position where he could help the boy.

As the bandit leader walked out of the cabin, Nathan knew that he was in trouble. The man was as big as Soron, his father, had been, only bigger around the waist. In his armor and with sword and shield, there would be no help from Verin's arrows, which would be ineffective against this foe. His own weapons would be less effective as well. But armor and shields were heavy and slow, so agility was Nathan's advantage if he could survive the northerners attacks long enough to find an opportunity to use his speed to deliver an effective blow.

The bandit leader carefully walked around the corner, keeping his shield positioned to protect from Verin's arrows. The large bandit leader stopped and stood there, scowling at Nathan. He is man-sized but truly is a boy, Ungar thought to himself. How pathetic his men were for dying at his hands. "You never should have come here, boy. You may have killed this rabble, but I am going to cut your heart out and feed it to you. Then I am going to kill your archer. Once I am done, I going to find any family you have and do worse to them," the giant raged as he prepared for Nathan to attack.

Nathan knew the man was trying to goad him into attacking where the bandit was safe from any of Verin's arrows. Nathan was not falling for this. He also wasn't waiting for Verin either. This was his fight and he would meet it head on. Trusting in the lessons his father and uncle had given him, Nathan walked behind the cabin slowly to meet the outlaw who had caused so much pain and terror over the last few months.

Once Nathan was well past the corner of the cabin, Ungar made his attack. Coming fast, he attacked with a vicious downward swing of his sword. Nathan blocked the attack but Ungar used his shield to bash Nathan back. Nathan stepped back quickly but still was hit hard by the shield. He barely had time to raise his weapon and block the next attack. Ungar was relentless in his attacks. He wanted to kill the boy quickly before the unknown archer could join the attack. But Ungar was unable to get past the defenses of Nathan. While this boy was young, he was quick and almost as strong as Ungar. And he had skill with those damned daggers, thought Ungar. He would not go down. He had underestimated the boy and, as much as he was intending to kill him, he actually admired the boy's. *Yes,* he thought, *the little bastard has guts*!

It only took Verin two minutes to get down the mountain and into meadow where he could see the fight taking place. Verin did not fire on the bandit chief. Instead he walked up and just watched.

Ungar saw the man standing there and was baffled that he had not yet joined the fight. The boy has skill, but surely this man didn't think the boy would beat him. As much as he was glad for the reprieve of not having to fight this second man, he was further infuriated by him watching Ungar fight a boy. He would kill that one slowly.

Nathan sensed his body beginning to tire. He started to worry that he would not be able to defeat this giant. He was too strong, and Nathan was getting too exhausted. The relentless pounding of the giant man's sword was taking its toll, but Nathan began to breathe deep, despite being in constant motion. He was able to control his breathing and keep his adrenaline from releasing too fast. While Nathan breathed his way back into control, the giant man was starting to lose his. While bigger and stronger than Nathan, Ungar had heavy armor, a shield and a large sword to wield. The continued attacks were beginning to leave Ungar short of breath. He would need to end this quickly or have nothing left, with which to face the archer.

So Ungar surged forward, giving one massive effort into a downward swing. Nathan's instincts kicked in and, as he had learned to do against his father, Nathan pivoted on his right foot, swinging his body out of the way of the sword coming down at him.

Bringing both blades up, he crossed his daggers and let the sword strike the blades. But instead of trying to push the sword off to the side, he turned his daggers and forced the sword to continue on past his turning body to hit the ground. He pushed down on his daggers, keeping the sword momentarily pinned to the ground. He then used the momentum of his pivot to swing his left leg around and behind the legs of Ungar.

As Ungar pulled back on the sword to release it from the wedge formed by the ground and Nathan's daggers, his own momentum forced him back onto Nathan's leg. He lost his balance and took an awkward step back to try to regain it.

During this step back, Nathan kept his left blade on the sword, now pushing it off to the side. Still balanced on his right foot, he pushed up and forward bringing Nathan close enough to his opponent's body to strike him. While he had only tapped his father on the chest to finish the maneuver, this time he struck hard, sinking his dagger into the bandit chief's exposed neck. Ungar was dead before he hit the ground. Ungar did not even complete the thought going through his mind, that his awkward step would be trouble.

Now that the battle was over, Nathan looked over at Verin, then around at all the men they had killed. With the sun out, he could see the faces of the men. They weren't just dark forms in the dusk that needed to be killed, they were cold pale corpses. In the light, Nathan saw that the two sentries on the wall, were in fact the two bandits that previously attacked him on the road. This did little to make the sorrow that was building in him go away. He felt nauseous. Death was ugly. He looked at the blood spatters on himself. He felt remorse and satisfaction at the same time. His eyes showed their confusion when they looked toward Verin.

Verin embraced him, placing a hand on his shoulder, giving it a gentle squeeze. "Let it out, boy. It is okay to weep for the loss of life here today. Even bandits, thieves and murderous scum like this deserve someone to cry at the lost. There is no shame in feeling bad about having to kill. The shame comes when you no longer care."

Tears streamed down Nathan's face as he held his uncle tight. Adrenaline had carried him through the battle but now it was fading fast, leaving only sorrow.

"The number of lives you saved today and the number of wronged souls that you have avenged is worth that pain. Let it out now, so it doesn't haunt you later. Whenever you wake in the night and see the faces of dead foes, concentrate on their deeds and the lives that have been saved because of your actions," said Verin.

Nathan absorbed his uncle's words, and understood them. When he thought of Ava and the rest of the villagers who would be safe now, the emotional pain started to dissipate. He did what was needed here, nothing more. They started burying the bodies. Verin was tempted to leave them to rot but the mountain pass intrigued Nathan and he did not want to have to look at the bodies ever again. The battle itself took only a little time, less than half an hour from the first arrow till the falling of the northern bandit but the cleanup took a full day. By the time Nathan and Verin finished burying the bandits, it was almost dark.

Despite the availability of the cabins, they chose to spend the night camped outside where they could see the stars and not think about sleeping in a dead man's bed. Someday, the cabins might be useful but it was much too soon to use them without thinking of the men that slept in them.

Chapter twenty five

HAVING SLEPT LATER than usual, Nathan woke to the smell of Verin cooking breakfast. He looked around to see where the aroma, that wetted his appetite, was coming from. He stretched. A few muscles protested. The soreness in his arms was from grave digging, not fighting.

Verin saw the wince Nathan made as he stretched his arms above his head. He made a joke that next time they should let a few bandits escape so there would not be so much digging.

Nathan looked apologetic. He had insisted on burying the men. He appreciated his uncle's attempt at humor. Dealing with the emotions of having killed these men was hard. He wondered how his father had felt after his first kills. Would his father have been disappointed that he had hunted down these men?

Verin watched Nathan carefully; he could see the range of emotions he was struggling with. The boy would make it through this, but it would change him. "Should we head back to the village, check on the potion making?" asked Verin. He did not want to camp here any longer than necessary; doing so would keep Nathan focused on death, something Verin wanted to avoid. Going back and seeing the people he was fighting for would be a good reminded of why they had come here.

Nathan thought about this, he remembered Ava's last word to him. He wasn't ready to deal with it yet. "Actually if it is okay with you I kind of want to try this path over the mountain. The nearest pass through the mountains dad had mentioned was weeks of travel to the west." Nathan paused to see Verin's reaction, when no negative response came he continued "This would be a good opportunity to get into the northern lands and gather some witch oak, there are some projects I want to make before we leave the village for Balta. I am going to need some for them. I also want to try making a bow out of a witch oak."

Verin nodded, he knew a bit about making black steel from Soron. Verin knew the value of witch oak, the strongest and most dense wood known to man. It was only found in the northern lands and was vital to getting the forge fires hot enough to work the graphite and phosphorus into the metal. "Making black steel are you? Well, I'm okay with that. I would like to watch you do it. I have seen black steel blades like yours before but never seen it made." Verin had no problem with the idea of spending a few days traveling through the north. New country always intrigued him and a quest for the rare wood would keep the boys mind off more unpleasant things.

"Black steel?" asked Nathan, unfamiliar with this term.

Verin explained to Nathan that while in the east the metal was simply called northern metal after the men who forged it. In the south, it was simply called black steel, for the dark tinge the graphite added to the metal. Steel was a rare commodity throughout the land, black steel an even rarer commodity.

Preparing for the journey into the north, Verin and Nathan went through the bandit's supplies. While they had not wanted to sleep in the beds the previous night they had no problem taking some of the food supplies on hand for their trek over the mountain. Being that it was late summer, it was a perfect time to travel north. Despite the cooler weather they would encounter at the summit, they would likely be dropping to lower elevations right away and would not need to worry about freezing. With restocked supplies and no real time table for the journey, they began the trip to the summit.

Normally to get to the northlands one would traverse over several large mountains with very hostile conditions. The altitude, high winds and barren rocky lands made travel near impossible. In a few places like this one, there were natural breaks in the groups of mountains. One only had to travel over a small mountain top and down a much less forbidding path than what most of the mountains had to offer.

The weather was clear and Nathan could see for miles. He had never been this high before and was taken aback by how far the eye could travel. Mountains and more mountains comprised the view to the east and west. To the south, he could look past the woodlands that he called home and onto the plains beyond. He wondered how much farther the plains went beyond what his eye could see before you got to the coast. To the north, all he could see was the mountain rising above. They journeyed above the tree line now and were rapidly approaching the rocky summit. While the mountain itself rose much higher on both sides the pass was low and not so steep that they could not walk up. On this side of the mountain, they could easily use horses or mules to travel with. What the other side of the mountain looked like remained to be seen.

By early afternoon, they reached the summit of the mountain pass. Nathan took a moment to survey the northern lands. His first impression was that   the land seemed more patchwork than the south. While the south had a gradual transition from mountains to hills, woodlands to prairie. The north seemed to be quillwork of valleys forests and dry barren looking land.

Verin interrupted Nathan's musings on the different land formations with an important question "Where do you expect to find witch oak, Nathan?"

Nathan had been thinking about this when not absorbed in the raw beauty of the land they looked upon while traveling through the high mountains. "The mountain pass father used is to the west of here, but he mentioned that witch oak was fairly common all over the northern valleys. So if we keep heading north into the valleys we should find some. If not we can just keep heading west until we reach the lands my father mentioned." Soron had given several descriptions of the landmarks he used traveling the north to Nathan growing up. He had described the twin mountains, that marked the western pass, well enough that even from the north side Nathan thought they should be recognizable.

When darkness fell, it found them camped under a ledge. The ledge had been formed by an outcropping of rock, which jutted out from the otherwise slow slopping mountain. Under the ledge, they had plenty of room for a fire. They were sheltered from the cool winds that hinted the changing of seasons was about to come. The fire danced, shooting sparks up every now and then. It was a comfortable camp. It was a perfect time for conversation, a perfect time to ask Verin more questions as they sat eating a meal of dried meat and fruit. Nathan asked Verin what he did back in Balta; there was so much he wanted to know about his mothers' family.

Verin finished chewing a piece of jerky before explaining, "in Balta I am a ranger. When I was a boy not much older than you Balta was attacked by Morthon. Morthon is a smaller neighboring kingdom only separated by a narrow patch of desert, and the forests. From the coast of Balta, you could view almost Morthon. Morthon besides having a large cattle and sheep industry did not possess much wealth. The king of Morthon looked with envy on the comparative wealth that blessed Balta. With mines of gold and silver along with a healthy agricultural base, we were and still are considered a wealthy nation."

Verin paused taking another bite of jerky. "The biggest differences between Morthon and Balta are political though. In Morthon the king owns the majority the land in the kingdom and its entire population is subject to the king, only a few select lords are allowed to buy property. In Balta, your grandfather and great grandfather have changed the structure of our own laws. Property rights have been given to our subjects. A farmer can own the land he works, a fisherman chooses when and where to sell his products without consulting the king. This has worked great in Balta, people are happier. They work harder and pay fewer taxes. The kingdom has grown because of it. And while our families' wealth initially decreased quite a bit from giving up our land to the people we have actually gained a lot as well."

Nathan thought about this while listening to the story. Balta sounded like a good place.

"The people are more loyal than ever before, they are happy and live better. Freedom and hope are powerful tools in running a kingdom, but the rulers in Morthon don't see it that way. They think our kings have grown weak, that we give up our lands because we cannot hold them. That the gods created kings to rule over the masses and only a true king can own land. This is why Morthon attacked Balta and the wars began," continued Verin. "I was a squire at the time, training to become a knight. I served Sir Edmont, the red. He was very brave and noble man. Like you and I, he was my uncle on my mother's side, and he taught me much about warfare and fighting. When the Morthon army struck it was Sir Edmont and his battalion of knights that turned back the initial wave of attacks. His knights were so fierce that they were defeating three Morthon soldiers for every knight that fell. Which was excellent except Morthon's soldiers outnumbered Sir Edmont and his knights five to one. Sir Edmont died in that first big battle but not before slaying the commander of the Morthon forces. Leaderless and with the majority of their troops dead the Morthon army retreated. But the Morthon leaders have no intentions of letting us live in peace so they send small scavenging outfits in to harass and scare the free landholders. We developed a network of scouts and rangers keep an eye on our lands for further attacks and track down any scavenging outfits we could find. Because of my status as a prince of Balta I became the leader of the rangers and still am. But I prefer to be out in the field with my men not in a castle. The last couple years have been relatively quiet so I have been home to the capital more often. It was on one of those visits to the capital that we received word of your parents' death" said Verin.

They talked more about Balta that night. Compared to life in Elderwood it sounded exotic and mystical. Nathan was excited. He had decided that he would join Verin and take the journey to see the land of his mother's people. He would miss Elderwood but now that he had taught the Dollans basic potion making and dispatched the bandits he could leave without feeling guilty. He thought about Ava and her parting words. They still stung. He wondered if she missed him. Perhaps it would be good to stay away longer, till her temper had truly cooled off. That red hair of hers was as fiery as her tongue. He missed it. He decided he could miss it just a little while longer. She hated goodbyes so he would save them from having to say another goodbye. It just seemed logical. He decided he would go back to Elderwood after visiting Balta. Before he went to sleep he thought about the strange directions his life was taking, the mystery shrouding his parent's lives. A warrior prince and a princess living incognito in a small village: it was like a fairy story his mother had once told him to help him settle down and sleep at bedtime. Had it really been a fable? Life was changing too fast. Nathan had pictured himself being a blacksmith as was his father. Now it seemed not so cut and dried. He could skip the royalty thing. However, the idea of being a protector seemed noble.

Nathan did not want to abandon his smithing. Working with metal reminded him of his father. He missed working the metal. Then he realized perhaps he missed his father more. Life was getting more confusing. Nathan sighed before he drifted off to sleep. Verin had assured Nathan than in Balta he would have all the access to blacksmith materials he wanted so that wasn't a problem. The issue being, in order to make the black steel, he needed to have graphite, phosphorus and witch oak. The first two weren't that rare and could be found in Balta, but witch oak was a different story. As far as anyone knew the only place it grew was on the north side of the Applomean Mountains, the land of the Pellians.

Chapter twenty six

NATHAN AND VERIN continued their journey down into the valleys of the north. As they got lower out of the high mountains Nathan started to see some subtle variations in the vegetation and landscape different from the south. While the area they were in was forested it was sparse. Instead of thick clumps of cedar, pine and birch there were towering red oaks that were so big that small trees didn't grow around them. The undergrowth was rocky and mossy with less vegetation altogether.

For two days, they traveled west. They were taking their time, hunting and enjoying the scenery as they went. It was new land to both of them and they were savoring the experience. They had been following a small creek when they came up to a deep pond. It looked promising for fish, as it was dark and deep. When the first trout jumped out of the water in front of them Verin insisted they stop. Nathan laughed, thinking that catching fish would be a fine idea, so they stopped and built themselves fishing rods out of a couple oak branches and thread from one of Verin's old shirts. Nathan was too reluctant to rip the fine clothing he had purchased in Birchone. Nathan carved small hooks and attached them to the newly made fishing rods. They used small bits of dried fruit for bait and had a most successful and fun day. By nightfall, they had caught and smoked a dozen good size fish and eaten three more. With bellies full and replenished food stores for travel, they continued their journey in relative comfort.

On the fourth day in the north, Nathan and Verin came to a village. They were not sure how the northerners would react to strangers, but it would be better to walk straight up then be found lurking in the forest. So they took their chances and entered the village. It was a small village, eight houses of modest size with a large main lodge in the middle. The houses and lodge formed a horseshoe around a relatively open space only with a well in the middle.

When Nathan and Verin walked into the village there were a few children playing in the open space by the well. When they saw Nathan and Verin, they scattered into various houses. As Nathan got closer to the well he could sense that all the eyes on him were not just in the houses. While they had walked up into the village someone had come up behind them. Slowly Nathan turned to find a towering older man with a large spear standing not over ten feet behind them. The old warrior walked as quiet as a soft wind to get that close without being noticed.

Nathan thought about the old warrior sneaking up behind them, if he had meant them harm, he likely would have already done so. Nathan smiled and raised a hand in greeting. "Hello, we have been traveling west when we came to your village. We thought it best to come in and announce ourselves before continuing on our way."

The old northerner looked over the two men. Verin with his blond hair and slender build was much smaller than the most from the north and stood out as being from the south. Nathan with his dark hair and large frame was harder to place until you noticed the blue eyes that marked him as having at least some southern blood. "I didn't think you were very war like yesterday when you two spent half the day fishing. Otherwise, I would have killed you in your sleep, what are you doing here?" The old warrior's words sounded harsh, but the smile on his face and twinkle in his eye showed he was having a little fun at their expense. Letting them know that they had been watched for at least a day without their knowledge.

Nathan laughed. "Well, I meant war on those fish. Northern trout is mighty tasty."

"Come with me, the men will back from the mine soon. We will eat then you can tell me how two southerners ended up in Arith.The old warrior led them to the main lodge. Inside the lodge were two long tables with a large fireplace on the far end. The old warrior walked to the far end of one of the tables and took a seat at the head of the table. He gestured for Nathan and Verin to sit beside him. "My name is Burinn Oggson; I welcome you to my table," said the warrior.

Verin having had some dealings with Soron and other northern men relaxed a bit. Now they were safe as Burinn had declared them guests. They were under his protection as long as they were in the village.

"My thanks, Burinn. My name is Verin and my young companion is Nathan," said Verin, giving a small formal bow as he spoke.

As the introductions were completed a woman came into the room with a pitcher and three mugs. Burinn told them a little about the village as they watched the room begin to fill with men woman and children. Soon all the curious villagers were in room and dinner was brought in.

The meal was delicious, roast duck, elk steaks, yams and wild asparagus. The villagers were polite yet wary. Mainly Burinn, and a few of the men at his table, spoke with them while the other men talked amongst themselves. This changed when one of the men, Manyal, noticed Nathan's black daggers.

"Fine looking knives you got there boy, where did you buy them?" Manyal was one of the men who were being friendly and his voice held a curious tone, so Nathan did not take this as a threat and replied honestly, "Actually I made them."

The room went silent and everyone focused their attentions on Nathan. "That is a lie," spoke a man from the opposite table. He stood from his seat and walked over towards Nathan. "You are here as a guest of Burinn, but if you disrespect me again by lying in my presence, I will take out your lying tongue."

Nathan wanted to be polite and make sure nothing bad happened, but to be called a liar made his blood to a boil. He had never been so insulted and he would not back down to appease this man. "The blades are mine, I made them myself and if you call me a liar again I will show you how good I am with them." Nathan smiled at the man but did not look happy. He looked more like a predator about to strike.

Before the man could say anything more Burinn raised his voice "Enough Magnus, sit down. I will deal with this." Burinn turned and stared at Nathan. "You are my guest, but no southerner can forge the black metal. To continue this tale would be disrespecting me, and as such, I would have to end my hospitality and let Magnus continue this conversation. It would not go well for you."

"I am not sure I like the hospitality of this village anyways, calling guests liars without knowing that of which they speak and I will not change my claim. The knives were made by me." Nathan was fuming, this was so insulting! He just wanted to lash out and hit someone. He stared hard at Magnus, wishing the big man would attack him.

While Nathan argued with the northerners, Verin was surprised. He had never seen Nathan lose his cool before, even in battle he had remained calm. So before things got too far out of hand, Verin decided it was time to calm things down and explain who the boy truly was. The explanation could be useful or very dangerous if Verin had read the men wrong. He hoped, as he had gathered from their earlier conversation, gleaning bits of information, that these villagers were friendly to the clans that called Stoneblood their king. Verin gambled. "Nathan, sit now!" Verin commanded in a sharp tone that Nathan had not heard before.

Surprised by the sharp authoritative command, Nathan momentarily forgot his building rage and took a seat.

As Nathan sat Verin continued to address the northerners. "Burinn, we are grateful for your hospitality and do not wish to cause trouble. The boy is speaking the truth. The fault lies with me for not giving a proper introduction. My full name is Verin Albin, from Balta, and this is Nathan Stoneblood, son of Soron Stoneblood."

The entire room started to mumble at this, Soron Stoneblood, son of Theron Stoneblood, a king of the north. While Nathan sat ridged, seething in anger and waiting for someone to call this a lie, Burinn started to laugh. "Well that certainly does explain the knives and the temper. I've never heard of a Stoneblood who could take being called a liar." The tensions in the room disappear with Burinn's hearty laughter. "Hell boy, why didn't you say so earlier. We would've cooked something fancy for you."

Nathan, while starting to cool down, was obviously still furious so Verin answered for him, "Young Nathan and I are not familiar with the north. But we do know that not all the tribes are loyal to Theron Stoneblood. I thought it prudent to not mention it."

Burinn and the others all could see the logic in this, as there was many northern chiefs who would gladly take the life of a Stoneblood, any Stoneblood. "Well you picked the right village to wander into. This village owes a lot to Theron Stoneblood."

Magnus came over to Nathan again, "My apologies Nathan. I should have recognized by your size that you had some northern blood in you, but those damn blue eyes are so southern." This was finally the moment where Nathan's anger dissipated. He joined in with the villagers in their laughter "I, too, am sorry Magnus. I lost my temper."

The rest of the night went much smoother and many laughs were had as the food was taken away and the mead got stronger. As the night went on more and more of the villagers returned to their houses until only Burinn and Magnus were left with them.

"Time for sleep now, we have a long day ahead of us tomorrow." Burinn announced as he and Magnus stood up. "You will sleep in here tonight. There are furs for you to sleep on beside the fireplace. Then tomorrow the four of us are going to see Theron Stoneblood. At which time you will be given an opportunity to prove yourself or die for impersonating a Stoneblood." Burinn winked at Verin before giving Nathan a friendly slap on the arm as he headed to the door "Sleep well, boy."

Chapter twenty seven⁊

EARLY THE NEXT MORNING, Magnus came and brought Nathan and Verin outside. Burinn was already outside, standing with four horses. Nathan gave the older warrior a funny look that Burinn noticed right away. "What, you don't have horses in the south, boy?" he laughed as he mounted his horse.

Nathan had seen plenty of horses. He had even helped take care of a few for traders coming through Elderwood, but he had never actually ridden one. "Sure, we have horses. But, that doesn't mean I have ever been on one." Nathan laughed and the men joined in the mirth.

Verin, an excellent horseman, who had been around horses his whole life, gave Nathan a lesson on horsemanship. "Put your left foot in the stirrup, climb on its back and grab the reigns." Nathan did as he told, climbing on the animals back and quickly grabbing the reins. "There, now you are a horseman," Verin quipped.

Nathan laughed as they took off at a canter. There certainly was more to being a horseman than getting on and not falling off, but for now he was grateful that he was still on the animal's back. After a few hours, Nathan felt a lot more comfortable about not falling off and making a fool of himself. His mount was well-trained and responsive. When Nathan asked the beast to change direction, by pulling on the reigns, it did so with no hesitation. It was a relief the animal was very well trained. Nathan didn't use the reigns, hardly at all. The horse was good at picking out the easiest path and sticking with the rest of the horses, so all Nathan needed to do was stay on.

Verin could see that Nathan was finally comfortable enough on the horse that it was time they had a little talk. Verin brought his mount alongside Nathan's. "Your ass sore yet?"

Nathan laughed. He certainly was not used to this type of travel. "Yes, thank you it is. "

"Speaking of asses..."

Nathan cut Verin off before he could continue the thought. "I'm sorry, Verin. I know I behaved like an ass. I don't know what came over me. I have never been that angry in my life."

Verin could see that the boy was being sincere. "It happens, you probably have never been called a liar before, but that is not the point. The point is as you grow into a man you are going to need to control all your emotions. That is why your father spent the time to teach you those breathing techniques. They are not just for controlling your heart rate and adrenaline. They will also help you control your emotions. So next time your emotions get out of control just breathe," said Verin.

It was late afternoon when the four men road into the town of Amradin, the home of Theron, the king of the north. It was the largest place Nathan had ever been. Hundreds of houses surrounded a main street where blacksmith shops, taverns and assorted buildings lined both sides of the main street. At the end of the street lay the Great Hall. As they entered the town, Nathan stopped his horse. "Wait. Before we go and see my grandfather, Burinn, you and Verin need to go have a drink or two. Magnus and I have to settle something."

The men peered at Nathan and could see he was serious. "All right, we will go eat and drink. You two just don't go killing each other while we gone" replied Verin.

After Verin and Burinn left for a tavern know to Burinn to have the honey mead he favored. Nathan turned to Magnus, "You know any of the blacksmiths in this town?"

Magnus said he did and took him to one just down the road. Dismounting, they entered the shop where Magnus introduced Nathan to Sur'ath the blacksmith. Nathan explained that Magnus had questioned his abilities to smith northern steel and Nathan wanted the opportunity to prove himself. As it was Magnus who had questioned his abilities, he needed to witness them for himself.

Sur'ath asked to see Nathan's daggers and after a quick inspection of the weapons simply said "The shop is yours." The large burly northern smith handed Nathan his hammer and went and stood beside Magnus to watch.

Nathan felt at home in the shop. Its setup was very similar to his father's shop, so Nathan was quickly able to find the materials he was searching for. Out of the corner, he picked out a small iron rod, and then with Sur'ath's tongs he inserted it into the flames. Sur'ath had been working on making horseshoes when they had entered the shop so the fires were hot. But the heat necessary for horseshoes was not the same as for making northern or black steel as Verin called it.

Nathan let the tongs sit on the edge of the forge keeping the iron heating up while he turned to Sur'ath. "Witch oak?"

Sur'ath simply pointed to a large sack, sitting against the opposite wall. Nathan went to the sack and took out two small pieces of the witch oak. He threw the two pieces into the fire. He waited a few minutes to let the reaction start to take place. Now the fire was exceptionally hot. The iron rod was glowing red and orange. It was ready to be worked.

Nathan used the tongs to take the rod out of the fire and place it on the anvil. He took the hammer in his right hand and began to strike the metal. It felt good to be working in a smith shop again. Nathan worked like in a trance. He really didn't have a plan or the time to do anything too involved. That said, he did intend to show Magnus, and anyone else that cared that, his father had taught him well.

Suddenly, inspiration came to Nathan. Using the tongs, he put the now flatter metal rod back into the heat of the forge. He needed the metal to be very hot for this to work.

For two hours straight, Nathan worked and Sur'ath and Magnus stood silently, watching as the metal began to take shape. For the first hour, it didn't look like much other than Nathan turning the thick foot long iron rod into a much longer, narrower rod. He worked the graphite and phosphorus flakes into the iron. Nathan once again put it into the flames. Now the extra heat from the witch oak would be essential. As the iron reacted with the graphite and phosphorus, it would turn incredibly hard. The high heat delayed the process allowing Nathan to mold the metal into something new.

As he hammered on the metal, he gave it a twist giving the rod a curl. Once the entire rod was curled he bent the rod in half and began twisting it so that the two pieces intertwined into a weave. Once he had this weaved he put it back in the heat for a moment. Next he began curving the woven rod into a circle the size of a fist with two ends crossing and extending past each other. Then he hammered the two ends together flat and began to shape the end. Finally, he put the metal into a bucket of water to cool. While the metal cooled Nathan found a leather strip. Taking the circle out of the water he strung the leather strip through the small hole and tied the ends of the strip together in a knot. He quietly walked over to Magnus and placed the newly made medallion around his neck. The medallion was of a dagger within a woven circle.

Magnus and Sur'ath had not spoken the entire time Nathan had been working. Now, as Sur'ath examined the medallion hanging the other man's neck chest Magnus spoke. "Well I suppose you have a little skill. I guess you got some northern blood in you after all. "

Sur'ath gave Magnus a look that suggested he thought the man a little daft, before finally speaking. "Magnus, next time you call a man a liar for saying he's a smith, look at his hands and forearms, not his eye color. I would've told you this boy was a smith the second he walked into this shop." Sur'ath turned to Nathan "That was some of the finest work I have ever seen. Anytime you want to borrow my shop, be my guest."

Nathan thanked Sur'ath for the use of his shop, offering to pay for the metal he had forged and bade him farewell. Sur'ath declined payment, thanking Nathan for a lesson, stating, "You very skilled, watching you work

was a pleasure. If you ever need work I would hire you...
just don't' set up a shop in competition with me."

Nathan smiled, "Wouldn't dream of it, sir." He had no
interest in shoeing horses and making mundane things.
He could and would if he had to but he took more
pleasure in making beautiful objects. His father's
influence had been very strong.

When they got to the Inn, Burinn and Verin were happy
to see both alive and no physical marks on either man.
But both were annoyed that they had been gone so long.
Before walking into the Inn, Magnus had tucked the
medallion inside his shirt so no one could see the piece
yet. Instead of telling the story he simply said, "We are
good, I am satisfied that Nathan here has more than an
ample amount of northern blood in him. Now, someone
bring us some food. I'm starved."

Nathan and Magnus sat down and ate while Burinn and
Verin teased Magnus. They tried to coax out of him the
story of why he now believed Nathan, but the proud
northerner would say nothing about their trip to the
blacksmith shop, only that Nathan had proven his claim.
Now that the men were sated and full, the time had
come to go see the king of the north.

Chapter twenty eight

AS THEY ENTERED the Great hall, the guards stopped them at the entrance, making them wait for a steward to come to the door. When the steward reached the door Burinn addressed him. "Tell the king Burinn is here to see him."

The steward recognized Burinn but was not going to let them in immediately. "The king is eating his dinner at this moment and does not wish to be disturbed. He will have a few moments for you later if you would like to wait."

Burinn growled at the steward, "No! The king will see me now, or I will stick my spear right up your pompous ass. Tell the king he has waited long enough for the news I bring. And take us to him or you will regret it."

"One moment please," the steward gulped. He could tell that Burinn was serious so he moved hastily, almost running, to see the king and tell him Burinn's message.

Burinn shook his head as he watched the steward leave. "Put a fancy coat on them and they start thinking they're special. I ought to skin that pompous jackass."

Shortly the steward returned. His back straight and head held high in a haughty expression. It seemed that the king had found time for them. "Follow me please."

Down the hall, they went until reaching a small dining area. The king sat by himself at the table. As the men entered the room he spoke to Burinn. "There had better be a damn good reason you are interrupting my meal you old goat. I was enjoying the silence."

Burinn had known Theron for as long as he remembered, well before the man became a king, and was immune to his insults. They hardly ever spoke to each other without an insult or two thrown in for color. Burinn went to the king's table, grabbed a chicken leg off his plate and started eating it. "Fine, if you don't want to meet your grandson today we can come back tomorrow," said Burinn between mouthfuls of chicken.

At this Theron looked sharply at Burinn, then at his three companions. Magnus, he had seen before and the small blonde man was obviously no kin to him. The one in question was the dark haired boy with the blue eyes. Theron studied him for a minute without saying anything. Looking him over, head to toe the way he might inspect a young colt, finally he spoke. "Sort of looks like Soron did at his age, excepting the blue eyes of course. I don't suppose you can prove it."

At this Magnus took a step towards the table. "Excuse me my lord, but I can be of service in this matter. I can't say if the boy is truly Soron's offspring or not, but what I can show you speaks for itself...I met the lad last night and I called him a liar for saying that he forged the daggers that he carries now. This afternoon, Nathan and

I went to Sur'ath's smith shop and he made this in two hours."

Magnus pulled the black steel medallion out from under his tunic and placed it on the table so all could see it. The king picked up the medallion and examined it closely. The metalwork was flawless, a full circle of braided metal with a tiny dagger in the middle. An extremely talented smith could make this out of steel. Only a northerner with giant blood heritage had the strength to forge the black steel. To do it into such a beautiful piece was the work of a true artist. Very few smiths were able to produce something like this. Soron, his son, had been one of them.

The king smiled, the medallion brought back pleasant memories. "Your father used to love making jewelry and fancy artwork when he was younger. It was a sad day when your father left for the south. I have always regretted letting him leave on bad terms. Even more I regret not taking the time to fix it.

Nathan was relieved to hear the king's words. He had not been sure of how he would be received by his grandfather.

"When I received the letter explaining his and your mother's deaths it was a terrible blow. When the letter mentioned that there was no news of whether you were alive or not, I realized it was the first time I had ever thought about getting to know you. I mourned the loss of a son, a daughter and a grandson I never knew. Today,

I am happy beyond imagine meeting you, Nathan Stoneblood," spoke the king, gesturing for Nathan to come sit at his table. "Now tell me about yourself."

Nathan gave his grandfather an accounting of life in Elderwood. He spoke of his how his mother and father lived, the training they gave him; he went on to talk about the duke's attack, and how life had changed for him since that tragic day. When Nathan became emotional at the memories, Verin continued the story, telling how he had come to Elderwood. He told how Nathan helped the village by teaching his mother's skills then leading the excursion to find the bandits.

Theron was impressed with his grandson; his story was one of love and happiness followed by tragedy. Life in the north could be sudden, violent and filled with turmoil. Soron had struggled with that. His son had found peace and joy in Elderwood, even if his life had been cut short, it was comforting to know he had many years of peace. Verin's telling of the story was more eventful and showed that his grandson was following his father's example. The young man was a warrior but one with a kind and gentle soul.

The next day Theron took his grandson for a walk around the town. Amradin was a very interesting place to Nathan. He was learning a lot about his father's people. One of the first things he noticed was that while some of the men were incredibly large like his father had been, not all were so. On average everyone was certainly a little taller than people on the south sides of the mountains, but he didn't see any true giants either. He asked his grandfather about this.

Theron laughed, "I remember how those southerners talk about the north. They like to think we are all fierce, scary giants and the weather is freezing all the time and we devour children if they don't eat their vegetables."

Nathan smiled; this wasn't far from the truth.

"The truth is, there barely are any giants left in this part of the world and most of our people only have a little giant's blood in them. Occasionally you see a throwback, someone who exhibits giant traits; someone who is exceptionally big and usually as strong as an ox. But for most part, our people are not much different than those south of the mountains. Some of the bloodlines are a little stronger. Our bloodline has more giant blood than most and it is very likely you will grow to your father's size. Even for a northern boy you are exceptionally strong for one your age. Sur'ath told me how you forged the medallion. Two hours straight without a break, and barely broke a sweat. That is strong; it is no wonder your father chose sword breakers as weapons for you."

Theron and Nathan walked towards the stables and looked at the horses within. Even Nathan who had little to do with horses understood that these were magnificent creatures. "Beautiful aren't they. Besides blacksmithing and fighting, raising quality horses is one of the things we do best in the north." Past the stables towards the fenced off pasture they walked. One horse, in particular, caught Nathan's eye. It was a large, well-muscled stallion with a deep night black coat, and thick long jet black mane and tail. It walked with a majestic pace and seemed to stare right back at Nathan. Theron watched as Nathan and the horse eyed each other up. Some of Theron's thoughts about Nathan were now starting to make sense.

Theron decided to put his theory to the test. "Nathan, I want you to close your eyes and don't open them until I tell you. Now picture that black stallion you were looking in your mind. Focus on the stallion and without talking call it to you. Just picture the stallion walking towards us. Keep doing it until I tell you to stop."

Nathan was not sure what was going on but he knew there was something special about this horse. He closed his eyes and focused hard, imagining the stallion standing there looking back at him. He thought about the horse walking up to the fence and putting its head over the fence close enough to rub his nose. He could almost feel the animal in front of him now.

"Now without moving or saying anything I want you to open your eyes," said King Theron.

Nathan continued to humor his newly found grandfather and opened his eyes only to be staring right into its eyes of the magnificent stallion. Nathan was amazed, he had never done anything like this before, but then he remembered the wolf and had a flashback to the fox dropping the rabbit.

As Theron watched, the stallion walked up to the fence. He knew that he guessed correctly. Nathan was a throwback, but not to just giant's blood. The Stoneblood family tree did not just include giants but also members of the ingla, an ancient race from the far west. Many of the ingla had lived in the north hundreds of years ago, enjoying the company of giants. Ingla were some of the strongest users of magic ever known. But as the currian people who had already populated the southern part of the continent began to move north the ingla people began to return home to the far west.

Currians, for the most part, were a decent people. But they held a deep distrust for the supernatural and rarely reacted well when an ingla of any real power was around. Of the few ingla that stayed in the north, most had very weak powers or chose to hide them to make staying in their new home easier. Theron had heard of ingla who that had an affinity for nature. Some were simply attuned with the weather and would tell you days and weeks ahead what was coming. Other more powerful ingla would control or communicate with animals. Ingla mages were often talented with controlling fire or water. Theron did not have any of the ingla traits, but his father had shown the affinity with animals. He could not control them, but certain animals had been drawn to him and understood his wishes and thoughts. Knowing his own bloodlines were strong in giant and ingla blood it did not surprise Theron that his grandson would show the same talents.

Theron had briefly wondered if Nathan has some of the ingla abilities when Sur'ath had described the way Nathan had forged the black steel medallion. Forging black steel took giant strength but what Nathan was doing went beyond strength. Sur'ath had described the way Nathan focused on the metal as if he was in a trance. With each blow of his hammer, the metal seemed to move exactly where Nathan wanted it, as though the metal wanted to be changed. It was very uncommon for a smith to make detailed work like the medallion out of black steel. The graphite and phosphorus made the metal very hard and difficult to work with. Nathan being able to produce detailed medallion was an indicator of possible ingla powers. When Theron saw the stallion focusing on Nathan he had guessed this was another indicator of the ingla abilities. "Come, Nathan, let us go find Verin. The three of us have much to discuss."

They found Verin with Burinn and Magnus waiting for them at the steps of the Great hall. Burinn and Magnus were getting ready to leave. Magnus tried to give back the medallion to Nathan. Nathan refused and told Magnus it was a gift to remind him that Nathan did not lie. Once Burinn and Magnus were gone the three went to the king's private chambers and sat down around the small table.

King Theron started the conversation "Verin, what do you know of the ingla?"

Verin looked at the king then over at Nathan. "There are still a few ingla on Balta. They often possess some degree of magic. The ingla name for people with magic is a'kil. At one time, they were rather common in Solotine, but like giants in the north, few remain. Back in Mithbea the a'kil are much more common."

"Forgive me if this is rude but were there any ingla among your family's lines?" asked Theron.

"Actually, there were several. Several of my relatives have some sort of magical power. Nathan's mother Velaina had the unusual ability to tell when someone was lying. It was why she hated living in Venecia and dealing with all the royal politics. Everyone lied and it would give her migraines. It was also one of the reasons she loved your Soron so much. He never lied to her.

Nathan, surprised to hear that his mother had magical powers, thought back to how she always seemed to know how he was feeling and when he was lying. This certainly made sense.

"You've noticed the boy has powers then." Verin was speaking to the king but looking at Nathan. The king was also looking at Nathan while he spoke. "His metal craft had me wondering, it was a little too good, but today at the stables a stallion was attuned with him."

Nathan was starting to be a little uncomfortable with the way the conversation was going but held his tongue. Verin saw that Nathan was getting frustrated. "Basically it comes down to this. Both of your parents families have ingla bloodlines, and you boy are going to have special abilities. The only question is how strong they will eventually be."

Have I magic power? Nathan thought to himself. I guess that explains some of the things that I can do. "So what do I do now?" Nathan asked with earnest. Weird magical sounded terrible and yet intriguing at the same time.

Verin smiled "You can relax. These abilities are a blessing, not a curse. So far all you have shown is a rare connection with nature. Certain animals seem to respond to you and your ability to work with metals seems to be enhanced. You are not going to turn into a dragon…. Well I don't think you will." Verin winked at his nephew.

Nathan chuckled at the thought of turning into a dragon, now that was a little absurd, but the rest seemed possible. If it was true that his mother was a'kil then it certainly wasn't a bad thing, and he did not feel any different. Having the stallion come to him was very cool. Nathan decided being a'kil might not be so bad after all. It was time to go see his magical companion again. "Grandfather, is it okay if I take the stallion for a ride?"

Chapter twenty nine

WHEN NATHAN GOT BACK to the stable, Taneal, the stable master, was waiting for him. "The king said you would be coming. I warned him the beast of a horse isn't rideable but he gave instructions to let you try. He seems to imagine you are just going to jump on and go for a jaunt" said the man with a small smirk.

Nathan could sense the stable master was hesitant to let him ride the stallion. "He seems gentle, what is the problem?"

Taneal gave Nathan an incredulous look, "Gentle? Are you crazy? That horse is wild. It has only been in the stables for a month and no one has been able to ride it. Three good horsemen have nearly died trying to get on that black devil. But you go ahead boy, I will not argue with the king's grandson. He is over there in the big corral."

Nathan walked up to the edge of the corral and hopped over the rails. He continued a gradual walk towards the magnificent black stallion. The horse was standing in the middle of the corral, as if waiting for him. It did not move as he came up to it and started rubbing its chest. Not sure how the connection between him and the horse was supposed to work Nathan thought back to earlier, when King Theron made him close his eyes and visualize the horse coming towards him. Nathan did the same now. He closed his eyes and imagined himself jumping up onto its back while the stallion stayed still.

Nathan opened his eyes. He grabbed a handful of mane in his left hand and jumped up. He swung his right leg across the animals back until he was sitting on the stallion's back. So far so good he thought to himself. Next Nathan closed his eyes imagined the horse slowly walking up to the corral gates and then going off at a trot. He added some detail to his thoughts this time, visualizing the stallion responding to gentle steering by pulling on its mane to the left or right. As Nathan opened his eyes once again the stallion started walking towards the corral gates.

Taneal watched as the boy walked right up to the wild horse, his jaw nearly hit the dirt. He was surprised that the animal did not move. He was even more surprised as the beast stood its ground while the lad jumped on its back. As the boy rode the horse towards him, he silently opened the gates and let them out. Taneal was flabbergasted; amazed how gentle the stallion was with the young boy. Never would he have believed it had he not seen it with his own eyes. And even then he doubted what had had witnessed. It was as if the boy had magic. Taneal's face grew concerned. He worried. He looked about to make certain no one else had seen what he saw. He muttered some more about fools and kings that ought to warn a body. Taneal was loyal to Theron but it could not be said the same of everyone in the kingdom or the castle. The castle oft had ears and eyes unseen.

Nathan rode the stallion for hours that day. Despite having no reigns or saddle, he was so excited by the ride that he ignored the pains in his bottom side. After a short time Nathan realized that he did not to close his eyes and visualize. As long as he kept his thoughts about what he wanted the stallion to do, the animal responded. Being ak'il was amazing. The stallion was amazing. Whatever concerns he previously had about magic blood evaporated into thin air.

The cool northern wind felt good on his skin as they galloped aimlessly along. Riding a horse, especially one like his big black stallion was exhilarating. But his bottom really was getting swore, so Nathan thought about heading back to Amradin. As he finished the thought, the horse began to curve to his left bringing them around to head for the town. As they made their way towards Amradin, Nathan decided that he needed to have a conversation with Taneal. A saddle was going to be necessary.

While Nathan was out riding the stallion, Theron and Verin were discussing Nathan's future.

"There is not much love for the a'kil in Solotine. Even here in the north the boy would have problems. In Amradin, I rule by bloodlines. The surrounding clans accept me as king because I am the strongest chieftain. When my rule is over, the next king won't be chosen by bloodline but by power. The clans will gather and if one chieftain is strong enough to enforce his will on the majority then he will be king, if a king is not chosen then there will be fighting amongst the clans until one emerges." Theron paused for a second before continuing, "If Nathan stayed in the north, he would one day be chieftain of Amradin and possibly king of the north, but not without much hardship and shedding of blood. Nathan would be seen as an outsider because he was not raised in the north. His being a'kil would further the distrust that many would have. Amradin does not need Nathan here to thrive. I have other strong family members that will be capable of leading our people. Nathan should go with you to Balta. In Balta, he can be accepted for being a'kil. That won't happen anywhere in Solotine even the north," said the king with a hint of sadness in his voice.

Verin was in agreement with Theron. As much as the boy might enjoy growing up in the north with his grandfather, he would be much safer in Balta where being a'kil was not frowned upon. "I'm afraid that regardless of where he goes Nathan is going to see war and bloodshed. Balta has been at war with Morthon for many years and that is not likely to change. But it is true that in Balta being a'kil will not make him an outsider. In Balta, he can learn about magic so that his abilities don't become a danger to himself or others."

Theron sighed, he was not pleased to think that Balta was safer, but he would not jeopardize his grandson's life for his own selfish reasons. "Then we are in agreement, the boy stays with you and goes to Balta," said the king.

Verin nodded, he could see that Theron was not happy to make this decision; he would like to have the boy grow up with him, but was making a decision that was best for Nathan.

Glad that Verin agreed with him, Verin continued, "magic blood may be more common on Mithbea, but there are still very powerful ingla in the north. To the east of here lives an old ingla mage that is very adept at reading the powers of others. I would like you to take Nathan to meet him on your way south. There is a pass to the east of here near where the ingla mage lives, so it would not be out of your way. I marked down a grove of witch oak that grows just to the east of the pass so you will be able to get the wood as you head back to the south."

Theron handed Verin the map." I will be giving Nathan the stallion; you will accept a mount for yourself and two packhorses as my gift. When Nathan returns from his ride, I will take him for a walk and tell him of our decision. You will leave in the morning. I would like to spend more time with the boy but fear the longer he stays in the north the greater the danger for him."

True to his word, Theron was waiting at the stables for Nathan when he returned from his ride. While he waited for Nathan, the stable master filled him in on Nathan's success with the wild stallion. "Walked right into the corral, sauntered on over to the big beast and jumped on his back like he had known the horse his whole life. He rode him out of here without a bridal or saddle. It was like riding a pet pony. I've never seen the likes. It was almost like magic…"

Theron gave a half-hearted smile, the boy certainly shared a connection with the glorious stallion. "Don't worry old friend, I know how some around here feel about magic blood, I will be sending the boy away. Besides, he is too much like his father to truly thrive in the north."

When Nathan returned he was grinning ear to ear, ignoring the pain in his lower buttocks region and his inability to walk straight, Nathan found his grandfather. "Oh, Theron he is wonderful. I could ride him forever."

"Well, if you did that you would want to use a saddle."

Nathan laughed and rubbed his sore posterior, obviously his grandfather noticed his funny walk. "Yes, a saddle sounds like a good idea."

Theron gave Taneal a nod "I'm sure we will be able to come up with a decent saddle, now come with me Nathan, we have much to discuss." As Theron and Nathan walked, the king filled Nathan in on the conversation that he had had with Verin about going to Balta. The king explained the dangers for him in the north and why he wanted him to go to Balta with Verin; he also announced his gift of the stallion.

Nathan was torn; he understood the logic and agreed that going on to Balta was the right decision. He was sad that he would be leaving Theron so soon and sadder to think of not seeing Ava while he was in Balta. "Now tell me, Nathan, you have your very own horse. It is a beautiful black beast. But what are you going to name it?" Nathan looked at his grandfather "His name is Thorn."

That evening the king hosted a great feast, and they spent the night laughing and hearing stories of a young Soron, and his bride Velaina. The time of mourning had passed. To mourn longer would dishonor the dead. As custom dictated the departed were to be celebrated and honored with stories of victories and tellings of attributes; after the mourning period. It was a fitting tribute to Soron and Velaina.

The next morning Nathan and Verin spoke with King Theron one last time before they left to complete their journey. Besides the horses, King Theron had one last gift for Nathan.

"Here take this," said the king as he handed Nathan a small leather pouch. Nathan gave Theron a look silently asking permission to open the gift, which the king granted with a smile and slight nod. Inside the pouch were a large handful of gems. There were at least two each of diamonds, rubies, sapphires, and garnets. Nathan could see a half dozen emeralds and amethyst at the least. The small pouch contained a small fortune.

Theron explained his gift, "When your father was a boy, his favorite thing to smith was jewelry. I used to get mad at him and tell him that pretty things didn't win wars. That swords and spear were the only thing worthy of a blacksmith's time. Sometime after Soron left the north I started to realize that being king was about more than winning wars, it was about providing my people with a better quality of life." The king paused, reflecting back on his past. "Your father always appreciated beauty and knew its importance. It wasn't until I grew old that I began to understand what Soron knew all along. So a few years ago I started collecting these jewels. My intention was to give them to your father as a late wedding gift. My way of explaining that I came to understand why he chose to leave the north. Now that he is gone, these are yours. Do whatever you like with them. But I would ask that at least some of them you make into jewelry. I would like to see them again one day. In addition, you should show the jewels to the mage. He is trustworthy, and will be able to teach you something special about gems.

Nathan thanked Theron for the wonderful gift. Thinking of his lost parents was always tough and now leaving his grandfather was proving to be difficult. Nathans voice was wavering as he spoke. "They are beautiful. I promise to make something worthy of such a wonderful gift."

Theron was very pleased by Nathan's reaction to the gift. "In the supplies I also included a large bag of hexin. It is a rare mineral, which can be used like graphite except instead of making iron into steel it makes it into a softer metal. Your father used to try making jewelry out of it. But he rarely had enough of the mineral to make it work. See if you can make something of it."

With one last embrace Nathan with his grandfather, Nathan mounted Thorn and got a feel for the new saddle that Taneal had found for him. Satisfied that traveling for long periods of time would now be much more comfortable Nathan gave a last way and headed out of Amradin.

Chapter thirty

FOR SEVERAL DAYS, they traveled east following the directions and map that Theron had provided. Thorn carried Nathan effortlessly. Horse and rider moved as one. If a scent on the wind alerted Thorn, Nathan knew it. If Thorn saw a movement, or picked up a suspicious sound, Nathan knew it. As they headed east the land became drier, the vegetation sparser. Even the air seemed different to Nathan, almost acidic. However, the dry flatter land made for easy travel for the horses so they made good progress. On the third night, they were making camp when that changed.

The campsite they had chosen was a good one. A small clump of alber elm provided cover and firewood in an otherwise barren and exposed area. Verin tethered and unloaded the horses while Nathan gathered dry twigs and branches and then started a fire.

As they ate their supper, the horses were acting a bit unusual. Filled with nervous energy, the animals were jostling about with heads high, noses into the wind.

"They smell something out there, either a storm is coming or they have picked up the scent of a predator. If they don't calm down soon we will take shifts keeping watch," said Verin as he gave a cautious watch over the camp. Verin rose and took a long walk around the perimeter of the camp but failed to notice any obvious signs of anything moving out in the night.

By the time Verin was finished his walk around the camp the horses had already started to calm. Whatever had bothered the animals was gone or no longer worrying them as much. Despite this, Verin was wary. "Forgive me if this offends your ears, but I am going to sing to the beasts for a while. Singing always seems to calm herd animals, even bad singing." And with that, Verin began to sing. His voice not nearly the calamity he had insinuated it to be.

Fair lady I remember thee

Heart bound by in fire

I burn every time you get to close to me

Darkness of night and time past has taken my besot heart and turned it to stone

But even the stone heart burns every time you get close to me

Fair lady I remember thee.

Fair lady I come for thee

My broken stone heart still searches for it home in the fire of your love

Distance and time matter not for one day a time will come

Fair lady I will come for thee

As Verin sang his love song, the horses calmed and stopped moving about. The sad melody put Nathan into a contemplative mood. Afterward, Nathan asked about the song. "Mother used to sing to me all the time. I never heard that one before."

"It is not one of the popular songs of Balta. In fact, very few have ever heard it. It is just a song a lonely ranger wrote for a girl he knew long ago," said Verin in a reflective tone as he stared off into the distance.

Nathan could tell from the sound of Verin's voice that it was most likely that he was the lonely ranger and the song was a reminder of a lost love. Not wanting to embarrass his uncle or reveal that he had figured out where the song originated from Nathan simply replied, "It was lovely, your singing on the other hand..." Nathan drifted off into sleep dreaming about a certain village girl with freckles like the nights sky.

It was after midnight when Nathan awoke with a start. The camp was quiet. The fire had died down to just coals. Verin was asleep, as were the horses. Wait, all the horse except Thorn slept. Nathan sensed that Thorn was awake and was scared. Not many things scare a wild stallion so something dangerous was close to the camp. Nathan quickly added a handful of wood to the fire hoping that some flames would scare off whatever was out there, or at least provide more light to see the danger with. Nathan grabbed his daggers and quickly walked towards the horses.

Before he could get to the horses, dark terrors sprung out of the shadows in all directions. Only a movement, spotted out of the corner of his eye, saved Nathan. A large beast had sprung from the bush at him. Nathan instinctively jumped back and the large projectile flew past him. But not before a vicious set of claws caught him across the shoulder. The next attack came from a second beast trying to bite his leg while the first one corrected its path and turned back to attack Nathan again.

Nathan struck the second beast hard. He slashed it across the chest, but the blade made no cut. The beast's skin was incredibly hard and did not yield. As Nathan slashed at the seemingly invincible beast the first one again pounced at Nathan. This time the attack was successful. Nathan was knocked to the ground.

The beast was on top of him and about to sink its razor like teeth into Nathan's neck, when in one last desperate counter-attack Nathan drove his blade into the beast's mouth. This time the blade did not bounce off but pierced into the brain, killing the monster immediately.

Nathan pushed the beast off of him and looked around. The second beast was on him just as Nathan finished shoving the dead one off himself. Nathan felt a searing pain as a set of claws sliced through the back of his leg. Nathan spun to his side and jabbed his dagger into the second monsters mouth. The animal reared in pain before dying beside the first dead beast.

Nathan lunged to his feet looking around. The fresh pieces of wood had caught ablaze and in the light of its flames Nathan saw Verin trying to fight off three of the beasts. Another was attacking Thorn. The wild stallion was raised up and striking down with its hoofs, keeping the monster at bay. Nathan yelled at Verin "Strike them in the mouths. It is their weak spot." Nathan ran to help Thorn.

The monster, trying to avoid the ferocious strikes of Thorn's powerful front legs, failed to see Nathan coming up from behind. Nathan struck the beast to get it to face him. Nathan's dagger pierced through its mouth and into the brain of the ugly beast. The jaws of the beast had almost snapped close fast enough to immobilize the blades of Nathan's dagger. Had the beasts' mouths been deeper Nathan's hands would have been cut by the razor sharp teeth. Now that Thorn and the other horses were safe from immediate danger, Nathan turned and rushed back to help Verin against the remaining beasts. Verin had killed one of the beasts while Nathan had been looking to Thorn's attacker. But still faced two of the beast, while a third one was coming around behind him. Nathan ran towards the beast behind Verin hoping to distract it before it could jump on his uncles exposed back. As Nathan ran at the beast, Verin struck one of the two in front of him killing his second monster. Suddenly the two remaining attackers turned and ran off into the night.

Verin hobbled closer to the fire before collapsing to the ground. Nathan quickly came to him, checking to see the severity of his wounds. Verin had a deep wound in one leg were one of the beasts had bitten him and several claw marks over the rest of his body. The leg was bleeding profusely and Nathan noted with concern that Verin had lost a lot of blood.

Grabbing a piece of cloth Nathan made a tourniquet and tied it around the leg to stop the bleeding. As he worked, Verin talked "I have to say waking up to a vraber bite is not as pleasant of an experience as it sounds." He grunted as Nathan gave the tourniquet another tug to tighten it more. "I am taking a dislike to the north. Not a friendly place at all." Verin coughed, already weaken by the loss of blood.

"Vraber? I've never heard of one before," said Nathan as he worked on the wounds.

"While you were visiting with the king, Magnus and I were having a drink of ale and he was telling tales of the north. Magnus warned me about these god awful creatures that looked like a cross between a wolf and a lizard. He said they have scaly hide that supposedly makes great armor. I can see why now. They are a pack animal who live in the desert, and will attack anything. I thought Magnus might be exaggerating his stories a bit for my enjoyment. If I ever see him again I will have to apologize. They truly are a dangerous animal." Verin was rambling a bit at this point. Nathan suspected that the vraber wounds were causing a reaction in his body.

Nathan cleaned up the rest of Verin's wounds and fed him some water. "Go to sleep uncle. You have lost a lot of blood. Water and rest are essential now." Verin mumble in agreement before closing his eyes. In moments he was passed out. Once Nathan was finished with Verin, he worked on cleaning his own wounds up. Washing them out with water and applying salve. The rest of the night Nathan stayed awake to make sure the vraber that had fled did not return. As Thorn settled, Nathan knew he too could relax. He would trust Thorn to raise an alarm.

When the soft morning sun started to rise in the east Nathan finally got a good look at the dead vrabers that had attacked during the night. The description of a wolf crossed with a lizard was not far off. The murderous beasts were a combination of gold and black color with a hide that resembled scales. The mouths were short and wide, the mouths full of razor like teeth. The eyes were sunk back into the head and the ears were tiny, not a pretty creature at all. The bodies of the beast stank. The smell bothered the horses; he would have to do something with the bodies soon if they were to stay here.

Done with his inspection of the dead creatures Nathan started sorting through the packs of supplies Theron had sent with them. He started to boil some water to make soup. When Verin awoke, he would need to replenish his fluids and gain strength. A good soup was an excellent way of doing this. Once he had the soup started, Nathan checked on the horses then began walking around the area of their camp. Looking to see if he recognized any plants that would help Verin heal quicker.

After an hour, Nathan found some bai cacti. He had never seen the plant before but from his mother's lessons, he recalled the distinct purple and pink flowers that protruded from the prickly plant. The cacti were very fibrous and good at retaining moisture. Chunks of the cacti in the soup would help the body retain water. Nathan chopped up a few pieces of the bai cacti and returned to the camp. Once he finished adding the cacti pieces to the soup, Nathan sat down and quickly fell asleep. Exhaustion had finally over taken him.

When Nathan awoke a few hours later, Verin was awake but not moving much. He still seemed weak but at the least was now fully coherent. "I've been awake for almost an hour now but too weak to get up and get some of that soup that's being cruelly teasing my nose. I don't suppose you would mind handing me a bowl." Nathan smiled, Verin might be weak, but his sense of humor had not disappeared. The soup was nourishing but with the healing herbs he had put into it the smell and taste was rather awful. Once he had finished the bowl of soup Verin weakly thanked Nathan and went back to sleep.

Nathan assessed the situation. Verin would be too weak to travel for at least a day or two as his body recuperated from the loss of blood. As long as he didn't catch a fever he would start recovering soon. After that, he would be fine but for at least another day he would need plenty of sleep, and drink lots of water and eat more soup.

Since he was going to be there for a while, Nathan decided it was time to do something with the vraber bodies. The vraber hide was incredibly tough. The one he had slashed several times showed almost no damage, only small marks where the blade had passed across its chest, nowhere deep enough to penetrate the tough hide. If he could find a way to skin the beasts he could definitely use the hides for something. Going through Verin's gear, Nathan found his skinning knife, a small curved blade tool.

Taking the skinning knife, Nathan went to work on the first animal body. Nathan found that while the hide was incredibly tough where the scales of thick hide were, the chest back and neck, the areas around the belly and legs were thinner. Even these thin areas were extremely tough but with a lot of work Nathan was able to remove the hides. As he finished Nathan took the carcasses far away from the camp so the scent of blood would not linger and bother the horses. Finished with that unpleasant task, Nathan made a small stand to hold the hides. Once they were secure, he scraped clean the insides of the hides. Once the hides were cleaned Nathan crushed some alber elm bark into a paste he applied this to the skins then left them to dry.

Nathan checked on the sleeping Verin. His wounds were healing nicely with no signs of infection, or fever and some of the color was returning. Verin would likely be on his feet again soon. When Nathan cooked supper that night Verin awoke and got himself up to eat without any assistance. He would be weaker than normal for a while but Verin was ready to travel once again.

Chapter thirty one

WHEN MORNING CAME, Nathan loaded his vraber hides onto one of the pack horses and finished reloading the rest of their gear. After a quick breakfast, they were once again riding their way east towards the mysterious ingla mage that his grandfather, King Theron had sent them to see.

At first they almost missed the mage's dwelling. Theron had described a cave near the bottom of a steep mountain of dark red rock beyond the third creek to the east. Finding the mountain had been easy enough. But the entrance to the cave was well hidden by an overlap in the rock and a few bushes in front of the opening. They had ridden past it twice before Verin noticed the way the rocks overlapped and moved closer to find the cave entrance.

Making a small torch, they carefully entered the cave. While the entrance to the cave was a narrow and dark tunnel, after about fifteen feet they began to see light. Soon the tunnel opened into a large main cavern. The cavern was a surprisingly comfortable looking dwelling. Furs covered a large part of the floor and glowing rocks gave off a strange warm light that filled the space. In the middle of the cavern at a large table sat an old man. The old man was reading a parchment and hadn't even bothered to look up at them

"Well don't just stand there looking like idiots. Put out your torch and pull up a chair Stoneblood. "Nathan, surprised by this greeting, did as he was bid. He took one of the two chairs across the table from the old ingla mage. Finally, the mage looked up and examined Nathan. "You are too young to be Verin's boy, his grandson perhaps?" Nathan nodded, curious as to how the old man knew that he was a Stoneblood.

"I could tell you are Stoneblood by your magical aura; it is similar to that of your grandfather... only much stronger. Your father must have married someone with a strong magical presence." The mage took in Nathan's blue eyes and then looked over at Verin. "Judging by your blue eyes and the look of your companion, he married a southerner. Baltan if I am not mistaken, strong ingla bloodlines in Balta."

"Yes sir, my name is Nathan Stoneblood, son of Soron Stoneblood, son of Theron Stoneblood. My mother Velaina Stoneblood was born in Balta and this is my uncle Verin Albet."

The old mage gave a small smile. "Greetings Nathan Stoneblood and Verin Albet, my name is Amaden Blugroson. What can I do for you?"

Nathan appreciated the old mage's warm, friendly greeting. "Grandfather told us to come here. He said that you would have an idea of what type of magic I am capable of and help me to understand some of my power."

The mage got up from his chair and walked around the table. He took both of Nathan's hands in his own, examined both sides then let go, then he examined Nathan all over before placing one hand on Nathan's chest. He closed his eyes and stood like that for a minute. Without a word he removed his hand, went back around the table and sat down again.

"It is good that Theron Stoneblood sent you to me. He is partly correct, I can tell you some about the innate magic you possess, but magic, like any other skill, can be learned, strengthened and honed. So what magic you can perform in time will only come from what you learn and practice." Amaden paused a moment to study Nathan before continuing, "I can teach you about being a'kil, and how magic affects you and the world around you. First, we need to each lunch. From the looks of him your our uncle is still weak from his wounds and could use some rest." The mage looked at Verin, "Forgive me for looking into your mind. I needed to know your intentions towards young Nathan here. Even in Balta there are those who frown upon the a'kil." The mage touched his bony fingertips to Verin's forehead.

Verin gave a weary smile, "Theron Stoneblood trusts you, it is enough for me, and it's not the first time a mage has snooped around in my mind." Verin knew a lot about mages. Magic was much more common in Balta, and he had some training in how to shield his mind from such invasions but had chosen to allow the mage to look into his mind. Verin had nothing to hide.

As they ate a stew that Amaden had already been cooking, Nathan took the time to study the old mage. A gray and white beard covered a pale and wrinkled face. He possessed bright green eyes with a twinkle that made guessing his age very difficult. As Nathan tried to figure out the mages age, Amaden interrupted his chain of thought. "How long have you been connected with the stallion?"

Nathan thought back over the last few days of travel and the time spent in Amradin. It seemed to him the time had flown faster than possible. "I first laid eyes on Thorn a week ago."

Amaden nodded, "That makes sense. The bond between you two is still somewhat weak. As you spend more time with the animal the bond between you will grow." Nathan understood that he had a bond with Thorn, but he still didn't understand how it worked, so he asked Amaden about it.

"There is no easy way to explain magic. It is something like the energy within all living things yet magic can also be in none living things as well, stored like energy. The glowing rocks that give off the light in this room are an example of that. In your case, the magic within you has an attraction to the magic within your horse, Thorn. It creates a special connection between your minds. You will be able to feel its emotions while it can also feel yours and understand your wants. You will be able to tell where each other is even over long distances and be able to find each other. You will not likely have a connection like this with another animal, it is hard to say. Some with this ability only connect with one beast, others with several, but if you have strong feelings for another person, it is likely that a bond can develop. I actually sense that you have already started to form this bond. Eventually you will be able to talk to that person through your minds if the bond becomes strong enough, but that is a dangerous thing and you shouldn't try it without the training of a master. You also have a very strong bond with the earth. From your hands, I would say you have taken on the family trade and are a blacksmith. I would guess that smithing comes easy for you. Am I correct?"

Nathan told him that he was correct.

Amaden continued his explanation of magic to Nathan. "The earth bond is very powerful. It opens the door to many different types of magic. With training, you will be able to potentially call upon the elements. At the least learning runes and imbuing jewels will be within your powers."

With the mention of jewels, Nathan opened up the pouch of gems his grandfather had given him. "Theron said to show you these."

Amaden inspected the gems. "Ah, these are perfect, but we will get to imbuing another day. Today, we will work on your connection with Thorn. Verin, would you please go outside and untie Thorn." Amaden waited for Verin to return before giving his next command. "Nathan, tell Thorn to go for a run. Don't specify a direction just tell him to go fast."

Nathan focused on Thorn and told him to go for a fast run in any direction.

"Now I don't want you to communicate with Thorn, but just feel where Thorn is." After a few minutes, Amaden continued, "Tell me which direction Thorn is going right now."

Nathan was focused on Thorn and could tell which way the animal was headed; he turned and pointed out towards the northeast.

Amaden smiled, Nathan was picking up things very quickly. "Excellent, now how far away is Thorn?"

This took Nathan a while but once he focused just on Thorn's location he was able to feel the stallion moving away from him. "He is about half a mile away and getting farther away. He turned and is heading more towards the east now."

Amaden clapped his hands together. "Excellent young Stoneblood, you will now always be able to tell which direction Thorn is from you. Over longer distances, you will not be as precise but still you will have a scope of the range between you and if it getting smaller or larger. Enough talk about magic for one day, tell me how my old friend Theron is doing."

Nathan was pleased by the first lessons he was receiving but at the same time was disappointed the day's lessons were already finished. He would have stayed up all night to continue learning from the old mage. He thought to himself this was well worth the dangerous trip, as they chatted about his grandfather and the events in Amradin.

The next few days were a bit of a letdown for Nathan. Amaden did not spend a lot of time talking about magic. Instead, he would have Nathan do breathing exercises like his father had done. Sometimes they just did stretches or went for walks. Nathan was ready for more magic. Finally, he could not help himself, he asked, "Why are we just walking and stretching? I thought you were teaching me about magic?" Nathan and Verin had been there a week, and other than working on his bond with Thorn, they had not done much new.

"Magic is not for the impatient. You are still young and need to understand that magic can be dangerous. I needed to be sure you had the right temperament before I shared more. But you are correct. It is time that we did more work." Amaden signaled Nathan to follow him. "Your patience lasted longer than I thought it would, but you could have waited a little more young man. Patience is a power unto itself."

Amaden walked to a small shelf and grabbed a bowl and a small knife. He returned to Nathan and ordered him to hold out his arm. "I shall require a measure of your blood, son of Soron."

Nathan held out his arm. I hope the knife is sharp and quick he thought. He steeled himself to show no emotion or fear.

The old mage made a small cut on Nathan's arm. Letting the blood drip into the bowl, he then selected a small rock up off the ground. As he put the rock into the bowl of blood he spoke to Nathan. "Like your connection with Thorn, you also have a connection to the earth. While the earth can't talk to you it does hold a strong magic. Even this small rock contains it, but it is inert. Only by soaking it in your magic filled blood do you gain the ability to use its power. Put the rock in your hand. Focus on the rock. Imagine it is as heavy as one the size of your head. Keep focusing on that idea until the rock actually does feel that heavy."

After a few minutes of focusing on the rock Nathan felt the rock getting heavier. He looked up at Amaden who took the rock out of his hand. It took Amaden two hands to remove it. "Oof, next time think of a lighter rock. That is the basics of imbuing. Different types of materials have different abilities to help create magic. Stones are excellent for weight or heat. Gems are particularly good as a storage device. You can transfer some of your magical energy into gems to use later or with other materials like steel or gold. You can make an iron sword stronger by imbuing it with your blood. But make an iron sword with a blood stone gem in it and you will have a much superior weapon. The ability to imbue relies on your imagination as much as it does the energy within you and the stones. And remember magic takes a toll on the body. You can't go endlessly imbuing every rock and jewel you see. Always try to have energy left for an emergency."

For the next couple days, while Verin continued to heal, Amaden had Nathan work on imbuing. There were more areas of magic that could be explored but mastering a few was better than spreading oneself too thin. Although Amaden had much that he could still Nathan he was satisfied that the boy had enough training to control his powers. Nathan had strong magic and the sooner he left for Balta the better.

After almost two weeks of living in the cave with the wise old ingla mage, Nathan was ready to go make the journey through the mountains once more. Before they could do that they still needed to find the grove of witch oak trees. It seemed forever since they had defeated the bandit chief and hiked over the mountain pass into the north. But in actual fact, they had been gone for barely over a month

Chapter thirty two

DUKE EVOLLAN WAS LIVID. His face was red. His nostrils were flared and the deep furrow in his brow was a sure sign to those around him they had best not cross him, question him, or even speak unless spoken to. Not only was his wilderness campaign to gain favor with the king a failure, but there was actually talk that the king was recalling him to Progoh for a trial.

The idea of being imprisoned for killing a bunch of low bred rabble that were not even part of the kingdom was beyond the duke's comprehension. It wasn't his fault a southern princess fell in love with some northern tribal leader's son and decided to live incognito in the woods like peasants. Living life like a peasant was as bad as going to prison and neither option was acceptable to the duke.

Bailmont, the duke's captain, walked into the library where he found the duke staring out a window while playing with a dagger. "You summoned me, my lord."

"Tell me Bailmont, how many of our men are going to disappear into the forest and become bandits when they find out that the king is calling us to Progoh for a trial." Bailmont thought about it for a few seconds before replying, "I would say of the hundred men under your command that about a dozen will disappear. The rest consider themselves loyal subjects of the king and will show up at the trial declaring their loyalty to the king. They will beg forgiveness and remind the king that they were following your orders."

The duke had thought the number would be close to that. That would give him a dozen men similar to Bailmont. Men that enjoyed killing and pillaging, but found it prudent to do so in the name of the king instead as outlaws. They were exactly the sort he would use. Men smart enough to see the value of serving under a lord but still ruthless enough to do whatever was asked of them.

"Okay then, inform the men of the king's decision to hold a trial. Assure them that it is only a formality. Also let them know that the only one likely to receive any punishment is me, and that I am fully confident that our actions were justified and will be proven so. I intend to show the king that the village was indeed a gathering point of bandit" said Duke Evollan.

"Yes, my lord. I will give the order. May I ask how you intend to prove this to the king?" said Bailmont with a bit of a smirk on his face.

The duke gave Bailmont a hard look, "I don't intend to. When you inform the men send them at a slow march towards Progoh. Have them stop half way and wait for me to arrive so I can lead my men into Progoh. Let the men know that I am waiting upon vital news that will prove our innocence and will make towards the capital with all haste once my messengers return. I will keep a small number of men here as a personal guard, about a dozen will do."

Bailmont saw where this was leading, "When the main troops are gone what are the orders for the dozen that remain?"

"Ransack the estate. Take all the gold and anything else small enough to worth taking. Then send one of the men to Salma to tell Count Mavane that the king has found out that I am leading my army towards Progoh and intend to lead a rebellion against the king. The king wants Count Mavane and all his men to ride to Progoh immediately. Once Count Mavane has left Salma, we will enter the city. We shall ransack the king's coffers and make our way south. By the time Mavane reaches Progoh, we will be half way to Venecia and then Morthon."

"Morthon?" Bailmont had no issue with betraying the king of Progoh, nor with leaving the kingdom for new lands. He was simply curious towards the direction the duke intended to lead them.

"Morthon and Balta have been at war for years. In Morthon killing a Baltan princess does not make me a criminal it makes me a hero. Morthon is far enough away from Progoh that the king can't waste time or men to chase us down. Once we are in Morthon, I will be able to buy land with the king's gold. Then we will find some use for your particular skill sets."

Bailmont was pleased to hear this. "Oh and what skill set is that my lord?"

"Raping, pillaging and murder of course. Speaking of which, we will be making a stop in a certain village on our way south. We have unfinished business in Elderwood."

Days later, when Duke Evollan walked his men into Count Mavane's estate it was unguarded and practically empty. As he had arranged with his misleading message the count and all his men at arms had left to help thwart off the false attack on Progoh. Besides a few cooks, servants and stable hands that remained the only person of interest to the duke was Bannah the count's main steward. When the duke entered the estate he had his men gather up all the servants, cooks and stable hands. Bailmont was sent to find Bannah.

Bailmont soon returned to the main hall of the castle with Bannah in tow. The duke wasted no time setting the tone for this encounter. "Ah, Bannah, there you are. We have been waiting on you. Now shhh, please don't talk. Just listen carefully. Before you stand nine men and woman." The duke pointed to the lineup of servants against the wall of the room, hands tied behind their backs with a gag over their mouths. "How many of them live to see the morning is completely up to you. But to prove how serious this situation is might I provide a small demonstration."

At this point, the duke gave a signal to one of the men standing beside the group of prisoners. The man without a word pulled out his knife walked up to the nearest hostage, an older male cook, and slit his throat. The man wiped his blade clean on the fallen cook's housecoat and returned to his previous position. Bannah stood rigid, appalled by this senseless act of violence.

"Right then" the duke continued his speech "now there was nothing you could do Bannah, to save that poor soul. He was going to die regardless of your actions. Now the other eight, if they live or die completely relies on how you answer my questions. If you answer truthfully and are co-operative, then you and these fine people will all live to see the morning. If you lie to me then everyone here will wish they had died as quickly as that poor soul."

Bannah was terrified and his eyes showed it. Yet he managed to keep his composure and answer in a strong voice "I understand completely your lordship, how may I assist you?" said Bannah.

"Excellent Bannah, that is just excellent. I was hoping you would take that approach to this situation. Now what I need from you is all the tax money that you store on the kings behalf put in a large chest and brought to this room as soon as possible. Oh and while you are at it bring any gold or jewels that the count might have with you as well." The duke's smile and pleasant tone did little to hide his traitorous, evil intentions.

Bannah could not believe his ears. The duke, the very man who the king sent to rid them of robbers, murders, and thieves, was now murdering and robbing from the king. But again Bannah held his facial expressions and simply replied "would it be possible for you to spare two men. I'm afraid the chest is going to be quite heavy."

With a large grin that Bannah would later describe as that of a mad man the duke replied, "That my good sir is absolutely possible. Almod, Marthin please assist the good steward in retrieving our gold."

Once Bannah and the duke's men returned to the hall with the large chest filled with gold and an assortment of jewelry the duke was most pleased. "Bannah, you are a man of your word, and so shall I be. You and these fine people deserve to live. Now I have one last condition that must be met for this to happen. I am confident you will see the wisdom of agreeing to it. When my men and I leave, I will be leaving one man behind. If even one soul tries to leave this room before morning he will kill you all." With that final warning Duke Evollan left the estate of Count Mavane, having committed murder, treason, and robbery. It also made the duke very rich, which was the only fact that mattered in his mind.

After the theft of the kings gold, Duke Evollan wanted to get south as quick as possible to escape any attempt by the king the retrieve his gold. He also needed some time for his intended stop in Elderwood. Elderwood was where his plans for becoming king of Progoh had come burning to the ground. It was only fair that Elderwood burned with them.

When the duke entered the village, he did it at the break of dawn. He had his men break down every house door and had the villagers gathered in the center of the village. When his men finish gathering the scared and confused villagers, the duke spoke to them. "Greetings villagers of Elderwood, I am Duke Evollan. I apologize for getting you all out of bed so early on this fine morning but I am in urgent need of your assistance. Among you is a child of a north man and a woman from Balta. I need to speak to this child. Someone please point the child out so we can all move along in our lives."

The villagers all looked around at each other. Everyone knew who he was looking for, but the boy had been gone for nearly a month, if not longer.

The duke paused and waited for someone to point the boy out, but no one moved or spoke. "Come now, does no one know who I am speaking of? Big man, a blacksmith, with a Baltan woman and a child? Does this not sound familiar?"

Tomas spoke up. "Sir I believe you are speaking of the Stoneblood family. Nathan Stoneblood is the boy you seek."

The duke clapped his hands together and smiled "There we go. Nathan Stoneblood, alright, now we are getting somewhere. So which of you is this Nathan Stoneblood?"

Again Tomas was the only one to speak up, "I'm afraid he has been gone for weeks. He left with uncle to hunt bandits." The duke was not pleased by this bit of information. Having the boy alive was a loose end that he did not want to have to deal with.

"Okay, so the boy is hunting bandits. That is rather bad timing. I was looking forward to meeting the young man. I don't suppose you know a way I can get his attention?"

The duke and the sadistic looking Bailmont terrified Tomas. He recognized that these were the men that had raided the village before. He did not want to die. Far better for Tomas to try gain the favor of the fearsome duke. Join them, rather than gamble that the duke would not finish what he had started before. Tomas had no problem giving up Nathan to the duke. It would serve two purposes, save his life and get rid of Nathan. The prospect of doing harm to Nathan outweighed any fear of the duke. Tomas spoke up, "The girls. If you took the girls, he would come to you."

"And what girls would that be my lad?" said the duke, pleased this young man was so willingly giving up the information. "Ava and Rose," spoke Tomas as he point to the two girls. Sharon could be silent no longer.

"Tomas, you sniveling little coward. How could you? Nathan is our friend," cried out Sharon.

The duke looked at the attractive girl who had spoken out. "Another friend of Nathan Stoneblood? Bailmont, we will be taking these three girls with us." As Bailmont and two of the duke's men grabbed the girls and tied them up Tomas spoke once more. "What about me my lord, I mean what about the rest of us my lord. I have answered all your questions?"

"Oh forgive my rudeness. I thank you all for your assistance, especially you boy, most helpful. But I am afraid that it is time for us to part ways.Bailmont burn everything, kill them all, starting with him."

Tomas shivered and cowered on his knees sobbing, "But I told you everything."

The duke gave Tomas one last look before giving the signal to destroy Elderwood. "Nobody likes a traitor or a coward, boy, at least die like a man."

Ava, Rose and Sharon could only watch in horror as their families, and the rest of the villagers died before their eyes. The bodies were thrown into the Inn to burn like the rest of the village. The girls screamed and sobbed for mercy, but none was to be found.

The next day, while travelling south Bailmont had a thought, he asked the duke how he intended to find Nathan now.

"Oh when he finds out we kidnapped his girlfriends I am sure he will come to us" the duke replied.

Bailmont wasn't so sure, "But we killed all the villagers, who is going to tell him?" The duke thought about this for a moment, he had almost made a grievous tactical error, "It would appear that killing everyone wasn't as prudent as it seemed at the moment. Perhaps we should have let the coward live after all" mused the duke. "Oh well, nothing we can do about that now. The count seems to like involving himself in the affairs of the boy, so send a note to the meddlesome count that we have taken the girls with us. And If Nathan Stoneblood would like to see them again then he should come to Venecia to rescue them."

Bailmont gave a sadistic smile, "We are going to wait in Venecia for the boy?"

The duke looked at Bailmont as if he had grown a second head. "Gods no, we are going to continue on to Morthon as planned. We will simply spend a little of the kings gold in Venecia to hire assassin to do our waiting for us. They can kill the annoying young man for us."

Chapter thirty three

NATHAN WAS READY TO return to Elderwood, say goodbye to Ava, and begin the journey to Balta. He knew after seeing Ava again it would be ever harder to say goodbye again. Would she be hurt and angry? Would she understand and wait for him if he left her behind one more time? After many years of listening to the warnings that magic was dangerous and evil from those outside of his home, it was strange to find out that he was a'kil and that because of that, he was considered evil and could be hunted and killed. The sacrifices his parents had made to protect him did not escape him anymore. Obviously, the warnings of evil were false. His heart told him he was not evil, his mind told he was not evil, and his mother certainly had not been evil.

Those who hunted a'kil, he decided, were evil. To hunt a being that was different, just because it was different was abhorrently wrong in Nathan's mind. He wondered about hunting them. Then he realized he would be no different than them. However, he concluded that he would not run, nor avoid those seeking to destroy him because he had gifts of magic they feared or hated. Nathan thought about his father. Soron had taught peace, avoided violence, and still had been slain. Nathan reasoned that avoidance failed. His heart argued with his mind constantly. He wanted justice. It felt like justice when they killed the bandits. It troubled him that it also felt a bit like vengeance. He wished he could go back in time, be an innocent child once more, ask advice of his father. He let out a deep sigh. A tiny voice inside said, Verin will give good counsel.

After thanking Amaden for all his help and hospitality, Nathan once again mounted Thorn, who seemed more than ready to get moving again. Thorn snorted and pawed the ground to show his impatience at standing while the men said their farewells. With Nathan mounted, the horse flicked his tail wanting to gallop. Nathan laughed when he realized he had heard the silent voice of his horse. He nudged Thorn's sides as he silently gave the stallion permission to run.

Verin smiled, and urged his mount to keep up to the young warrior. Nathan was fast becoming a skilled rider. This pleased Verin to no end. Nathan was eager to learn, he absorbed as much as he could from every lesson given him. He showed no signs of arrogance. If he made mistakes he owned them. Outside of his outbursts of anger, Verin could find little wanting. His sister would be proud to see that her efforts held strong. That Amaden had taken the youth as a pupil spoke volumes, for Amaden had been known to turn away would be apprentices, and cursed them for vanity, greed, and malice. Amaden had taken Verin aside and told him he foresaw great things and great sorrows ahead for Nathan. The old mage told him to be prepared, to help guide Nathan with the difficulties ahead.

As they rode towards the grove, Verin and Nathan discussed what lessons Nathan had taken from his time with Amaden. "Besides learning about imbuing the gems the most important thing was to control the magic. Just like my temper with Magnus if I don't control myself the magic can become out of control and dangerous to me and people around me. Breathing and focus are as important in magic as they are in battle."

Verin who for the last couple weeks spent with Amaden had been a silent observer was glad that this was the main piece of knowledge that Nathan had absorbed from the lessons. In the future Nathan could learn many powerful uses for magic, but as long as he remained centered and focused, he would be safe. The king had been right to send Nathan to Amaden Blugroson.

The towering trees of the witch oak grove they sought were visible from miles away. It took longer for Nathan and Verin to reach the trees than it did to find them. Once they reached the large grove of majestic trees, they set up camp. After they had the camp setup complete, Nathan and Verin talked in more detail about what they wanted to find. "The more dried branches we find the better. Any dead branch bigger than your wrist and smaller than your arm is perfect for using in a forge."

Besides wood for the forge, Nathan still planned to make a bow out of the strong witch wood. This was Verin's area of expertise. "We want to find a live sapling, slightly smaller around than your wrist, but it also has to be at least a year old. Going through winter hardens the core of the tree and gives it the strength needed for making a good bow.

For the rest of the day, they walked through the forest picking up dry wood and bringing it back to the camp. By nightfall, they had a large amount of dried wood ready to be cut and three pieces of sapling to make into bows. While Nathan cut the dried wood up into chunks the size of a fist, Verin was peeling and shaping the saplings.

The next day, while Nathan continued cutting the branches, Verin worked on carving and bending the strong and supple saplings into the shape they would dry into. By the time Nathan was done cutting the branches up for the forges, the three bows were drying and ready to be transported. After one more night in the witch oak grove, they began the journey over the mountain and back into the eastern kingdom of Progoh.

From the grove it was only a few short miles before their path started to rise up into the mountains. By mid-day, they located the twin peaks marked on the map. And by late afternoon were high into the mountains pass on a small winding path. Too narrow for a wagon, the path was easy for the four horses as long as they rode single file. That night they made their last camp on the north side of the Applomean Mountains. As they slept in the crisp, clean, light mountain air Nathan wonder if he would ever return to the land of his father's people. He liked his grandfather, gruff and intimidating at first but by the time he had left he had been very comfortable around him.

Once they were over the top of the mountain pass travel down the mountain was easier. The path gone but the southern slope of the mountain had a gentle decline and without the need for switchbacks the way down was simple.

When they reached the bottom of the mountains they stopped for lunch and to decide if they should make their way towards Progoh or Salma. By going to Progoh they would be able to talk directly to the king and find out what had been done in the name of justice for the village of Elderwood and Nathan's parents. On the other hand, Salma was closer to home and it had been a letter from Count Mavane in Salma which brought Verin to Elderwood. After a brief discussion they agreed that while knowing what happened to the duke was important, it was likely they would find out what transpired in Salma. Regardless of that, it was the count they both wanted to thank for his compassion in the way he dealt with the tragedy that had befell Elderwood.

As they rode into the small city Nathan admired the view. Built on the shores of Salman Lake, it had a thriving fishery and has the home base for several mines in the nearby mountains. Walking the horse up the trail towards the town, Nathan looked out onto the lake. Between the reflections of the setting sun and the town buildings along the lakeshore, it painted a serene and beautiful picture, he thought to himself, I wish Ava could see this; she would want to skip rocks along the water, just to shake things up. He felt happy, for he was eager to see Ava and share his adventures and secrets with her. It would not be long before he could hope for another kiss. That kiss felt like it had a magic of its own. Would kissing get better with practice? He wondered and anticipated. If it did it would sure beat the hell out any other magic he had learned. Nathan was happy. However, his happiness was soon to be shattered.

When they arrived at the estate of Count Mavane and identified themselves to a steward, they were quickly led to see the count.

"Count Mavane, may I present Verin Albet of Balta and Nathan Stoneblood." As Bannah gave them the formal introduction Nathan was studying Count Mavane. Slender and stately, the count appear to be in his mid-forties if gray hairs and laugh lines could be trusted. Nathan noticed that while the count's clothing looked be of a very high quality and traditional, there was no great amount of jewelry or furs. There was nothing pretentious about the way the count dressed, Nathan noted. So far, his first impression of Count Mavane was a positive one.

The count greeted them warmly, "Nathan Stoneblood, I am so glad to see you here today. First, I wish to offer both of you my condolences for the tragic loss of life of Soron and Velaina. I had the pleasure of knowing both of them and two finer people I did not know. Your father was a good friend."

"On behalf my brother, King Verbon Albet of Balta, I would like to thank you, Count Mavane for your timely letter after the death of our sister and her husband Soron. Without your assistance we may never have been acquainted with young Nathan here. For that you have my eternal gratitude."

Nathan observed the formal tone his uncle was taking when speaking to the count. Nathan would have to get used to the careful wording and tone used among royals. Even among friends the conversations always seemed to start formally. Nathan wondered to himself if this was for each other's benefit or for the audiences that would see them. It did not take long for the conversation with the count to take a more friendly and relaxed tone. Nathan was grateful for this.

"Thank you, Verin, sending a letter was the least I could do. I spoke true when I said that I was saddened by the loss of Soron and your sister Velaina, but I must confess I had a secondary motive beyond notifying you of the tragic events. I hoped, and still do, that my transparency in the matter would help prevent a war."

Nathan, surprised by this talk of war, had not considered that the death of his parents could cause such an event to occur. He was equally surprised by his uncle Verin's reply.

"I appreciate your honesty, Count Mavane, now let me be equally honest. The possibility of war remains a real threat. When I make my report back to my brother, the king, he will decide what course of action Balta will take in reprisal for the death of two members of our royal family. My role here in Solotine was simply to find the boy and to find out more about the attack."

The count nodded his head; he had not expected the problem would go away easily. "Verin, all I ask is that you let me be of whatever assistance necessary in avoiding a war. The kingdom does not want war with Balta nor the north for that matter. The attacks on Elderwood will not go unanswered."

Nathan knew that despite the friendly tone this conversation was very serious and that it would be best if he did not interrupt. But the way the count had said attacks... "Excuse me, did you say attacks?"

The count paused for a moment, did they not know about the second attack? Carefully, he answered. "I am afraid I did say attacks. When is the last time you were in Elderwood?"

"We have been gone for over a month. We took care of the bandit problem and then went north. We are just returning now." Nathan was getting more than a little worried now.

Count Mavane was now also a little nervous. Whatever goodwill he had gained with his prompt letters could be going out the window when they found out that once again Elderwood had been wronged. "I am afraid once again I am the bearer of bad news. It is time we spoke in detail of the activities of Duke Evollan. I think it is probably best if I start at the beginning and work forward."

Verin sensed that Nathan did not want wait to hear of the recent news of Elderwood. But it was very important to have a clear idea of what was happening so letting Count Mavane take his time and tell the back story would be the right way to go. Placing a hand on Nathan's shoulder Verin spoke out, "We are anxious to learn of Elderwood. But I agree, start at the beginning."

A chill went through his body and Nathan's eyes were starting to become moist. He could barely hold his emotions in as the fear of the worse seeped into his mind. The way they were talking was bad, really bad.

Count Mavane began his story about bandits being a problem for Salma and how he had tried to deal with it.

But with Salma being on the outer reaches of the kingdom, the king had been very hesitant to send troops into the west. Only when entire caravans were being robbed did the king allow troops to be sent out beyond the lands of Broguth. Duke Evollan and his soldiers were the men assigned to deal with the problem.

The count, knowing the dukes reputation for violence and his lack of knowledge of the area, tried to convince the duke to use some of his local scouts who were familiar with the villages and people beyond the kingdom. But the duke saw this as meddling and an attempt to diminish the amount of credit he would receive for ending the bandit problem. He refused all offers of assistance.

The duke had then come to Elderwood and his scouts saw Soron and Nathan training in the meadow. While that happened, a large group of tribal warriors from the south rode up the trail towards Elderwood. Scouts reported all this to the duke and he mistakenly assumed that the warriors were re-enforcements coming to protect the bandits, which were using Elderwood as a base of operations. The duke decided, against the warning of his scouts, to attack Elderwood. His orders were to kill anyone who fought back. From reports of the soldiers there the attack almost failed due to the ferocity of Soron after seeing his wife slain trying to help a wounded villager. But eventually Soron fell to the multiple arrows wounds that he received.

After slaying the villagers, the duke, and his men, retreated to the forest to await the horsemen riding up the road. It was then he found out that they were from Venecia and coming to Progoh to investigate the death of an emissary. At this point, the duke came to Salma to brag about so quickly ending the bandit issue. When the count heard the story he sent the letters to Balta and Amradin, and then sent his own scouts to Elderwood to see what happened and to help any of the villagers still remaining. Once this was done the count sent word to the king of the tragic events.

The count paused for a moment before continuing his story, "After the duke realized that he had not solved the bandit problem but possibly started two wars through his stupidity he returned to his estates in the east. When the king sent for him to come to Progoh, he decided to forgo the trial. Instead, he became a traitor, taking with him a dozen soldiers of the worse kind. The bastard then sent the rest of his men towards Progoh, setting up a ruse to get me and my men out of Salma. He then raided the king's gold, along with my own." The count took another deep breath; he hated to have to deliver this news. "After the duke left Salma he headed to Elderwood where he killed every living soul." The count paused letting this sink in before finishing his terrible news. "He is now headed south, as far as we can tell."

Verin took a deep breath, instantly thinking of Amaden's warnings of great sorrows ahead. Could the mage have seen this coming? Was Nathan cursed to a life of misery? Not if he had any say in the matter.

Nathan was stunned. The news hit him like a hammer, stealing his breath away. His chest felt empty as if someone had ripped out his heart and lungs. The only thing he could think of was the words He killed every living soul...Dead. Everyone was dead, Rose, Bends, Ava...

Ava was dead.

Chapter thirty four

AVA WAS GRIEF STRICKEN, devastated by the loss of her loved ones. Had it not been necessary to be strong for Rose she would have completely lost her mind. It had been horrifying watching her mother and Bends being killed by the duke's men. Flashbacks of the horrific slaughter plagued her each time her eyes closed and she tried to sleep. The only remotely good thing to happen that day was that bastard Tomas getting what he deserved. She had been missing them like crazy for the first couple of days. Thank the gods I still have Rose, Ava thought. Rose was her reason to be strong, without her Ava would fall apart, without Rose and Sharon she would have lost everything close to her heart. For days now, they traveled south, locked in a carriage, away from Elderwood. Now her mind was wondering towards Nathan. Was he alive? Would she ever see him again? Why was the duke so fixated with him? Nathan, with his goofy smile and the way he was always bleeding. Ava smiled at the thought, well most of his bleeding was her fault, she thought to herself.

Sharon noticed Ava's small smile. It was the first one that she had seen since they left Elderwood. "What are you thinking about?"

Ava looked at Sharon for a moment. She thought about how to answer. She checked to make sure Rose was still sleeping before confessing to her friend. "I was thinking of Nathan. I miss his goofy smile."

Sharon smiled; talking about boys was a good way to stop thinking about the terrible images that had been filling her mind. "I'll bet that is not all you miss. Tell me, did you guys ever have sex?"

Ava's eyes popped open wide. Sex! With Nathan? That was ridiculous... wasn't it? "What? No! Why do you ask that?"

Sharon laughed at her friends discomfort talking about sex. "Well he loves you, would spend all his free time with you and let's face it your boyfriend is hot. That dark hair, those blue eyes, I'd totally be all over him if he wasn't yours."

Ava stammered "My boyfriend? He's not my boyfr— you think he loves me?"

Sharon could not believe how oblivious her friend was to the feelings Nathan obviously had for her. "Hey, I was there when Tomas was on top of him beating his face in. Tomas would have stopped if Nathan agreed to leave you alone. Nathan told him to piss off. And when the village was attacked the first time, what was the first thing he did? Save you and Rose, taking you out into the forest." Sharon paused recalling the other evidence of his affection. "Then after he leaves the first thing he does when he gets back? Teach you, Rose and your mom how to make perfume and medicine so your mom can support you without leaving the village. Face it, Ava, that boy is yours. Are you telling me you never even kissed him?"

Ava thought back to all those moments. Nathan had always been there for her, and now that she thought about it, his blue eyes were more than a little fascinating and she could admit it he was very cute. "I kissed him a few times, but we were just friends..." She thought back to the last kiss, maybe they were more than friends now.

Ava closed her eyes and thought where are you, Nathan? I need you, we need you, please be alive, please come for me.

...

While Ava was talking to Sharon Nathan was sitting by himself, in front of Salman Lake. He sat there throwing rocks into the water to watch the ripples make their way towards the shore. Salma truly was a beautiful spot, but all Nathan could think of was Ava. He thought he had done enough to keep her safe by killing the murdering bandits responsible for bringing so much death to Elderwood. But while he was off adventuring in the north, that bastard the duke had come back and killed her, killed her and everyone else remaining in the village.

Nathan wanted to get away from all the killing. What good was being a warrior, when he wasn't there to protect the ones dearest to his heart? His heart was heavy and his mind in turmoil. What good was magic when it came too late to protect Ava? He decided to go Balta with his uncle and start over. Elderwood had too many ghosts. He steeled himself not to shed any more tears. His knuckles went white as his fists curled and tightened. His blue eyes looked cold. But one day... One day he would meet this duke. He gripped the handles of his daggers. One day...

Nathan lay back on the pebbled beach. He pictured Ava's face. He remembered how her hair looked all messed up from wrestling and tree climbing. He imagined looking into her eyes, and the last kiss that held so much promise. Suddenly, Nathan noticed something change in his mind. He focused on Thorn for a minute to see if the animal was in danger. No, he was back in the count's stables nothing amiss there. Then Nathan realized there was another presence, he was connecting with something else, a distance pulse, weak but distinct from Thorn's. Then it hit him, he was connecting with Ava, he could barely sense it, but it was her. His heart soared. She was alive.

Nathan rushed to back to the counts estate to find Verin. Ava was alive!

Nathan found Verin in the courtyard talking with the count. He ran up them "Verin, Verin... she's alive she's alive." Nathan was so out of breathe from running all the way back from the lake that his words were hard to understand, but Verin caught the last alive.

"Take a few breaths, and then tell me what you talking about."

Nathan took a few deep breaths before exhaling loudly. "Ava is alive. Verin, I can sense her the way I sense Thorn."

The count gave a skeptical look. Verin could see the count thought Nathan was grasping at straws. Verin, thinking that the count could be trusted, explained that Nathan was a'kil and had a connection with his horse, Thorn, that allowed him to sense the horse and allowed him to send it thoughts. Verin explained that while they were up in the north they stayed with Amaden, an ingla mage, who told them it was possible for Nathan to develop the same connection with some people.

Verin turned to Nathan "Can you sense her location?" Nathan shook his head." No, it's like she is just barely there. I can sense she is alive, but I can't tell direction or distance. Maybe she is hurt or too far away, I don't know. But we have to get to Elderwood and look for her right away. Nathan's voice conveyed the urgency he felt.

The count spoke to them both "go now; if you hurry you can get there before nightfall. Don't worry about your things. I will have a rider bring your pack horses and gear with you in the morning. If you haven't found her by the time the rider comes back I will come to Elderwood with my men to help you search."

"Thank you, Count Mavane. You have been a most gracious host. We will talk again soon." While Nathan had already taken off for the stables to ready the horses, Verin spoke to the count for a few more seconds. Cautioning him that Nathan's powers, his magic, was to be kept a secret. The count agreed to secrecy, knowing how his people felt about magic.

They departed Salma at a gallop. Nathan rode Thorn, the big black wild stallion, and Verin on the beautiful bay mare that Theron had given him. The bay had nice lines and good endurance, but it did not have the speed of Thorn. Several times Nathan had to slow Thorn to give Verin a chance to stay close. Once they were close to Elderwood, Nathan gave up on this and pushed Thorn ahead. He wanted to get there as quick as possible.

Nathan rode into Elderwood at a full gallop. Thorn was breathing hard at the exhausting trip but showed no other signs that they had just rode hard for two hours straight. Nathan jumped down and began yelling "Ava, where are you? Ava."

Nathan ran from building to building, desperately searching for her. Most of the wood homes had been partially or completely burnt. Places built out of stone and masonry like his father's blacksmith shop were still standing, but none of them contained Ava.

Nathan was just finishing looking through the empty buildings when Verin rode in. He could see from Nathan's expression that he had no luck so far. "First let us build a fire. If she is hiding in the woods, it is possible she will see it. If she is out there somewhere hurt, she will need the warmth when we find her. Nathan worked fast building a fire. That night they walked all through the forest calling out her name but with no results. An hour before dawn, Verin made them stop looking and return to the village to get some rest. "Sleep for a couple hours, then when there is enough light, we will look for tracks. If she was alone there could still be sign of her movement.

In Salma late that same night, a trader arrived with a letter for the count. "I'm not sure who it was, but he said it wasn't urgent and to take my time getting here. But I thought that it was strange. Any letter for the count is important. So I made my way here as quick as possible."

Bannah thanked the trader and quickly brought the letter to the count in his office. "Someone headed south asked a trader heading east to drop off this letter sir. I thought with all the goings on as of late that it would be prudent to bring it to you right away."

Count Mavane thanked his loyal servant and opened the letter

Dear Count Mavane

As you read this letter, I will be half way to Venecia. I do apologize for spilling blood in your great hall. I hope the stains come out.

If you would do me a small favor, I would appreciate it greatly. The next time you write a letter about my actions in Elderwood could you be a dear and address it to Nathan Stoneblood. I would like it if he knew that I have his wonderful little friends with me, and if he would like to see them again, he should join us in Venecia at his earliest convenience.

p.s. If the king has not been informed yet do let him know that I officially resign from my position in court. I have taken the liberty of helping myself to a small sum of gold from your stores to offset the cost of my future endeavors.

Your dear friend

Duke Everode Elmore Evollan the third

The count was shocked, Nathan was right the girls were still alive. "Bannah have my horse ready to go at first light, I will be taking the pack horses to Elderwood myself."

When the sun came up the next morning, Nathan had hardly slept a wink, but now was no time to catch up on sleep. With the full morning light, he and Verin would be able to search for tracks. For hours, they searched in a circular pattern around the village. They started at the center and make the circle ten feet bigger each time. Nathan would go in one direction Verin in the other. Each time they completed a circle they would switch the direction, so that they were both making circles in both directions. The hope being that looking at things from different angles would help them find her.

By noon they stopped and returned for a bite of lunch. As they ate, Verin thought about the lack of tracks around the village. If Ava was indeed alive, she was nowhere near Elderwood. As he thought of a tactful way to discuss this with Nathan without upsetting him further he gained a reprieve as Count Mavane road into town with their horses.

Stepping down from his horse the count greeted them. "Gentlemen, I swear that someday I will bring you good news."

Verin knew well the next line in this conversation, "But not today."

The count simply handed the letter to Verin, "No, not today."

Once Verin had read the letter, he passed it to Nathan to read for himself.

When Nathan was done reading the letter he didn't know if he should be happy or terrified. Ava, Rose and he assumed Sharon were alive. His senses had been correct; His magic had sensed Ava. Of course, the being kidnaped by the Duke part was not an ideal situation to say the least but despair had been replaced with hope and purpose.

Chapter thirty five

VERIN THOUGHT ABOUT how best to catch the duke. The man only had a few days head start and he would not be expecting them to get his letter so quickly. "We shall stay here today. We rode our horses hard last night and the pack horses have been going all morning. The trip to Venecia takes almost a week by horse. That gives the duke only a few days head start on us. Either way, the duke has no way of knowing that we have received this letter so fast. He won't harm the girls yet if he plans to use them against you." Verin looked to Nathan to see if he agreed with this assessment of the situation.

Nathan nodded. Pushing the horses hard now would help no one. Besides neither he nor Verin had slept well the night before and were exhausted.

Verin address the count, "Thank you for personally bringing the note to us. Once again, you have done our family a service. While I cannot speak for my brother, the king, let me assure you that I will reporting of the help we have received in this matter. I will tell my brother the only war we need is with the duke, not the Kingdom of Broguth."

"Thank you, Verin. That is a great relief to hear. Duke Evollan has gone quite mad it seems. I fear his actions will cause even more death if a war started. Now I can only hope that Theron Stoneblood sees it the same way."

Nathan realized then how difficult of situation the count was in. Trying to avert war, while dealing with the destruction left in the wake of the duke, was a delicate position for the count to be put in. The count was an honest and good man, so Nathan decided to try to help the count. He only hoped the count would not dismiss his efforts because of his youth.

"Count Mavane, how much trade does Salma do with the north? "

The count thought about it. "Very little, we used to have good trade with the north. But over the years the distrust grew faster than the trade and with the increase in bandits the last few years there has been almost none."

"If you could have Salma trade with Amradin would you be interested?" Nathan asked.

"I would love that. Salma would benefit greatly from trading with Amradin." The count was confused though.

With kidnap and a possible war, trade was the last thing on his mind.

Nathan could see the counts confusion, "If you wait here for a couple hours, I will give you a message to take to my grandfather. If you do, it may mean peace and trade for Salma."

Count Mavane looked closely at the young man, "Nathan I would personally take your message if it only meant a chance at peace. I will wait gladly."

Nathan turned to Verin. "I will be in the blacksmith shop for a couple hours. Would you draw a map from Salma to Amradin using the mountain pass at the bandit hideout?"

Verin had a pretty good idea of what Nathan was thinking and even if it didn't work out it was well worth an attempt. And right now that gave his nephew something to think about other than Ava and the girls. He agreed to draw the map.

Before going into his father's workshop, Nathan went to the packhorses and grabbed a couple chunks of the witch oak along with the small bags of minerals.

Once in the blacksmith shop, Nathan started a fire in the forge and got his tools ready. It frustrated Nathan sitting around in Elderwood while the girls traveled farther away. But Verin had been right, leaving today would not gain them anything, and this way he would fulfill a promise to his grandfather while possibly helping Count Mavane at the same.

Now that Nathan understood that part of his ability to craft steel was not just from his father's lessons but from his magical energies, his bond with the earth, it made things so much easier. Instead of thinking about what he was trying to accomplish, Nathan just focused on the image in his mind. The hot iron moved and flowed like never before.

Nathan finished his project and headed back out to see Verin and the count. As he walked, he thought of his father. He would have approved of the broaches, for their artisanship and the symbolic gesture towards peace they represented. Nathan hoped the count would feel the same. Verin and the count were quietly relaxing while they waited to see what Nathan was up to. Before he revealed his latest project, Nathan needed to write a letter. Grabbing parchment, a vial of ink and a pen he sat down to write.

To King Theron Stoneblood

Grandfather, I have safely returned to Elderwood, but things are not well here. Duke Evollan has betrayed his king, stolen from him then came to Elderwood and murdered the rest of the villagers except for my friends Ava, Rose and Sharon, which he has kidnapped. Verin and I are going after them.

Before I leave for the south, I would like you to get to know Count Mavane of Salma. He has been very helpful to me and done his best to account for the duke's actions. I have sent him to you in hopes that you will get to know him and consider him a friend as I do.

I have suggested to the count that trade between Salma and Amradin is a good idea, I also ask you to consider this as well.

Nathan Stoneblood

p.s. the count has a trinket for you. As promised I tried to make something pretty.

p.p.s you never told me the hexin makes iron white. I think it is rather beautiful. It is no wonder dad liked it.

Done with his letter he handed it to the count and told him to read it in case something happened to the letter. Then he pulled out the two brooches he had made. Both were exactly the same size and style, a rose with a jewel in the middle. The difference being one was made with the dark black steel with a small diamond in it and the other was made with hexin. This one was a soft white color and had a ruby for a gem.

"The black rose brooch is a gift to you Count Mavane. The white rose brooch is for my grandfather if you would please give him it to him when you deliver the letter I would be most thankful."

Count Mavane accepted the gift and letter with as much grace as he could. He was very moved by the wording of the letter and the beautiful brooches. The fact that Nathan spoke of him as a friend meant much to the count. The young man showed wisdom beyond his years; a desire for peace and peacemaking when he could have easily focused on his own losses. If the boy survived his encounter with the duke he would surely go on to great things. "Nathan, Verin, it has been an honor to meet the both of you. I will wear my brooch with pride and hope that I can do as much for you one day as you have for Salma. I pray that you find the duke and save those girls."

As Count Mavane left to return to Salma Nathan returned to the blacksmith shop, calling out to Verin as he went. "I have one more thing to make today. "

With the count gone, and Nathan occupied in the blacksmith shop, Verin decided to finish making the witch oak bows. The curves of the bows were already completed. All Verin needed to do was carve the ends, grip and arrow nook then sand the bows down before applying linseed oil. Verin made two of the bows this way and left the third in case Nathan wanted to do it himself.

When he tied on the hemp string, the bows looked great. Verin tried to pull draw back the bowstring. Pulling as hard as he could Verin was only able to pull the string back a few inches. As he had suspected only a northerner would have the strength to use the bows. Frustrated but glad to be busy, Verin went out into to the forest to find some good wood to make arrows of.

While Verin worked on the bows and made arrows, Nathan was making weapons. When Nathan and Verin defeated the bandits, they had surprise and luck on their side. Not to mention the only really well trained warrior was the bandit leader himself. All of Duke Evollan's men were trained veteran soldiers and they knew Nathan and Verin were coming. Better weapons might be the only advantage they would get.

First, he made a new sword for Verin. This sword was almost identical in design to the one Verin already had, same length and blade size with exactly the same grip. But Nathan gave the new sword a few key changes that made all the differences in the world. First Nathan forged it out of black steel and made the blade thinner and sharper. Normally this would also make a blade more fragile and susceptible to breaking. However, the combination of being made of the harder black steel and the magical nature of the blade countered that effect. To give the blade its magic Nathan inserted one of his blood gems into the helm, a blood emerald that would attune the sword to its owner, making it lighter and stronger when its owner used it.

After Verin's sword was completed, Nathan restarted the process to make new weapons for himself. Taking a short break, Nathan headed back outside. Verin was nowhere to be seen, still out collecting wood for arrows. Nathan noticed that while he had been working on the blades Verin had completed the bows. Once done, Nathan took his whetstone to the swords. He spent a lot of time while forging the swords on getting the edges flat so it would not take long to work the edges until they were extremely sharp.

Taking one of the bows up, he pulled as hard as he could, but the string barely moved. The witch oak bows were too stiff. Perfect Nathan thought to himself, this will do nicely. Then Nathan went to their supply packs and got his stack of vraber skins. On the return trip from the north Nathan had thought of a way to cut the skins so that they could make use of the extremely tough material. Grabbing the skins and the two bows, Nathan headed back into the blacksmith shop.

When Verin returned to camp Nathan was still hard at work in the blacksmith shop so he kept making more arrows. Barking and straightening the wood until he had a large bundle of arrow shafts ready to go. While gathering the wood, Verin had come across a wild turkey. The turkey provided all the feathers Verin needed and was going to make a tasty supper.

It was almost dark when Nathan finally came out to see Verin. "All done in there?" asked Verin.

Nathan had come out only holding a small bowl and dagger. "Well actually I am almost done I just need one more thing. Hold out your hand." Nathan pricked Verin's arm and let the blood drop into the bowl. Once a small pool had formed in the bottom of the bowl Nathan stopped. "There, put some pressure on that and it will stop bleeding in a minute. I'll be back in a few minutes."

Verin did not know why Nathan was taking his blood. Apparently, he should have been paying more attention to what Amaden Blugroson was teaching the boy.

True to his word, Nathan came back out of the shop only a few minutes later. This time he carried a handful of gear. "Here try out this bow and then this sword." Nathan handed the weapons to Verin.

First Verin tried the bow. It looked exactly the same as before with the exception of a small gem carved into the handle. Verin lifted the bow and tried to pull the string back "It feels heavier than before and I can't even pull the string back."

"hmm, okay now try the sword." Nathan could feel Verin's disappointment start to mount.

The sword looked beautiful. The thin black blade was razor s with an emerald in the helm. "It is beautiful and I've never seen a blade so thin and sharp but it is really heavy and awkward feeling." Verin put the sword down and shook his head. "I'm afraid I can't use either of those weapons." Verin did not want Nathan to feel too bad. He had obviously put a lot of effort into making the weapons.

"That is because those are my weapons. Now try these ones." Nathan handed the bow to Verin. This bow felt completely different. It was so light that it hardly even left like he was lifting a thing. Then when he pulled back on the string he was surprised by how easily the bow bent and he was able to get the string back to his cheek.

Nathan smiled, the magic he had put into the weapons was working as planned. "Ah, much better right, now try this sword."

Verin put the bow down and accepted the second sword. Like the first it was a thin black steel blade with a small gem in the helm. When Verin took the sword it was just like the bow. Super light and well balanced, the sword felt perfect. He could not believe the quality of weapons his nephew had made him.

Verin turned to Nathan, "They are perfect. How did you do it?"

Nathan explained the bloodstones and how the bow and sword were now attuned to him. If Verin used the weapons, they were light and easy to use. If anyone else tries to use them they would be heavy and unyielding.

Verin marveled at the weapons, they were truly wondrous. It then hit him like a bolt of lightning. "Blood stones, Stoneblood, you are not the first of your line to do this."

Nathan nodded "No, I'm not. Amaden said that for hundreds of years the Stoneblood family used magic to imbue stones. But as the use of magic died off in Solotine it became a forgotten art."

"I almost forgot, here try these on" Nathan passed Verin a pair of pants and a sleeveless shirt. "I figured out how to cut the vraber skins. I made a cutting knife out of a diamond. I imbued them as well. They will feel light and soft to you but no normal blade will slice through them. "

Verin remembered all too well how tough the vraber skins were, those deadly beasts had almost killed him. "These are excellent Nathan. We are well prepared to take on the duke and his men. Now get some sleep tomorrow is going to be a long day."

Nathan agreed, yawning. He was tired, very tired.

Chapter thirty six

AT FIRST LIGHT, they were off. Refreshed from a decent night's sleep, they pushed hard. The last time Nathan had gone from Birchone to Elderwood he had walked it in three days. Today, they rode into the village before noon. When they got into the small town Verin explained that he and the count had spoken about the journey and how to make it as quick as possible. The count had come to Birchone yesterday and arranged for two fresh packhorses to exchange for their own tired ones.

As they arrived at the stables, the owner had the horses ready for them. "The count explained the situation; these are my best two horses, grained and ready to go. The count also said to tell you he sent a rider to Kerth last night and two more horses will be waiting there."

Nathan and Verin quickly removed the packs from their tired horses and switched them to the new ones. The kindly stable owner also gave them each a loaf of bread and a couple chunks of cheese, telling them to eat as they rode. They thanked the man for his kindness and were off once more.

As they headed off again Verin explained that while the road to Venecia was long, most of the journey was through the plains. Thorn, and his own mount would have little trouble keeping up a fast pace all day. The packhorses, on the other hand, would be working harder and tire quicker. By changing out the pack horses here and in Kerth they would be able to push hard and cut days off their travel time.

Nathan was glad his uncle and the count had thought of this, he hadn't given any thought of the burden the packhorses would have been enduring. The time savings made by switching packhorses along the way would be substantial. Nathan filed this away for future reference. He wondered what other things he would learn from his wise uncle in time.

Onward they rode. Nathan had never been south of Birchone before and while they rode at a fast pace he was still able to notice the changes in the landscape as they went. With each hour they rode, the land seemed to flatten out more. Instead of always being in the forest like the road between Birchone and Elderwood, now they were going through small forests into large, open, hilly land and then back through lightly treed regions once again. If Nathan had not been so focused on Ava, he would've enjoyed the different landscapes.

Kerth was a decent sized town. It was built at the mouth of the Elmon river, where it joined into the bigger Betine river. When they made their way into Kerth, it was late afternoon. With haste, they made their way to find the stables. The stable hand took one look at the two of them and knew these were the men that would be exchanging horses. "You got here quick, the count's rider only got here an hour ago himself."

While they exchanged the packhorses, Verin let Nathan know that they would go as far as possible that night, then camp till dawn. Nathan did not complain about the amount of riding. He would ride as long as possible to get to the girls. Besides, riding the wonderful stallion was no hardship now that he had a saddle to alleviate that issue.

When they finally stopped riding that night, Nathan was tired. Even Thorn, who never seemed to tire, seemed grateful for the reprieve. The spot where they were camped was one Verin had camped at once on his way north to Elderwood. They were more than halfway to Venecia and would arrive the next night.

Verin asked Nathan if he was getting a stronger sense of Ava.

Nathan had been trying his hardest to gain a better sense of her but nothing worked, the connection was still too weak. "It comes and goes. It is still very weak but is getting stronger." It was like catching a scent, but not quite being able to recognize it.

...

When the duke got to Venecia the first thing he did was find a small cottage on the outskirts of town. He paid the owner to go visit family. In reality, the cottage owner simply went up the street three blocks and rented a room. The leftover money he spent on drink and a woman. This mattered not to the duke he simply needed a quiet place to hide the girls for a few days, while he arranged for a boat to take them across the narrow sea to Mithbea and the port of Pailtar. From Pailtar, he would travel on to Morthon. Pailtar was much like Venecia; a port city that did not owe allegiance to any of the kingdoms in Mithbea. Being a port city and a natural gateway for travel, it attracted great amounts commerce, as well as a healthy amount of shady enterprises. Whores, thieves and slave runners were common in Pailtar.

The question now was what to do with the girls? Bailmont wanted to use and then give the oldest one, Sharon, to the men as a gift and kill Rose and Ava. Prisoners were an inconvenience. In Bailmont's twisted mind, women were to be used and thrown away, not kept as bargaining chips.

The duke took a more practical approach; he cared not for the lives of the girls only the results that keeping them alive would achieve. "No, for now the girls are the bait to bring the boy to us. If she is dead, we can't very well exchange him for her. Besides, once we kill the boy we can sell the girls in Pailtar as slaves, but you can let the men use the oldest one. It won't matter as long as no one roughs her up too much."

Bailmont smiled at this. He had been pushing the duke to let him have the girl. The men might get a turn, but he was to be first.

It was late when Bailmont came and grabbed Sharon from the small bedroom the girls were tied up in. When Ava started to yell at him to leave her alone Rose started to wake up in a panic, wanting to know what was going on. Sharon calmed her, despite the fact she was being pulled out of the room. "Nothing my dear. Go back to sleep. Ava was just having a bad dream." Sharon wanted to scream, but Rose had been terrified enough. Her eyes darted from Rose to Ava appealing her to be calm. Bailmont was ugly, leering. He smelled of sour wine, and his touch, as he untied her, was rough and indecent. Sharon shuddered as he shoved her outside the bedroom door.

Ava stopped yelling, Sharon was right. There was nothing she could do, and yelling just scared Rose more. If Sharon could be that strong in the face of such evil, so would she. She would not cry in front of Rose, even though she was terrified that they would take her next. Frantically her mind raced, searching for some way out of this situation. Where was Nathan? He rescued her before. Where was he now when she needed him again? Where are you, Nathan? She yelled in her mind.

•••

Nathan awoke at that very moment, sensing her distress. Something was happening and it was bad. But he had her in his mind now, something had strengthened their connection. He could feel where she was. Nathan forced himself to go back to sleep. In his mind, he kept saying the same words over again. I'm coming, Ava, I'm coming.

•••

A few hours later, Bailmont returned Sharon to the room, her dress torn and her face stained from the constant tears. After Bailmont finished tying her up beside Ava and left the room Sharon spoke in a cracked voice. "Just tell me we are going to live. I can manage the pain of them using me... but I don't want to die, Ava."

Ava leaned into Sharon giving her as much of an embrace as she could while being tied up. "We are going to live. Nathan is going to come for us. I swear I can feel it, we are going to live."

Sharon thought it was a lie, but a sweet one, and right now any lie sounded better than the true of the nightmare they were living. Neither girl got any sleep that night, too terrified Bailmont would return to take one of the girls again.

...

Before dawn, Nathan was up and getting the horses ready to go. When Verin awoke, Nathan had already packed everything and was waiting to go. Nathan passed Verin a hunk of bread to eat and simply said "Let's go."

Today they took a slightly slower pace. There were no villages between here and the coast, so the packhorses would get no reprieve today. As they rode, Nathan focused his concentration on Ava. He could not push his thoughts towards her, but he was getting a better sense of her location, they were getting closer. Nathan picked up the pace a bit, they were getting closer.

...

Bailmont entered the cottage. "I found a ship, sir, and I spoke to the captain. A secured cabin and no questions asked. It has enough cargo room for the men and horses as well. "

The duke was pleased, the previous day they had no luck securing a ship across the narrow strait, the ships had no room, or captains that asked questions. "Excellent work, Bailmont. When does our ship set sail?"

Bailmont grinned. "Couple of hours, sir, for an extra gold piece the captain adjusted his schedule."

"And did you manage to find someone to keep an eye on the Dew Drop Inn for our young friend?" asked the duke.

Bailmont smile got bigger. "Got that taken care of as well, the desk clerk is a crooked sort with very questionable friends. If young Stoneblood shows up, he will be taken care of."

The duke was pleased by the turn of events. Things were going well. Soon they would be in Morthon and he could focus on working his way into power in this new land. With a large supply of gold and men like Bailmont working for him, anything was possible.

Chapter thirty seven

NATHAN AND VERIN were close enough to Venecia to see the cities shadow when Nathan felt movement from Ava. "She is here, but they are moving." Nathan wanted to push the horses to go faster, but after the long days ride, they were exhausted and could go no faster. Once they made it to the outskirts of the city, they slowed to a walk.

When they were about four blocks into the city, Verin went to turn right onto a side street. "If I remember correctly the Dew Drop Inn is about a block up this street."

"Okay, but Ava isn't there. She is this way and still moving away from us."

Verin processed this information, what was the duke up to? "The wharfs are down there. He is not staying in Venecia he is taking them across the narrow strait to Mithbea."

Nathan was confused. "He is taking them to Balta?"

"No, he is probably taking them to Morthon. He will be sailing to Pailtar. We cannot let him get there or we will never get the girls back. "

They hurried to the docks but even as they got there, Nathan could tell Ava was still farther away. He looked up and seen a ship making its way across the strait. "There, in that ship, Ava is there. Are we too late?"

Verin looked at the ship. "No, it is a merchant ship. Big and it can carry a lot of cargo, but is not the fastest of ships. How strong is your sense of Ava right now? Can you track her now?"

 Nathan nodded. I've been able to since last night. Something bad happened and seems to have triggered a stronger connection. I won't lose it now."

"Okay then, we are going to need to get across the strait. Come with me." Verin led Nathan away from the docks towards a large estate on the ocean shoreline. As they walked the horses up to the gates of the estate two guards stopped them and asked them to state their business. "Lord Verin Albet of Balta, I am here to see Paulo Ventego." One of the guards excused himself to go announce their arrival, while the other escorted them to the stables.

"Lord Albet?" Nathan questioned his uncle. It was the first time he had ever heard him use the label. Verin simply shrugged. "They like their titles here in Venecia, even more than in Progoh. Dropping the lord in is a friendly reminder that my brother is the king and helping us is a good idea. Paulo is a good man. He would help us regardless, but servants talk and it benefits Paulo if the rumors are that he entertains foreign dignitaries who refuse to see anyone else. Royal politics is a pain in the ass, but necessary sometimes."

Nathan saw that while Verin disliked the nature of politics it did not prevent him from using to his benefit. Nathan could see the prudence in the subtle methods Verin used to strengthen his ally.

Paulo came to the door. "My old friend, Verin, what brings you my humble abode? Come in please."

Once inside and sat down with an offer of tea and pleasantries out of the way, Verin gave Paulo a brief explanation of the situation from the attack on Elderwood, to his arrival all the way up to following the duke to Venecia.

"I actually know of the attack on Elderwood. Bandits killed my brother, Raul, on his way to Progoh. The horsemen that the duke encountered were Chundo warriors sent to find out what happened to my brother. After they met with the king and were told that Raul never made it to Progoh they began to scour the country sides in search of the bandits. Eventually, they tracked them back to a mountain hideout. But by the time Ashuna and the Chundo got there the bandits were all dead. The scouts say two men killed them all. This was your doing I presume?"

Verin nodded. Nathan nodded in unison.

"Well, you did Venecia a service. Those bandits were costing us a lot of money, not to mention the loss of lives. Now you are here. The duke is sailing across the strait. Obviously his letter to get you to Venecia was a trap. The girls are still alive, so he is keeping them for insurance... for now. But for how long? We need to get you across the narrow strait as soon as possible and make sure that the girls don't disappear into a slavers camp. "

Nathan shivered at the mention of slavers camps. He refused to consider that a possible outcome. He would die before letting that happen.

Paulo rose and walked to the doorway and called out for Peter, his servant. "Peter, send for Captain Berthal. Tell him to have the Lady Bonita ready to sail within the hour. Then have someone find Ashuna and send him here immediately."

Peter left without a word, matters of intrigue were common in Venecia and Peter had proven his value many times over. He always came through for Paulo.

"Peter is going to get captain Berthal. He will take you across the strait tonight. The Lady Bonita is a small cutter, you won't be able to take your horses across with you, but it will get you there fast. In fact, I would wager you will arrive in Pailtar before the duke. I have also taken the liberty of sending for someone who will be able to assist in the slaver issue. But I will explain that if and when he gets here, so for now let us discuss more banal topics."

As the conversation between Verin and Paulo drifted into the politics and trade of Venecia and Balta Nathan focused his thoughts on Ava. He felt her getting farther away, but the bond was not weakening. He was learning how to focus and not let distractions interfere with his silent focus. The trick in the future would be to be able to do both at the same time, be aware of everything around him and still focus on magical connection.

When Peter returned, he informed Paulo that the captain was almost ready and would be able to set sail within a half hour. Along with this news, he brought with him another man. Paulo greeted the stranger. "Ashuna, please come join us. I thank you for getting here so quickly. Ashuna, this is Lord Verin Albet and Nathan Stoneblood."

"A pleasure to meet you" Ashuna was impressed. A lord and a young boy were the ones who wiped out the entire collection of bandits that Ashuna had been tracking in Solotine. Ashuna would not have suspected that Nathan was so young from the scene of the bandit hideout. He had envisioned a seasoned warrior. Ashuna was glad that his mistaken judgment had happened in these circumstances, making that mistake in a battle would cost you your life. Likely, the bandits found that out the hard, way mused Ashuna. Paulo called Verin a lord but Ashuna cared not for titles; he knew these men were also warriors and very skilled ones. He respected that. "How can I be of service?"

Paulo explained how the duke had gone back to Elderwood kidnaped the girls and was now sailing across the narrow strait to Pailtar. Ashuna asked them what they would like him to do. Paulo addressed this carefully. "I was hoping that you would accompany them across the strait to Pailtar. If you were to spread the word that the Chundo were looking for the girls then no slaver in the city would dare take them. The duke would be forced to take them to Morthon."

Ashuna could see this working. Slavers were a cutthroat bunch and would do anything for a dollar. However, as much as they liked money, they lived living more. The Chundo were well feared in Pailtar. "This is a good thing, the duke taking the girls to Morthon?" was Ashuna's reply to the request.

Nathan, seeing what Paulo was suggesting, spoke up, "No, but the duke trying to take the girls to Morthon is a good thing. It is a long ways from Pailtar to Morthon. If the girls are all together it makes rescuing them easier."

Ashuna understood this logic. "Very well then, Ashuna will go to Pailtar with you." Ashuna liked the idea of traveling with the lord and boy warrior, they took on great odds with little fear. He would enjoy the prospect of joining them in battle.

With the matter settled, Verin arranged with Paulo to have the horses and the rest of their gear taken directly to Balta. Paulo let them know that Captain Berthal and the Lady Bonita were at their disposal for as long as necessary. They could sail to Balta once they finished rescuing the girls.

Paulo walked the men down to the docks where he introduced them to the captain. He explained to him that he was under the orders of Verin until no longer needed. Once they were on board the ship Nathan gave Paulo one last goodbye.

"Paulo Ventego, it has been an honor to meet you and I cannot thank you enough for your help. It means a great deal to me. I am in your debt."

Nathan was relieved that, thanks to the assistance of Paulo, the duke would not get far away before they could cross the narrow strait. "You are welcome Nathan Stoneblood, good luck on your journey."

The Lady Bonita was a cutter, a small but agile ship. It could not carry a large amount of cargo but was among the fastest ships in the sea the captain assured them. "No merchant ship would get to Pailtar before the Lady. Even with a couple hours lead. We will likely pass them in the dark. I'll sail a bit of a wide birth around them so they don't suspect we're following them."

Nathan didn't say anything to the captain but he knew that he was telling the truth. They had only been a sea for an hour, but Nathan could tell, through his a'kil bond with Ava, that the distance was closing.

Traveling across the sea was a very new experience for Nathan. The crisp salt water gave the air a different texture. The motion of the craft, as it cut through the ways took a while to get used to. He mentioned this to Verin. "The sea is a moving thing, the waves and swells of the sea cause the rocking motion. Many first-time sea travelers spend the majority of the journey getting sick. You are handing it well."

It had been late afternoon when the Lady Bonita had set sail from the port of Venecia, and now night was coming fast. Nathan asked the captain about sailing at night. "It is not a problem on a night like tonight. With no clouds, the stars give you enough light that tell by the shadows if you are close to hitting anything in the water. The narrow strait is deep water so no worry about running aground. Sailing all night will not be a problem for us or the merchant ship. We should arrive at Pailtar around dawn, and the merchant ship will be a couple hours after that."

By nightfall, Nathan was accustomed enough to the motion of the ship that he was able to get some sleep. Comforted by the fact that they were so close to getting the girls now, Nathan drifted off into a deep sleep. Around midnight, Nathan felt something change and awoke. They were no longer behind the merchant ship. They were now ahead of the duke, the captain had been right. Nathan relaxed and went back to sleep, he wanted to be refreshed for whatever lie ahead.

While Nathan was sleeping, the winds that had been moving them along quickly died off and it wasn't until an hour after dawn that Pailtar came into view.

Chapter thirty eight

PAILTAR, A DUSTY GOLD and dirty cream-colored canvas with speckles of minty green, was different from anything Nathan knew. Gone were the hues of blue and green that dominated the views of Solotine. Sand and adobe buildings were the prominent features of Pailtar, with strange looking trees and little vegetation.

When they left Captain Berthal and the Lady Bonita at the docks of Pailtar, it was agreed upon that the captain would wait there one week. If they had not returned by then it was likely they never would. As they gathered their weapons and gear, Ashuna told them of a small hill to the southeast that overlooked the city. He would meet them there later that afternoon. Ashuna went off to spread the word among the slavers that three girls were entering the city soon and if they liked living, would avoid doing business with the duke.

While Ashuna was scaring the crap out of slavers, Nathan and Verin went through a bazaar, purchasing water skins and food. Between Pailtar and Morthon were only a few watering holes. If they had to follow the duke and his men for long, they would need the skins to keep hydrated. Once they had the water skins and food, they went in search of the hill Ashuna had described.

The hill was about a half mile outside the city and gave a good view of it and all the roads out of the city. It was a good location to keep an eye on things. But, not close enough for anyone to recognize them as strangers. They were sitting on the hill waiting for Ashuna when Nathan turned to Verin. "They are here. Ava is in the city now. "

"Good, you being able to tell where Ava's location gives us an advantage. We can prepare an ambush or follow them until we get an opportunity to get the girls safely away. But for now all we can do is wait."

The time seemed to stand still as they waited. Finally, Ashuna came up the hill late in the afternoon. "I have seen the girls, all three are safe, but the oldest one has not been treated well.

Nathan did not immediately grasp Ashuna's meaning, but Verin did.

Ashuna continued, "I have spoken with all the slavers, none will accept the girls. Ashuna has done as he promised. But if you permit it, Ashuna would like to stay and assist you further." Ashuna was not one to sit aside while his friends fought.

Verin thanked Ashuna. A warrior like him would help even the odds out greatly. Ashuna volunteered to go back into the city and spy on them, but Verin explained that would not be necessary. Nathan knew where Ava was.

Ashuna gave Nathan a careful look. "You are a'kil?"

Nathan nodded.

Ashuna just grunted. "This is good, some Chundo are a'kil. Magic blood is useful for a warrior."

Suddenly Nathan had a thought "Ashuna you should go back to the city. We are going to need horses." He couldn't believe he almost forgot such an important fact.

Meanwhile as the Ashuna headed back to the city, the duke found his plans going awry. "None of the slavers will take any of the girls." Bailmont had spent the entire day working his way around Pailtar trying to find someone to sell Sharon and possibly Rose too, depending on the price offered, but it mattered not. Once any of the slavers realized that these were the girls that Ashuna had mentioned, they wanted nothing to do with speaking to Bailmont. They did not even want to be seen in the same street as Bailmont. It was as if he carried the plague.

"What do you mean none of the slavers would take the girls. Were you asking too much?" The duke was incredulous; a slaver not wanting young pretty girls was unfathomable.

"No I mean I could not give the girls away. There are Chundo warriors looking for the girls and no slaver will have anything to do with them," replied Bailmont.

Now the duke was worried. His plans were going awry. The Chundo were fierce warriors and if they were looking for the girls it meant nothing but trouble for him. "Alright, we take all the girls with us, I'm sure you won't mind keeping the older one around longer anyways. If the Chundo are in the city looking for us then we need to leave now. Have the men prepared to go as soon as possible."

"I already purchased horses and food sir. As soon as you are ready, we can leave." Bailmont was damn efficient. The duke should not have been surprised that his otherwise detestable servant would always be ready and prepared for any situation. As distasteful as the man was, he still served a purpose. The duke needed him now more than ever.

...

Ashuna returned to the hill with the horses. The duke and his men were already leaving the city with the girls. Nathan pointed out the group of horsemen, as they made their way out of the port city. "There, that group is the one." Verin counted the horses and riders. Fourteen riders minus the three hostages left eleven. The duke must have picked up a couple local guides.

While they rode, Verin explained some of the logistics of Mithbea to Nathan. "There are three main kingdoms in northern Mithbea. Pailtar sits at the most northern tip of the continent, the kingdom of Thune is far along the eastern coast, Balta along the western coast and Morthon in the middle, to the south of Pailtar. From Pailtar to Meron, the capital city, is mostly badlands, desert with little vegetation or water. There are a few watering holes along the way, tonight they will likely stay at the closest watering hole. This would be a good place to try retrieving the girls."

"Ashuna agrees. Tell me, when you attacked those bandits back in the mountains, at what time did you attack?" asked Ashuna.

Verin smiled knowing exactly what Ashuna was suggesting. "Right before first light, when the sentries are most tired. I think you are right. We will do it the same way."

Knowing where the water hole was and where Ava was, allowed Nathan and his companions to take a route that did not directly follow the duke and his men. By doing so, they avoided any chance of the duke's men noticing that they were being followed.

This was wise because Bailmont himself had dropped back to check the behind and see if anyone was following. When he caught back up to the duke and the others, they were already making camp at the water hole.

"Any sign of followers?" asked the duke.

Bailmont shook his head. "No my lord, there was no sign of anyone following, but from what our new scouts tell me, there only a few watering holes between here and Morthal. So if they are coming, we would not be hard to find."

The duke, still nervous about the Chundo, relaxed a bit when Bailmont reported no one following them. "Okay, we will have three watches, three men per watch. Bailmont you are on first watch.

It was almost midnight when Nathan, Verin and Ashuna closed to within a mile of the watering hole. Nathan had been working on a plan for a while, and was now ready to share it with the others.

Chapter thirty nine

"ASHUNA, WHAT ARE the chances of you sneaking into the camp, past the sentries?" asked Nathan.

Ashuna smiled. "The chances are very good. What is your plan?"

"Verin will sneak up and get close to their horses. He will find whatever sentries they post near them and shoot them. You will sneak into the camp, cut the girls free and take them to the horses. You and Verin put the girls on the horses and take them back to here, grab our horses then take them all back to Pailtar. Without horses, they cannot catch you going back to Pailtar."

Verin could not argue with the plan so far. Sneaking in killing a few sentries and riding out with all the horses sounded much easier than three men trying to fight eleven. "Alright, but what are you going to be doing while we are sneaking in and stealing the girls and horses. How are you getting back to Pailtar without a horse?"

Nathan had a grim look of determination on his face. "When Ashuna gets the girls to the horses, I will provide a distraction so you can get them out safe."

"As for getting back to Pailtar, it is not that far. I can travel on foot and only be a couple hours behind you" Nathan paused; he knew his plan had flaws when it came to his own part, but he was more concerned with getting his friends out. "Just get the girls to the safety. If I don't make it back, take them to Balta with you. They will need someone to look after them."

Ashuna shook his head. "You take too much of the risk, let Ashuna stay and fight while you ride with the girls."

Nathan gave a laugh. "I'm taking too much risk? You two are the ones having to sneak into the camp without getting yourselves killed. Besides, in the time it takes you to get the girls on the horses Verin will be doing a lot of damage with his bow. There will be hardly anyone left by the time you are gone." Nathan sounded more confident than he felt. He was nervous that he would not be up to the task and that either Ashuna or Verin were much better candidates for this dangerous mission, but Nathan simply could not ask a friend to take this risk. It was his job to do.

Verin was not so sure of this. But, he had witnessed Nathan fighting amongst the bandits without armor.

With his new vraber skin clothes and weapons, Nathan would be a formidable opponent for any number of enemies. They would do it his way.

Once it was time to move they split up and separately made their way towards the camp. Nathan was crawling forward until he was about a hundred feet away from the camp. He stayed in that position and watched, trying to see movement. From what Nathan could tell there were two sentries, one by the horses, and one walking a perimeter around the camp. Wait no; a third was sitting up in a tree.

Nathan carefully slid his bow up beside him and put the quiver of arrows beside him. When the time came, his first shot would be into the palm tree.

Suddenly, Nathan saw the sentry walking stop and bend down. When the sentry was bend down he seemed to disappear right into the ground it was still so dark out. The sentry quickly got back up and continued his rounds back closer to the camp. The sentry appeared to have a different gait now. Nathan realized that it wasn't the sentry. Ashuna had killed the sentry and taken his place! Nathan had been watching the whole time and hadn't noticed the change, and from the lack of noise in the camp no one else had noticed either. Nathan silently congratulated Ashuna. The warrior was stealthy, silent and deadly.

Ashuna, now pretending to be a sentry, walked slowly past the girls towards the horses. Then like it was an afterthought, he turned and went back to the girls. Putting his hand over their mouth's he gently woke each one in turn. Softly whispering into each girl's ear to stay silent and nod if they understood. Once each girl had nodded Ashuna whispered to all three. "I am with Nathan Stoneblood. When I rise quietly get up and walk with me to the horses. When I get on a horse you do the same, understood?"

The three girls were scared but at the mention of Nathan they knew that this was a rescue. So they nervously nodded and waited for Ashuna to rise.

Slowly Ashuna rose and started walking towards the horses. Ava then Rose and Sharon soon followed after.

When Nathan watched the group rise and begin to walk towards horses he quickly took aim at the sentry in the tree. He waited for the sentry to move or make a noise. When Ashuna and the girls got to the horses without being challenged the sentry started to sound out an alarm. Nathan released his arrow and silenced the man. Once the body started to fall towards the ground Nathan readied his bow for the next shot, waiting to see movement among the sleeping bodies. Chaos broke out as the falling body awoke the sleeping soldiers.

As Ashuna got the girls onto the horses, Verin was taking aim at the bodies of the sleeping warriors. The second Ashuna cut the rope and started leading all the horses away from the camp Verin began to fire. The imbued bloodstone bow was amazing. His aim and accuracy benefited from the lightweight and the arrows flew with far greater velocity than he had imagined possible. The bodies lying close to the fire made easy targets and he concentrated on these, firing as many arrows as he could. Soon a scream came from one of his targets, he put his bow away and quickly followed Ashuna and the girls. He had done as much damage as possible, now Nathan was on his own.

Duke Evollan woke to the sound of a scream. Shouting followed. Alarm coursed through his veins He peeked out of his tent. He searched for the source of the dreadful noise. One of the men was half sitting up with an arrow through his chest. Within a blink of an eye, a second arrow pierced the man's chest and he fell back to the ground. The duke panicked. He looked towards the horses only to see the cut picket line. Turning, he looked for the girls. They too, like the horses, were gone. The men were moving frantically around him trying to locate the hidden archers. Another man fell then another. The duke spotted one of the scouts they had hired in Pailtar; running up to him, he grabbed the man by the arm and hissed "Get me out of here."

Chapter forty

WHILE THE DUKE SLIPPED off into the night with the help of the scout, Nathan was busy firing arrows into anything that moved. As he heard the thundering hooves of the fleeing horse's carrying his friends he knew it was time to create his distraction.

Nathan let out a loud war cry, a fierce yell at the top of his lungs; the remaining warriors now had a target and began to move towards Nathan's position. Nathan fired his bow as quickly as possible. Between his position and the camp, the ground was soft sand. Despite their best attempts, the warriors were not able to make quick time in reaching Nathan.

Nathan could see one warrior moving off to the side keeping to the harder rockier ground. His path would bring him around to Nathan's flank. However, it was a wide approach and gave Nathan plenty of time to focus on the other remaining three warriors coming directly at him. He fired at the closest man, hitting him in the chest with his arrow.

Dropping his bow off to his side, Nathan pulled out his newly forged and magically imbued sword and dagger. The first warrior to reach Nathan swung his sword down hard at him; Nathan blocked the attack with his sword. The sun has started to come over the horizon but the light was still poor and attempting to block with the dagger would have been risky. This did not prevent him from using the second blade to attack with. Nathan sent the dagger into the warrior's chest.

A sharp pain in his side let Nathan know that the second attacker had swung his sword at Nathan's exposed side. Had it not been for Nathan's vraber skin shirt, he would have been sliced wide open. Nathan spun and attacked. The warrior, surprised that Nathan seemed uninjured, was barely able to raise his sword in time to ward off Nathan's attack. As the warrior back-peddled, Nathan pressed his attack using both sword and dagger to keep the man off guard. Before long, the warrior slipped in the soft sand and missed his defensive block. Nathan's sword sliced through his neck with no resistance.

Nathan turned. The last warrior was standing over Nathan's bow and quiver of arrows. The man was smiling at him "So you are the great northern boy that the duke hates so much. I have to thank you. If it were not for you, we would still be in Progoh and I would not have gotten to spend so much time with those lovely girls.

Sharon was nice but when I am done with you I am going to get Ava back and enjoy teaching her the ways of a sex slave before I sell her." Bailmont baited his youthful opponent. Anger made men make deadly mistakes. Moreover, the warrior before him was barely a man. He was mentally adding another kill to his credit.

The way the man was taunting Nathan almost made him lose his temper, but the many lessons on breathing had finally taught Nathan control. He kept his anger at bay and prepared to rush at the man.

Bailmont knew he would be able to pick up and fire the bow before Nathan could get close enough to be of any danger. As he reached down for the bow, he noticed the fine jewel in the handle. Only a silly boy would waste such a fine jewel in a weapon he thought. The bow would be a nice bonus once he finished with the lad. Bailmont growled deep in his throat like an animal. The sound intended to evoke fear.

Nathan, unaffected by the taunts, knew that his bow would be useless to the man. Seeing the man's eyes drop to the bow Nathan charged.

When Nathan rushed towards him, Bailmont reached down and picked up the bow. Gods, it is heavy he thought. The weight of the bow made his upswing much slower than anticipated and Nathan was gaining ground quickly. Bailmont slid the arrow into position and began to pull back on the string, but nothing happened. He was not strong enough. In frustration, Bailmont threw down the useless weapon to pull out his sword. He would end this the old fashion way, with a sword. He anticipated gutting him slowly and watching the life fade from his eyes. It fascinated him to watch death. It made him feel powerful. He was eager to feel that power again.

As Bailmont reached towards the ground, grabbing at the bow, Nathan was already moving. Confident that the bow would not work Nathan focused on getting close to Bailmont. When Bailmont threw the weapon to the ground Nathan was already in position. While Bailmont looked down to grab his own weapon Nathan threw his dagger towards the chest of the vile rapist. Bailmont grabbed the pommel of his weapon as the dagger pierced through his heavy leather armor and deep into his shoulder. His downward movement was the only thing that stopped the dagger from piercing into his heart. The pain and shock of being injured slowed the duke a fraction of a second. The short amount of time cost the man his life. Nathan still charging forward into him ran his sword deep into Bailmont's chest.

Bailmont looked down at the black sword that had penetrated into his chest, in a moment of clarity he noted the fine black steel, the thinness of the blade, the jewel sparkling in the helm. Magic, he thought to himself, never fight against magic. A rule he once had and should have followed. He looked up at the boy holding the magnificent weapon. One last surge of anger coursed through his body, a boy defeating him without suffering even one wound. Not in this lifetime he thought, knowing that that his time was ending. Bailmont, weak and fading fast, grabbed Nathan's sword hand and pulled him in closer. Bailmont raked Nathan's face with his gauntleted hand; the sharp metal sliced open Nathan's cheek despite the lack of power behind the move. Bailmont looked at the cut with satisfaction, smiled and coughed up blood before speaking "Something to remember me by." While he took his last few gasping breaths of air Nathan calmly removed his dagger from the man's shoulder then pushed the man away letting his sword slide out of his chest cavity. Bailmont looked into the Nathan's one last time. His last vision one of Nathan's icy blue eyes.

Nathan let out a deep breath and wiped a small amount of blood away from his cheek. Seeing the life fade in his opponents eyes was unsettling. He told himself that is was a death deserved, earned and long overdue. He wondered if he would ever not feel a chill when he looked into the eyes of a man as life faded. At least this time he did not feel the need to empty the contents of his stomach. Nathan refocused his thoughts back to the task at hand and surveyed the camp, no sign of the duke, or the last scout. Torn between the desire to hunt the man down and head back towards Ava, Nathan took one last look into the desert before making his way towards Pailtar. The duke had escaped, a regrettable outcome, but his priority was the girls, not revenge. Nathan picked up the pace as he moved across the desert towards his friends and family.

Chapter forty one

AVA WAS RELIEVED beyond imagination to be sitting on the Lady Bonita, safely away from the deranged duke and the vile Bailmont, but she could not stop worrying about Nathan. When Verin and Ashuna had taken the girls, she had assumed that Nathan would be hiding out in the desert, or possibly back in Pailtar, waiting for them to return. It wasn't until they reached the port city that she found out otherwise. Rose had asked Verin where Nathan was and when he explained that Nathan chose to stay back and provide a distraction while the girls escaped she wanted to explode. Didn't these stupid men know he was only a boy? That he would be killed and Ava would have no one.

Verin seeing the look she gave him tried to calm her down. "Relax Ava. Nathan is not a child. He has learned much in the last few months and those warriors who remained would give him little to worry about." Verin was not as confident as he sounded. But he wanted to reassure the girls that things would all workout. He believed Nathan could defeat the remaining enemies, but there was that shadow of a doubt. Should he have stayed behind with his nephew? What if he had miscalculated Nathan's abilities? As he kept his doubts to himself, he realized how fond he had grown of his sister's son.

Ashuna agreed with Verin, "Nathan's magic is strong, and he is a fine warrior. Those men are no more threat than the bandit chief that he defeated." Ashuna smiled down at Rose, he had held during the ride back from the desert and now the child seemed comfortable standing at his side. A spunky little thing he thought to himself.

Ava looked as Ashuna as if he was crazy. Had Nathan magic? Nathan killed the bandit chief? What was going on? Ava's mind raced with all the new information.

Verin took pity on her, he could see she still needed reassuring that things would be okay. It was obvious she was in the dark regarding his nephew's a'kil powers. He gave her a brief summary of all of his adventures with Nathan. "When we found the Bandit hideout, Nathan snuck in and led the attack while I provided cover. He single-handedly defeated the bandit chief. Afterward, we headed north and met Nathan's grandfather. It was there his magical heritage was revealed."

Ava didn't know what to think, it was all so confusing. Sleep deprivation and an overload of new information were messing with her mind. She just wanted Nathan back. She remembered the wolf in the forest, it seemed so long ago, but now she realized it must have been magic. But, it mattered not. Ava didn't care about magic, she cared about Nathan.

Verin thought about it for a moment. If Nathan could sense Ava, surely the girl could do the same. Verin thought back to how Theron had taught Nathan about his connection with Thorn. Inspired, Verin spoke to Ava, "Close your eyes. Think only of Nathan. Picture his face and talk to him inside your head." He saw her reluctance, her doubt. "Do it, trust me. Imagine him, talk to him. You and Nathan are connected; it is how we found you."

Ava wondered what good that would do. She was afraid she would just break down and cry, but Verin looked so insistent she gave in. Eyes closed, she pictured blue eyes, bronzed skin, and the warmth of his hand holding hers. Nathan Stoneblood, you get your ass back here! We need you and if you don't get back here soon, I'll kill you myself, you jerk! You are needed right here. I miss you. Rose misses you. Hurry, please! Nothing happened, but Ava was thinking back. Over the last few days, she had felt something different, like something was in her mind. She had attributed it to stress but what if that feeling was this connection Verin spoke of? Ava focused her thoughts again. The feeling was still there, like a dull reassuring pulse in the back of mind. Maybe that was Nathan and he was still alive.

Suddenly, Rose, who had been watching the shoreline, spoke out. "I see him, right there coming up the docks." She squealed and clapped her hands, jumping up and down for a second.

Ava looked up incredulously. She saw that Rose was right. Ava ran down the plank off the Lady Bonita and towards Nathan, with Rose close on her heels. Nathan grinning from ear to ear said, "Hey!" dropped his gear and quickly caught the flying girl, letting her momentum knock him over. Rose piled on top both of them.

"Oof," said Nathan as he enjoyed the girls embrace. "Am I always going to be looking up into the sky when you around, Ava?" said Nathan. His Ava appeared unharmed, just slightly disheveled and dirty. She never looked prettier to him than at that moment.

"Oh shut up you big jerk. I missed you so much." Ava looked closer at Nathan's face; the cut made by Bailmont's gauntlet still was caked in blood. She ran her hand over the wound "You've been bleeding again."

"It's just a scratch, a small price to pay for a good hug." Nathan remembered Bailmont's last words, but his memories would not be of the vile man, but instead what he regained.

Nathan and Ava sat up. Rose wiggled between them to give Nathan a hug. Nathan laughed. Rose was Rose! Nobody moved for a moment. Rose sighed, "Nathan, you rescued us again," Rose bounced. Nathan winced as his sore ribs took the beating. Ava noticed his pain and moved to get off him, taking Rose with her.

"I'm just glad you are all safe now," Nathan said sheepishly, not wanting the praise.

Rose looked at Nathan, her expression sad and serious. "Mom and dad and Bends are all dead. We don't have a home anymore."

Nathan took the sisters hands and gripped them tight, and looked Ava in the eyes. "You're coming with me. We are going to Balta. We will have a home in Balta."

Ava smiled. There was so much to learn about this new handsome version of her old friend. Her heart was more than happy as Nathan held her hand and led them back to the Lady Bonita. Nathan had a lot of explaining to do. He smiled as if he was reading her mind.

Authors Notes

Available now: THE MISSING MAGE Book two of the Stoneblood Saga

http://goo.gl/TbMY49

and SORON'S QUEST the prequel to Son of Soron

http://goo.gl/oEkAMv

twitter: https://twitter.com/robyn_wideman

webpage: www.robynwideman.com/blog